"You're the kind of lawman who must be every criminal's nightmare."

"That's exactly what I aim to be, ma'am," Zach said, but even his brave smile couldn't lessen the gravity of their situation.

"How *are* we going to get out of this?"

"We're not far from the road here, and just a few miles from a gas station with a phone booth."

"You've *really* planned for everything," she said in admiration.

"Be Prepared isn't just a Boy Scout motto."

C.Z. leaned over to kiss him on the cheek and Zach drew her into his arms. Their lips met in a lingering kiss. Desire sizzled along her nerve endings.

With a sigh of regret he released her. "Even if we weren't both well past the age of making out in the back seat, I plan on taking you to my bed when this is all over."

ABOUT THE AUTHOR

Saranne Dawson is a human services administrator who lives deep in the woods of central Pennsylvania. Her hobbies include walking, sewing, gardening, reading mysteries—and spending time with her grandson, Zachary.

Books by Saranne Dawson

Runaway Heart
Saranne Dawson

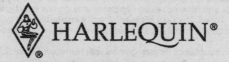

HARLEQUIN®

TORONTO • NEW YORK • LONDON
AMSTERDAM • PARIS • SYDNEY • HAMBURG
STOCKHOLM • ATHENS • TOKYO • MILAN • MADRID
PRAGUE • WARSAW • BUDAPEST • AUCKLAND

ISBN 0-373-22472-9

RUNAWAY HEART

This edition published by arrangement with Harlequin Books S.A.

Printed in U.S.A.

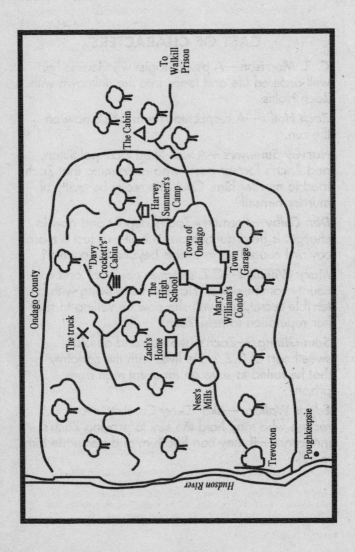

CAST OF CHARACTERS

C. Z. Morrison—A psychologist who leaves her well-ordered life and leaps into the unknown with Zach Hollis.

Zach Hollis—A respected sheriff who's now on the run.

Harvey Summers—A well-liked local politician, and Zach's former boss, who is claiming that Zach tried to murder him. Could he really be guilty of murder himself?

Dan Colby—Formerly Zach's deputy and now in charge. Is he a guilty man as well—or just a moral coward caught up in events beyond his control?

Mary Williams—C.Z.'s former neighbor and a county commissioner. Has she been living with a terrible secret, and will she now be willing to risk her reputation to help Zach?

Sam Gittings—Zach's attorney and an old sweetheart of C.Z.'s. He lives with the certainty that he failed to save an innocent man from prison.

Edgar Wallace—aka "Davy Crockett"—a recluse who may hold the key to proving Zach's innocence—if they can find him and persuade him to talk.

Prologue

Detective Zach Hollis leaned across the rose-colored Formica tabletop, and for just a moment, C.Z. was afraid she might drown in those eyes. She thought of a deep pond reflecting the pale blue of a winter sky, cold but compelling, with a hint of something else lurking within their depths.

"This is a small town. Everyone knows who the drunks are. What you do is round them all up and lean on them— *hard!* Check every one of their alibis and push them until they give up some more names. Drunks hang around with other drunks. It reassures them that they're okay. Believe me, someone knows—or has guessed."

Despite her intention not to be intimidated by those eyes or by his aggressive maleness, C.Z. drew back slightly, then compensated for that with an assertive tone.

"You're right, Detective Hollis, this *is* a small town. And that's why he can't do that. This isn't New York City. People take things personally up here, and my father has to live and work here. His ability to do his job depends on the goodwill of the citizens. He can't just lean on innocent people, no matter how reprehensible their personal habits might be, in order to find one criminal. *Your* methods won't work up here."

His wide mouth curved in a parody of a smile. "*My*

methods would bring to justice a drunk who killed eight children.''

She winced and tore her gaze away from his. Her father had shown her the news articles—and the photographs, the twisted, burned wreckage of the school bus that had been forced off the road and over an embankment.

C.Z. shared his rage—even admired him for it. But she continued to believe that his city methods wouldn't work here. Then she saw, with considerable relief, that her father was returning.

''I LIKE HIM,'' her father said as his gaze followed the departing Zach Hollis. ''He's single, too.''

C.Z. stared at him, shocked at that last comment. Her mother was forever pointing out likely son-in-law candidates—but her *father?* He'd never done that before.

''He thinks you should round up every drunk in the area and grill them until they confess,'' she said dismissively. She was trying to avoid responding to his comment about liking Zach Hollis because she didn't know what *she* thought about him.

''I know. He already told me that.''

''He says that someone knows—or at least suspects—who the pickup driver was.''

''He's right about that, too. The only thing he's wrong about is the methodology. I'm doing just what he said, but in my own way.''

He paused, then went on in a softer tone. ''You could do a whole lot worse, you know. Hollis is a good man. I've gotten to know him pretty well the past couple of years, since he built his cabin up here. He's got all the right stuff, brains, a strong sense of justice and integrity.''

''I don't believe I'm hearing this from you! You sound like Mom!''

''I sound like a father who wants the best for his daughter—and Zach Hollis is the best.''

Chapter One

Those eyes! Was it worse to see them in her dreams—or
to face them across the flimsy barrier of her battered desk?
C. Z. Morrison had about five seconds to consider that
question before the door to her office opened and he walked
in.

But Zach Hollis did not simply walk into a room. Instead, he instantly made it his own. Never mind the fact
that this was *her* office. Never mind the fact that she was
a prison psychologist and he was an inmate.

Her training made her adept at reading body language,
but it had *not* prepared her for the immediate and powerful
impact one body could have on another. Nothing could
have prepared her for that, not three years ago, and not
now.

He smiled with his eyes as he settled himself into the
chair on the other side of her desk. Three years ago, she'd
suspected that he knew full well the impact of those eyes,
ice blue, the color of a winter sky that when glimpsed from
the comfort of indoors seemed to promise warmth, only to
withdraw that promise when one stepped outside. Now, her
suspicion had hardened to a certainty, but it didn't lessen
the impact.

"So, Dr. Morrison," he drawled, with just the faintest
emphasis on her title, "have you convinced Sheckler that

all he really needs to do is to get in touch with his inner child and he won't beat his wife anymore?''

Robert Sheckler was the inmate who'd just left, and she had no illusions at all where he was concerned, though of course she couldn't tell Zach Hollis that.

He put up a hand as though to ward off her next words. He had large, strong hands, the backs dusted with black hairs. She noticed them because she noticed *everything* about him.

''I know, I know,'' he said in his rough voice that carried a hint of the Bronx. ''Professional ethics and all that. Just don't recommend him for parole.''

He settled himself more comfortably in the chair, his long legs stretched out before him, powerful thigh muscles straining at the ugly dun-colored prison twill. Then he folded his arms across his chest, all six foot two inches of him appearing to be totally at ease. She wondered if he was. It was only one of many things she wondered about where Zach Hollis was concerned.

''How are you feeling, Mr. Hollis?'' she asked, wincing inwardly at her cool, professional tone, certain he heard it for what it was—self-defense. ''Are you adjusting?''

He shook his head with exaggerated slowness, his eyes never leaving hers. ''Adjusting to a place like this means giving up your self-respect—and I won't do that. I'm not adjusting, I'm surviving. There's a difference.''

''How are you getting along with the others?'' she asked. She knew how difficult life behind bars could be for a cop. A *former* cop, she reminded herself, though it was impossible to see him as anything else—even here.

His broad shoulders moved slightly. ''They pretty much avoid me. I spend more time in the gym than I need to— just to make sure they know what they'd be dealing with.''

C.Z. thought they'd have to be fools not to know that, gym or not. At thirty-seven, Zach Hollis was in his prime, with no sign of incipient middle-age flabbiness. But she was sure that wasn't the only reason the other prisoners avoided him. She'd never before met a man who exuded such a strong sense of…what? Personal authority? Primitive maleness? Invincibility?

There were many men here, including many of the corrections officers, who tried to be what Zach Hollis was. On them, it came off as mere macho bravado. With Zach Hollis, it was genuine. And she guessed the others knew that.

"Do you have visitors?" she asked. She'd been curious enough to have wanted to check on it, but like everything else in the rigid prison bureaucracy, it was very difficult.

He shook his head. "My folks retired to Florida, and my sister is too upset about my being here without actually having to see me."

"But what about friends?" Surely there must be a woman somewhere. That was the real reason she'd wanted to check the visitor records.

"My friends are all cops, and it wouldn't help their careers to be visiting me."

"It isn't good for you to be cut off like that," she said, hiding her irrational relief at his failure to mention a lover.

Once again, he shrugged. "When I was in the army, we were trained to find ways to exist on our own—in case we were on a mission behind enemy lines or in case we got captured and held hostage."

"What did they teach you?" she asked curiously. She already knew from his record about his specialized military training.

"Mostly, they taught us not to dwell on the current situation—not to count the hours or days or whatever. Also, we weren't to think about the past—only about the future. Make plans and more plans, for after we got out or got released."

"And is that what you do now?"

He nodded. "I read a lot. The library here's not bad. And I think about how I can get at the truth when I get out of here—without risking getting myself sent back, of course."

"But isn't that thinking about the past?" she asked. She doubted that those who'd taught him had had revenge in mind.

He stared at her in silence for a moment, and she felt that telltale heat rising in her. She even imagined he could feel it, as well, or see it. So she couldn't look away. To do so would be a clear admission of the effect he had on her. It seemed all their sessions had been spent with her trying to find ways to make the essential eye contact with him— without letting him see too deeply into her. She was probably failing miserably.

"I'm a cop," he said finally. "And the only way I can ever be a cop again is to clear my name." He shrugged again. "But I'd want to do that, anyway, because I didn't try to kill Harvey Summers."

"Yes, I can understand that," she said. She only knew what she read about the case from Zach's file—and she knew there was more.

"Can you?" he challenged. "Has anyone ever questioned your honesty—your personal integrity?"

For the first time, she heard quiet rage in his voice. No, she corrected herself. Not for the first time. She'd heard it three years ago during that brief meeting, brief but unforgettable. She shook her head. "No, no one's ever questioned that."

"Then you can't know."

"I didn't say I knew, I said I understood."

"Don't play head games with me, C.Z."

It happened again, a moment when all that had gone before seemed only a pretense. Sometimes it was triggered by a look. Other times, it was a word or phrase laden with double meaning and all the more powerful for having been unintended. This time it was his sudden use of her first name.

She met his gaze and held it, but just barely. The drab office faded away to nothingness. The air—the space between them—crackled with an impossible life, vibrated with a sensuality that found its way deep into her and whispered darkly of the forbidden.

"I'm not doing that," she said, her voice embarrassingly husky.

This time, he smiled with his mouth as well as his eyes. He had a wonderful mouth, wide and perfectly shaped above a chin with a hint of a cleft.

"No," he said. "I don't suppose you are. Or if you are, you aren't doing anything I haven't done myself—many times."

"What do you mean?" she asked uncertainly.

"Half of police work is playing head games, with witnesses and suspects and then with juries, if you're lucky enough to get a case to court. It often seemed to me we were just shrinks with guns."

"Oh," she said, relieved. Her father had once said much the same thing. But she'd thought Zach had meant he was playing games with *her*. Of course, he might be. In all likelihood, he was. But she didn't want to think about that, couldn't think about it now, in his presence. She'd do that later, when she reviewed their session. She didn't need to record these sessions with him, or even to take notes. All she had to do was hit the replay button in her mind and it all came back, every minute, every word, every nuance of speech and body language.

Desperately trying to find her way beyond the moment, C.Z. asked, "Do you consider yourself to be a violent man?" She tried to sound as coolly professional as she could under the circumstances.

He didn't answer immediately, and she knew it wasn't because he didn't have an answer or because he was trying to come up with one that would please her—as so many of the others did. Instead, he was drawing a bracket around the moment just past, letting her know he'd been as aware of it as she had.

"I don't know," he said finally. "I guess it depends on your definition of violent. I'm not violent in the destructive sense, like most of them are here. But I'm not afraid of violence, either, like most people are. I wouldn't have been in Special Forces and I wouldn't have become a cop if that were true."

"So you just accept violence as being normal."

"Don't put words into my mouth, Dr. Morrison. I don't accept it, but I'm not naive enough to believe that it can't happen anytime and anywhere—or that I can change those who are violent by nature."

His last comment was a definite insult. Her contract with the prison was for a program that sought to intervene in the lives of inmates convicted of violent crimes. And it didn't help at all that she knew he was probably right.

"Why don't we cut to the control freak part," he said with an indulgent smile, as though encouraging her to speak.

"What do you mean?"

"Cops are notorious for being control freaks. Don't you want to talk about that? You must be familiar with it, being the daughter of a cop."

"Actually, my parents split up when I was twelve, and my mother took me to Rochester."

"He was a good cop," Zach said, and she knew he meant it.

They were silent for a moment. She was thinking of that day three years ago when she'd been visiting her father and had met Zach. At the time, her father had been chief of police for Ondago County while Zach was a New York City detective who had a cabin in the area.

A little more than a year after her father's fatal hunting accident Zach had gotten his job. Her father had liked Zach, and she recalled thinking at the time he might have engineered that brief meeting—or at least manufactured the phone call that had taken him away from the table for a while.

"Sorry," he said softly, breaking into her thoughts. "I didn't mean to bring it all back."

She looked at him, startled by the gentleness in his voice, half certain she'd imagined it. But it was in his eyes, too— or maybe around his eyes, a subtle change that suggested this man was also capable of tenderness.

C.Z. shook off the thought. She didn't trust her judgment where Zach Hollis was concerned. Since taking this job, she'd felt danger many times with the men here, but the danger represented by Zach Hollis was of a very different kind.

"You're trying too hard, C.Z."

"Wh—what do you mean?"

He shifted in his chair, making her more aware of his long, lean body. She tried desperately to concentrate on the regulation prison uniform covering that body.

He didn't answer directly. "It must be tough for you, dealing with the men here. I'm surprised they'd hire a woman for this job."

She very nearly sighed with relief. Knowingly or unknowingly, he was giving her a way out, shifting the conversation to a safer level.

"I don't think they knew I was a woman until it was too late. My résumé said C.Z., and I was hired by Jack Sanford, who contracted with the prison for this project. By the time they found out, it was too late for them to get rid of me without risking a discrimination lawsuit."

He grinned, too, and she felt the tension lessen to a sort of low hum that still vibrated through her but at least left her more or less able to function.

"You haven't told me what C.Z. stands for," he said, gesturing to the nameplate on her desk.

She made a face. "Charlotte Zoe. I was named after my two grandmothers." She couldn't help smiling. "Now do you understand why I use the initials?"

That drew from him a chuckle. It was a deliciously intimate sound that immediately conjured up an image of a candlelight dinner or a quiet conversation in front of a roaring fire. Why was she thinking such things? She'd never even read a romance novel.

"Charlie," he said, still smiling. "That would work. I think I like that."

"That's what my father called me sometimes," she murmured, plunged once again into the emotional morass of her memories.

"Sorry. I wonder if he might have mentioned that, and that's why it came to me now."

She had a sudden clear image of the two of them, big men swapping cop stories, laughing together, casually tossing out bits of personal information the way men so often did, then hurrying on before things got too personal.

"We seem to have gotten offtrack somewhere," she said. "I know you said you'd had special training to deal with...situations like this, but you need more personal contact, Zach. Withdrawing isn't a good solution to your problem."

He folded his arms across his chest again, his gaze steady. "And just where do you propose that I find it?" he questioned mildly in a tone that hinted broadly at her naïveté.

"In case you haven't noticed, I'm surrounded by scumbags who've been put here by people like me."

"The corrections officers?" she suggested, knowing immediately that was a foolish thought.

"Number one, they aren't permitted to fraternize, and number two, there's some resentment there. Some corrections officers are guys who wanted to be cops and didn't make it."

"Surely there must be some men here who aren't that bad," she said, wishing she'd never brought up the subject. It went against all her training and everything she believed in to know she couldn't help him. She'd become a psychologist because she wanted to help people, and now...

"Don't worry about me, Charlie. I'll manage."

Their eyes met and held. C.Z. held her breath. *In a different world,* said his eyes—to which hers replied, *Oh, yes. Yes.*

Her phone intercom buzzed, causing her to start nervously, as though she'd been caught doing something very wrong instead of just thinking about it. He glanced briefly toward the phone. The moment shattered. She got up from her desk.

"My next appointment is here," she said unnecessarily.

He stood, too, but he didn't move toward the door until she had come around her desk. Without it between them, she felt frighteningly vulnerable—and yet she knew she'd gotten up because she wanted, for one brief moment, to remove that barrier.

She looked at him, allowing herself for one crazy moment to imagine how it would feel to be in his arms, to nestle her head just under that square chin—to let it happen.

He knew. His gaze was steady. Not once during their sessions had he ever said or done anything suggestive, as the others invariably did. She almost wished he would, because then maybe she wouldn't spend her nights fantasizing about him.

"See you Thursday, then," he said, betraying his thoughts only with a slight, but undeniable huskiness.

"THERE WAS TROUBLE last night," Jack Sanford said by way of greeting C.Z. when she arrived at work two days later, her mind already on the session with Zach Hollis scheduled for this afternoon.

"Oh? What sort of trouble?" She wasn't surprised. The prison was in the midst of a pseudo-strike by the corrections officers. They weren't permitted to strike, so instead, they were calling in sick in great numbers.

"A fight. Michaels and Johnson from your group and two from one of my groups. The victim was yours, too—Hollis, the cop."

Very fortunately, C.Z. was turned away from him at the moment as she poured herself some coffee. "Zach?" she said, unable to prevent his first name from slipping out. "What happened to him?"

"He's in the hospital. The four of them ganged up on him in the rec room. The warden's ordered a lockdown until the sick-out's over. Michaels and Johnson are in the hospital, too. The other two were treated here in the dispensary."

C.Z. turned to him, having set down her coffee mug because her hands were trembling. "How badly is Hollis hurt?" she asked in a carefully neutral tone.

"Not too bad, I guess. A concussion is what I heard—plus some cuts. One of them had a knife." He shrugged. "I guess they went after him because he's a cop—or was."

C.Z. struggled not to let her relief show. It sounded bad enough, but certainly not life-threatening. Sanford ran a hand through his thinning hair. He was her boss and the man who'd sold the state prison authority on his idea for an intervention program.

"This could spell trouble for us, C.Z. We've got a six-month review coming up, and I'm afraid they could terminate the project even though I've got a one-year contract.''

She managed to murmur sympathetically, but her concern was for Zach, not for the project. She knew Sanford still had high hopes for their success, but she knew the program was doomed even before this incident. The prison environment just wasn't conducive to their program.

''I'm going to the hospital to see Hollis,'' she said, then added hastily, ''and Michaels and Johnson, too, of course.''

''Sure. Okay.'' He nodded distractedly. ''We'll talk about it after you get back.''

C.Z. PAUSED in the doorway, breathing a quiet sigh of relief. He didn't look as bad as she'd feared. In fact, the only visible sign of injury was a thick bandage on the upper part of his right arm. The nurse had told her the concussion was severe enough that they would probably keep him for a few days.

She thought about their conversation only two days ago, when she'd asked him if he considered himself to be a violent man. He'd said he wasn't afraid of violence, and now she understood why. He'd been attacked by four men, at least two of whom were as big as he was. And yet he'd clearly managed not only to survive the assault, but also to put two of them in the hospital, as well. She shuddered, then began to approach his bed.

''Zach,'' she said quietly, not sure if he was awake. His face was turned away from her and he'd given no indication he'd heard her come in.

When he finally turned toward her, she saw that his right eye was blackened and there was a small bandage on the left side of his jaw.

She sank into the chair next to his bed. Uncomfortable with the silence, she asked, ''What happened?''

"I'm a cop," he replied in a tired voice she barely recognized.

"It wouldn't have happened if it weren't for the sickout," she said.

He grimaced. "That only gave them a better opportunity. It would have happened sooner or later anyway."

"Is there anything I can do?" Though she knew there wasn't, she wanted desperately to let him know she cared.

He regarded her silently through his one good eye. The scrutiny went on for so long she became uncomfortable, hearing the echoes of her meaningless words.

"You can help me get out of here."

She stared at him as a chill slithered through her. "You mean out of the hospital?" she asked, even though she was certain that wasn't what he meant.

"No, I mean out of prison. I've got a plan. I was hoping you would come here."

She managed to meet his gaze but looked away quickly. "I can't. I mean, how—"

"No one would know you've helped me. I've got it worked out." His words tumbled out quickly, then he paused. She could sense his discomfort. She knew it wasn't the result of his injuries. It was that he was being forced to ask for her help.

"It won't stop, C.Z. And if I'm transferred, it'll happen there, too."

"But if you're transferred and no one knows you're a cop…"

"No one was supposed to know here. They can smell cops."

"What's your plan?" she asked, hoping against hope she could somehow prove to him it wouldn't work.

He gestured to the window. "That bottom part that opens is held in place with a couple of screws. There's a ledge outside, and from there, I can get to the roof of the ambulance garage, then to the ground.''

She got up and walked to the window. A part of her was pleased he obviously trusted her enough to tell her about his plan. But mostly, she was terrified—terrified of what he was suggesting and even more terrified of her ambivalence. She knew she should say no in the strongest possible terms—but she didn't.

"That ledge is awfully narrow, and it's a long jump to the roof—especially in your condition." She added that last as she remembered his military training. She couldn't begin to guess what skills he might possess.

"I don't intend to try it now. I'll be okay by tomorrow, but I'll pretend to still have the headaches and double vision so they keep me here."

"What about the guard?" she asked, turning to him and trying not to sound desperate. Her conscience and her professional ethics were screaming at her to say no.

He shrugged, then winced at the pain in his injured arm. "There's only one, and he's more concerned about the other two, who are down the hall. It's doable, but I need someone to bring me clothes and a screwdriver."

He reached carefully for the box of tissues on the nightstand, then dug into the bottom and withdrew a dinner knife. "I've already tried to use this on the screws. It would probably work, but it's going to take more time than I'm likely to have. But I can leave it behind and they'll think I used it. My prison clothes are in the closet. I'll take them with me so they'll assume that I'm wearing them."

Their eyes met, but after only a second, he looked away. She knew he wouldn't beg her—and she also knew she didn't *want* him to beg. He had lost so much already, and she couldn't bear to see him lose his pride, as well. Neither could she stand the thought he might be killed.

"All right," she heard herself say, even though the turmoil within her continued. She knew that, at the very least, she should wait and think this over—away from his overwhelming presence. She would be committing a crime that could not only end her career but send her to prison.

The enormity of those two small words washed over her like ice water, but she could not take them back. She could not deny Zach Hollis, and she'd known that from the very beginning.

Then she heard the voice that was hers again, calmly asking for his sizes. He gave them to her, saying he would need shoes, as well, since his had been taken away. She nodded and wrote that down. The whole scene had taken on a surreal quality. This couldn't be her, calmly agreeing to commit a crime to help a man who was convicted of attempted murder.

"I...I have to go now," she said shakily.

Neither his battered face nor his voice revealed anything as he nodded. "I'll ask them to call you tomorrow. I'll say I really need to talk to you. That way it won't look suspicious for you to be coming back."

She nodded and left his room. She was in her car before she realized she hadn't talked to the other two men.

After her visit to Zach, C.Z. talked herself out of her insanity. She would see him tomorrow and explain that while she certainly sympathized with his predicament, she just couldn't risk becoming involved. But an hour later, she was in her car and headed toward the mall.

"Reality-check time," she told herself as she tossed her purchases into the trunk and got into her car. "If you're really going to do this, at least be sure you understand *why* you're doing it."

There were good, solid reasons, of course. She believed in Zach's innocence, though a few doubts remained. She also believed he might well be killed if he remained in prison. But the truth was that those were good reasons to feel sympathy for him—and that was all. What transformed sympathy into action—*illegal* action—was far more complicated and frightening.

From the moment she had first laid eyes on Zach Hollis three years ago, something inside her had snapped. No, she thought, that wasn't the right word for it. Something had awakened—something she'd never felt before.

She'd been visiting her father, and the two of them were having breakfast in the local diner before she left. They had just sat down when she saw her father beckon to someone—and suddenly Zach was there and her mind went blank and her body began to do some very strange things.

And the memory of those ice-blue eyes and that indisputable maleness had haunted her all the way to New Haven, Connecticut, where she was in the midst of grueling graduate work. But she'd quickly immersed herself in her studies, and after a time had convinced herself it was a meaningless episode. She'd never see him again.

Following her father's death, his chief deputy, Tom Strasser, had been named to replace him as chief of the Ondago County force. But a year later, he was forced into early retirement by a heart ailment—and Zach had gotten the job.

C.Z. heard about all this from Stacey, a childhood friend who still lived in the area. With her father gone, she'd had no reason to go there. It was through Stacey she'd learned of Zach's arrest and conviction. Even then, she'd managed to convince herself she'd never see him again. New York State had many prisons, and surely he wouldn't be sent to the one where she had just begun to work, in upstate New York, several hours away from Ondago County.

But he was—and then she told herself he wouldn't remember her from a brief meeting three years earlier. He did, though, and she discovered that not even the fact that he was a convicted criminal made a difference to her treacherous body.

Lust, pure and simple, she thought. And yet there surely had to be more to it than that. Or was she only desperate to justify his assault on her senses—the way his mere existence had bypassed all her normal restraint?

C.Z. SPENT a restless night filled with dreams that were by turn frightening and erotic, but she did her best to get through a busy day at work. Jack Sanford enlisted her help in his meeting with the warden, who lost no time telling them their project was worthless. C.Z. remained quiet while Jack defended the program, then she asked what measures could be taken to protect Zach in the future.

"I saw him at the hospital yesterday," she told the warden. "And he's very concerned." As she heard herself speaking calmly and professionally, she knew she was already trying to justify his future escape—and her part in it.

"We'll do the best we can," the warden said. "But I can't give him any guarantees—and he knows that."

"Couldn't he be moved to another facility where no one knows his background?" she asked, hoping that the warden would contradict Zach's answer to that question.

"We could move him, but it wouldn't matter. Prison grapevines are pretty amazing, Dr. Morrison. They'd find out sooner or later. He was with the NYPD for some years, and he'd be bound to run into someone he helped put away or someone who knew he'd been a cop.

"In this case—and I think Hollis would agree with me— it's better to know where the trouble's coming from. We *will* be moving the others as soon as it can be arranged. But my sources tell me the real instigator wasn't involved. So there's nothing we can do about him—yet."

"Who was that?" Jack asked before she could.

"William Davis. We think he put the others up to it."

She exchanged a glance with Jack. They both knew Davis. He was in one of Jack's groups. He was serving time for manslaughter, a knife fight in a bar, she recalled. And he was from Ondago County, though she was sure he was already in prison by the time Zach was appointed. She'd have to mention the comment to Zach.

They left the warden's office, and C.Z. glanced discreetly at her watch as Jack bemoaned the bleak future of the program. It was nearly three o'clock, and Zach hadn't called before she met with the warden. Could he have changed his mind? She was more conflicted than ever after the scary picture the warden had painted of Zach's future.

She got her answer when they reached the small suite of offices shared by the psychologists and other counselors. Their secretary called to her, waving a pink message slip.

"I have an urgent call for you from the hospital social worker. She says one of the men is demanding to see you. He won't talk to her, and she says he seems really upset."

"Who is it?" C.Z. asked as her heart began to thud and then threatened to leap into her throat.

"Zach Hollis. He's that good-looking cop, right?"

C.Z. nodded, wincing inwardly. She didn't like hearing Zach's attractiveness being mentioned.

"He's probably worried about what he'll be facing when he comes back here," Jack said, shaking his head sadly. "I really feel for that guy, after what the warden said."

"You're probably right," C.Z. said. "I'll stop to see him on my way home." She didn't dare sound too eager.

Jack heaved a sigh. "TGIF—and not a moment too soon. If I ever needed a long weekend, it's right now."

C.Z. realized she'd completely forgotten about the upcoming Columbus Day weekend. But no matter how much Jack thought he needed it, she needed it more. If Zach *did* manage to escape, she'd have plenty of time to practice acting shocked before she returned to work on Tuesday.

IT WAS JUST PAST four-thirty when C.Z. stepped off the elevator and started down the hallway to Zach's room. She had tried to stuff his clothes and the screwdriver into her oversize shoulder bag, but in the end had been forced to use her attaché case, as well.

The guard was positioned as before, between Zach's room and the rooms of the other two men. Sweat began to prickle her skin as she approached him, knowing he would be well within his rights to ask to search her bag and case. She hoped to dissuade him with the excuse that she was taking work home for the weekend.

She walked toward him, smiling—flirting just a bit. His interest had been plain enough yesterday. But with each step, she became more certain that she was walking into a disaster.

"Afternoon, Doc," the guard said, his gaze traveling over her—but not over her big bag and the attaché case. The suit she'd chosen was as close to sexy as she dared for her job, a close-fitting jacket and a slim skirt that ended just above the knees to display the long legs she knew were her biggest asset.

"He's been asking for you about every five minutes," the guard went on, his gaze shifting from her face to her legs. "I expect he's worried about going back. They're planning to discharge all of them tomorrow."

C.Z. glanced toward the rooms of the other two. "Maybe I should stop in to see them, too."

"I wouldn't waste my time if I was you," the guard said with a grimace. "Just see Hollis and then go enjoy your weekend."

She managed a laugh that sounded genuine. "I think I'll take your advice. I'll be seeing them soon enough as it is."

She wished the guard a pleasant weekend, then forced herself to walk casually toward the open door to Zach's room. It was surely the longest twenty feet she'd ever walked.

ZACH HEARD her voice as she talked to the guard. He'd begun to fear she wouldn't come—that is, when he wasn't busy hating himself for having asked her to help him.

He still wasn't certain she *would* help him, of course. She might be coming only to say she'd changed her mind. He couldn't blame her for that. The risk to her was as minimal as he could make it—but it was still there.

He heard her approaching and held his breath, then released it slowly when she appeared in his doorway, looking terrified and carrying both a big shoulder bag and an attaché case. He sent up a silent prayer of thanks for an idiot guard who'd clearly been too busy staring at her legs to search her bags.

She stepped into the room, then hesitated, half turning to close the door. He was sitting on the edge of the bed, and she came over and sank into the chair with an audible sigh of relief, setting the bag and case on the floor beside her. He stared at them, still not completely certain.

"I've brought everything," she said in a low, breathy voice that was sexy as hell, even though he knew it was from fear, not from any intention to seduce him. She'd been managing that from the beginning, without any conscious intent.

"I owe you a lot for this, C.Z.," he said sincerely, wishing for the umpteenth time he'd met her under different circumstances. She didn't wear a ring, and he wondered if there was anyone in her life. Maybe when this was all over...

"I still think you're making a mistake," she said, her big gray-green eyes pleading.

"I don't have a choice."

"Where will you go?"

"That's none of your concern. The less you know, the better." His voice was intentionally harsh. He was letting her know she would probably be questioned.

"I just don't see how you can possibly clear yourself if you're a fugitive. Couldn't you hire someone to look into it for you?"

"What good would that do if I'm dead by the time they get it sorted out?"

She stared at him, then nodded. "How are you really feeling?"

"I'm fine," he lied. He was still having occasional dizzy spells and some double vision, but he knew from experience that would end soon.

"I wish you'd at least tell me where you're going," she said.

Zach climbed off the high hospital bed and reached out to her. After a moment's hesitation, she took his hand. His arm still hurt from the stitches, but he surprised himself by carrying her hand to his lips. He'd never done a thing like that before, and it felt weird—but also somehow right.

"Don't worry about me, C.Z. I'll be all right. And I'll get in touch with you as soon as I can—just to let you know that."

He let go of her hand rather self-consciously, and she let it drop into her lap, then stared at it. "I still can't believe I'm doing this," she said softly.

"I'm glad you are and..." He hesitated, then let the words come out. "And I'm really sorry we had to meet again under these circumstances."

She lifted her head and stared at him but said nothing for a long moment while he thought about all the times they'd sat in her office, with that desk separating them, and how he'd wanted to pick it up and throw it out of the way and—

"I'm sorry, too, Zach," she said softly, then dragged her eyes away quickly, as she'd done so many times before.

"What do you want me to do with the clothes?" she asked as she stood, her tone suddenly all business. It was a replay of the times before, when they'd edge toward the unthinkable, then pull back.

"Put the shoes and whatever else you can into the nightstand, then give me the screwdriver and the rest and I'll hide them in the bed."

She did as told while he edged closer to the door to keep an eye on the hallway.

"I thought you might need some money, too, so I put two hundred dollars in the pants pocket. It isn't much, but…"

"That's fine," he told her. "I'll see to it you get reimbursed for that and for the clothes."

"I didn't get you a jacket because there was no way to hide it. But it's gotten much colder out."

"I'll be okay," he assured her, wanting to get her out of there while he could still control himself. If he couldn't get things straightened out and had to spend the rest of his life as a fugitive, he'd never see her again.

"Good luck, Zach." She walked toward the door—and him—with a tremulous smile.

"Thanks." He started to move aside, to let her pass and walk right out of his life.

But they had come too close to each other. She hesitated, then moved sideways. He stopped. Their eyes met. And then they both stepped off the edge.

Zach's mouth was on hers even as his hands began to explore her curves, sliding beneath the jacket to caress her through the thin silk of her blouse, palming the soft fullness of her breasts. She hesitated for a moment, then surrendered with a small, strangled sound as his tongue found hers and began a sensuous dance.

He slid his hands down, cupping her bottom, wanting her to feel his hunger, his need. Then he smiled against the petal-soft skin of her neck as she gasped with pleasure.

Still holding her against him, he began to move them both toward the bed. The flames of his hot desire were fed by hers as she grasped his head and deepened the kiss with her demands.

And then, from the corridor, there was laughter. He raised his head. But no one was there. The laughter was coming from the next room.

She moved away from him and he let her go, shocked, now that reason had returned, to see just how close they'd come to forgetting everything but the roaring fire of their need for each other. He could see in her eyes, too, that volatile mixture of surprise and desire.

"I have to go," she said in a low, husky voice.

"I know. We just forgot there for a minute."

She hurried toward the door, then stopped at the last minute to comb her hair with her fingers and tuck in the blouse that had come loose. He picked up her bag and attaché case and handed them to her. They shared a smile that was, in its way, as intimate as what had gone before.

Her scent lingered for a few minutes after she'd gone. Zach breathed it in greedily. It suited her well—subtle, delicate, sexy.

He walked to the window, willing the darkness to come. He was far less certain of his future than he'd told her. He didn't have a plan beyond getting out of here. Plans had a way of going awry. He'd take it as it came.

Chapter Two

A horn blared. Brakes squealed. C.Z. saw something briefly in her peripheral vision, a car swerving. Then she was through the intersection and staring with horror behind her at the red light she'd failed to see.

Badly shaken, she pulled into the parking lot of a nearby office complex. Her hands were trembling as she pulled her fingers from their death grip on the steering wheel. She was a good driver and a cautious one. She'd never had an accident, not even a speeding ticket, ever.

She wondered uneasily if she'd run any other lights. She couldn't remember anything from the time she'd left the hospital—and Zach. She raised her trembling hand to her lips. She could certainly remember his kisses—and what had almost happened.

She could remember her thoughts as she'd driven away—fears for him and what he would do, where he would go, how he could prove his innocence when he was a fugitive. Those thoughts had blinded her to everything else.

Zach needed her help. He had practically no money, and she doubted very much that he had any place to go. She could help him with both. She had the money her father had left her, which she was investing until her job was more secure and she could think about buying a house. And she had the perfect place for him to stay, as well, courtesy of a friend who'd gone to Europe for a year.

Those had been her thoughts when she'd run the red light. But sitting in the aftermath of a near accident, she told herself to stay out of it. She had done enough. She was probably still safe.

She remembered her father telling her once about a murder case he'd solved. Sometimes, he'd said, people take one giant leap into crime, but most of the time, they do it in increments, descending by little steps until it's too late to get out again.

Already, the step she'd taken was more than a little one, but the chances were very good she could get out unscathed. But if she did more...

She shuddered, thinking about those brief moments in his arms when she'd completely forgotten who they were and where they were. Never before in her life had she felt like that, even though twice she'd believed herself to be falling in love.

And Zach was so very different from any man she'd ever known. She'd always dated men much like herself, cool, cerebral types who thought carefully before they acted. Zach, on the other hand, was a man who acted on his instincts, who'd never sit around calmly and rationally discussing any action or relationship.

But he made her body sing. He made her feel the vast, exciting differences between male and female in a way no one ever had. He sent shock waves through her with nothing more than a glance—then tore her completely loose from her moorings with his kisses.

People began to pour out of the offices, laughing and talking. Several of them sent curious glances her way as they got into their cars. She backed carefully out of the parking space, then headed home. Her decision was made, though a part of her still harbored the hope that she would come to her senses before the time came to put her plan into action.

SHE PULLED into the rear parking lot at the hospital just after nine o'clock. She had a clear view of Zach's room on the third floor. The lot was reserved for hospital staff, so she figured she should be safe until the shift change, which was probably at eleven or midnight. And she was sure he would make his move before then, to give himself as much darkness as possible to get far away.

His room and all the others she could see were dark. The only lighted windows were at the nurses' station at the far end of the hallway from his room.

She'd thought his plan had looked dangerous from up there, but it seemed even riskier from down here. The ledge looked very narrow, and the window frames didn't protrude to give him any handholds. To reach the corner of the building closest to the detached ambulance garage, he'd have to follow the ledge for about thirty feet. Then he'd have to jump at least twenty feet to reach the roof of the garage—but at least it was flat and probably no more than ten or twelve feet from the ground.

She kept her eyes trained on his window, then drew in a sharp breath when at last she saw movement. He was definitely there, just inside the window, but she couldn't tell if he was beginning to remove the pane or about to climb out.

Anxious moments passed when she very nearly forgot to breathe. Then she saw him climb out and straddle the windowsill for a moment as he reached inside. When he made a sudden move, she was about to cry out, thinking he was losing his balance. But all he'd done was to throw a bundle to the ground. His prison clothes.

He swung his body out and planted his feet firmly on the ledge. He was barely visible as a faint, dark silhouette against the dark red brick facade. She reached for the door handle, then stopped. There was nothing she could do to help him, so it made no sense for her to expose herself yet.

Once again, she held her breath as he began to move along the ledge. She couldn't see him that well, but his movements seemed very sure. Maybe he hadn't been lying about his condition, after all.

After what seemed like half her lifetime, he was at the corner. He hesitated for only about half a second before suddenly launching himself into the air, landing in a crouch at the corner of the roof. He didn't move for a few seconds, and she began to worry that he'd hurt himself.

She dragged her gaze from his shadowy figure and scanned the lot, then glanced at his window. No one was in sight in the lot, and his window remained dark. She opened the car door quietly, not wanting to startle him, then left it unlatched and began to run in a crouch toward the garage, concealing herself between the rows of cars.

There was still one row of cars between her and the garage when she heard a thud, followed by a muffled groan. When she peeked out from between the cars, she saw him picking himself up slowly as he clutched at his injured arm.

"Zach!" she cried in a loud whisper, at the same time standing and waving at him.

He ran toward her in a crouch, then dragged them both down between two cars. "What are you doing here?" he demanded, his hand clutching her shoulder.

She shrugged off his hand and ignored his anger. "Come on! My car's back there."

For a moment, she thought he would refuse. He raised himself to look around, and she saw him sway slightly, then put out a hand to steady himself against the hood of a car. She grabbed his other hand.

"Come on, Zach! If you pass out, I can't carry you!"

Still, he hesitated, even started to pull his hand from her

grasp. But she held on, and he stared at her, then nodded reluctantly. In his reluctance, C.Z. saw her foolishness as clearly as he did. But a line had been crossed. She was committed to helping him.

Staying low, she hurried toward her car, then turned when she reached it. He was gone! She knew one brief moment of indecision—and then she saw him coming toward her, running in a low crouch, carrying the bundle he'd tossed to the ground earlier.

Moments later, they were out of the lot and on their way. She felt a surge of triumph she had no right to feel—no right, that is, if she were being rational about it.

She glanced at him as he sat there silently, occupying far more space than he should. She saw beads of perspiration glistening on his face. He was clutching his injured arm, and when his hand came away, she saw blood.

"I ripped a couple of stitches," he muttered when he saw her staring. Then, after a brief pause, he said, "You're crazy, you know."

"I can't be crazy—I'm a shrink." Rather to her amazement, she began to laugh, and a moment later, his deeper laughter joined hers.

"Well, Clyde." She grinned. "Where do you want to go?"

He chuckled. "I don't know, Bonnie. This seems to be *your* show."

"Believe it or not, I have a plan—or at least a place where you can stay."

"You do?" he asked skeptically, turning in his seat to face her as she tried to keep her attention focused on her driving. "Look, C.Z., just get me away from here and drop me somewhere. That way, you'll still be safe. I can manage."

"No one could connect this place to me even if I were under suspicion. It's a mountain cabin that belongs to an old friend from grad school. He's in Europe for a year, and he asked me to keep an eye on it and use it if I want.''

"Where is it?" he asked, and she detected a wary sort of hope in his voice.

"It's off that old road that runs from Trevorton to route—I can't remember the number. The road from Neff's Mills over the mountain to the Thruway. I have the directions. I haven't been there yet. He left just last week.''

"The Warrior Ridge Road?" he asked.

"Right. That's it. You go on this gravel road and make a couple of turns, and then you're on a dirt road that runs to Scott's cabin and one other. His is at the end of the road. Scott knows the owner of the other cabin. He bought the land from him. But he travels a lot and only uses it during ski season, according to Scott. So he won't be there for a while yet. Scott says it's really isolated. He drew a map for me because he says it's easy to get lost back there.''

He remained silent as she drove through dark, quiet, residential streets, half expecting to hear sirens.

"Well, do you have a better plan—or any plan at all?" she demanded impatiently when his silence continued.

"No, I don't,'' he admitted reluctantly.

"Okay, then that's where we're going. We should be able to get there in about two hours or so, even if I stay on back roads.''

She glanced at him to see his reaction, but he was staring out the side window. There was a dark patch of blood on the sleeve of the shirt she'd bought him.

"I'd better stop somewhere and get you something to put on your arm so it doesn't get infected,'' she said.

He nodded. She was surprised and even a bit annoyed at his silence. She asked how long he thought it would be before his escape was discovered. Instead of responding, he reached over and switched on the radio, then began to punch his way through the stations.

"Zach!" She cried in exasperation when he stopped at a station that was carrying a baseball game.

"Just a minute. I need to get the score."

"What?" she sputtered, unable to believe he could be interested in a baseball game at a time like this. She was driving with one eye on the rearview mirror, expecting to see flashing lights and hear sirens at any moment. "How can you—"

He silenced her by pressing a finger to her lips. Her annoyance faded quickly, buried beneath the onslaught on her senses. The gesture seemed so absurdly intimate, so incredibly erotic.

Okay, she told herself. *So maybe he needs a diversion right now.* She was willing to give him that, even though she hated baseball. But a few minutes later, he turned off the radio.

"I think I'm safe for a while," he said as though no time at all had passed since her question. "Kenny, the guard, was watching the game in the visitors' lounge. It's a tie game, the top of the seventh. He probably won't check on me until it's over, so it could be an hour or more before they start looking for me."

She stopped at a convenience store at the edge of town to buy some antibiotic ointment. Zach put his seat into a reclining position and pretended to be asleep. As she waited to pay, she glanced out and satisfied herself that even if the clerk looked out, he would see nothing more than a shadow in the passenger seat. But he barely glanced at her, let alone her car. He was watching the game on a small TV behind the counter.

Then they were on their way again, taking back roads with little or no traffic. Zach pulled off his shirt and applied the ointment to the ugly wound on his arm. She kept her eyes on the road, but even so, she was totally aware of his lean, hard body so close to hers. His every movement sent tiny frissons of heat curling through her. And soon they would be alone in an isolated cabin.

Very little conversation passed between them except for periodic discussions of their route. He seemed relaxed, which annoyed her because she still expected to discover a roadblock around every curve.

He broke the silence to ask her to pull over at a dark and deserted service station. Then, after she had done as requested, he asked for her driver's license. She reached into the back seat for her purse and pulled it into her lap.

"Why do you need it?"

But her question went unanswered as he took the identification and got out of the car, then turned back and asked her for a quarter. She gave him that, and he went to the pay phone on the wall outside the station.

Who was he calling? Why did he need her license? C.Z. was becoming very annoyed at his habit of ignoring her questions—and answering them in his own good time. She could tell he'd reached whoever he was calling, and she waited impatiently for him to return to the car and explain himself.

The adrenaline rush she'd felt during the escape and the fear that they would be stopped were dying away. In their place came the harsh, implacable reality of what she'd done. And along with that came the belated realization of just how little she knew about him.

He returned to the car and handed her the license. "My folks will be sending some money in your name. They'll wire cash, so it'll be safer—no check to show up in your bank account."

"What did you tell them?" she asked curiously.

"Just that I've escaped. I can't tell them where I'm going because sooner or later someone might question them. But I need money, and I can't get at my own—what little I have left."

His final words held bitterness. While it was true she didn't know him well, she was slowly learning a few things, at any rate. He kept his own counsel, and he hid his feelings well most of the time.

"They must be very worried about you," she commented as they resumed their journey.

"It isn't the first time. They haven't stopped worrying about me since I went into the military. My father was a corporate lawyer, and they both wanted me to follow in his footsteps."

"Why didn't you?"

"Because I couldn't see myself spending my life in three-piece suits telling corporate crooks just how far they could go before they not only bent the law but also broke it."

She laughed. She couldn't imagine that, either. In fact, it was impossible for her to imagine him being anything but a cop. Her father had been the same way.

He lapsed into silence again, and before long all her fears came rushing back. She felt as though she was on some sort of emotional roller coaster, laughing with him one minute and gripped by an icy fear the next. And always there was that awareness of him, the way she felt his presence with every fiber of her being.

They raced on through the night while C.Z. imagined a huge search being mounted for him. Lights would be flashing, sirens would be wailing—and questions would be asked.

There were questions *she* wanted to ask, as well. But she didn't ask because a part of her feared hearing the answers. What if his story didn't ring true? And what if his stated intention to clear his name was nothing more than words spoken for her benefit, when what he really intended was to take the money his parents were sending and disappear?

Her doubts continued to nibble away at her. Each passing

mile brought them closer to their destination—and brought her closer to facing the fact that she might have made a horrible mistake.

He began to study the directions Scott had given her, and suddenly he announced that the turnoff should be coming up soon. She slowed for a sharp curve. Both of them were watching for the gravel road, but still they nearly missed it. She braked sharply, threw the car into reverse and turned onto the unmarked road.

"If this is it, we should come to a fork pretty quickly," he told her. And then, when they did, he told her to go left.

After several more turns, they were on a dirt road just barely wide enough for one car, with the woods pressing close on both sides. Nowhere had they seen any signs. She guessed it was one of those places where if you didn't know where you were going, you had no business being there in the first place, which pretty well defined her feelings at the moment.

"Where do those other roads go?" she asked, thinking nervously that it was like a maze back here. If they were on the wrong road, how would they ever find their way back?

"Nowhere, as far as I can tell," he said as he studied both Scott's map and a road map he'd gotten from her glove compartment. "Most of them are probably old logging roads or service roads into state lands. Or some of them could lead to other cabins."

"Scott told me that if I ever wanted to get away from it all, this is the place. But I didn't expect it to be *this* isolated."

They crawled along the deeply rutted road, and suddenly a cabin loomed ahead, directly in front of them at the road's end.

"That can't be it," she said unhappily as her worst fears were confirmed. "Scott's cabin is an A-frame."

"We're on the right road," he said confidently. "This is the other cabin he told you about. The road to his place must be here somewhere."

She cast him a sidelong glance, thinking every man she'd ever known refused to admit being lost. She was about to tell him just that as she pulled into the cleared space in front of the cabin, clearly the end of the road.

"Back up and aim your headlights in that direction," he told her, pointing toward the rear of the cabin.

"Why will men never admit—" She stopped her complaint as she saw that the road continued around the cabin and into the woods at the back.

"You were saying?" he asked dryly.

She didn't bother to reply as she let the car settle into the deep ruts and carry them perhaps another half-mile, where the pseudo-road ended at a small A-frame tucked against the base of a steep mountain and surrounded by tall oaks and hemlocks.

When she turned off the engine, total darkness descended upon them until Zach switched on the flashlight. She stepped out of the car into a cool, fragrant and very silent night. The beam illuminated only a narrow space as they walked to the door, and somehow that made the surrounding darkness seem even more threatening.

She unlocked the door. Musty air that smelled strongly of wood smoke rushed out at them. Zach stepped through the doorway first, then played the light over pale wood and a motley assortment of furnishings that had obviously been chosen for comfort rather than for esthetic purposes.

A disproportionately large stone fireplace and chimney rose from the center of the open space. In front of it was a bright, thick rya rug and an assortment of big pillows. Spotlighted by the beam, they gave off an air of sensuality and intimacy that made C.Z. look away quickly.

A sleeping loft extended from the rear of the house, and

beneath it was a small kitchen. Two areas were partitioned off, one at the rear and one along the right side, which she assumed must be the bathroom.

"I'll get a fire going," Zach said. "Why don't you see if you can find some matches to light those oil lamps?"

He set the flashlight on a table and moved toward the fireplace, stepping around the pillows to reach for a pile of newspapers stacked neatly next to the hearth. A large stack of firewood was fitted into a wrought-iron rack on the other side.

For a moment, C.Z. didn't move as she watched him, thinking again how little she knew about him. But even with the cold, harsh reality of what she'd done inundating her, she still felt that powerful attraction to him. She turned away quickly, before her imagination could get too carried away.

She found a big box of matches on the kitchen counter, together with several oil lamps. After lighting them, she carried one of them, along with the box of matches, to Zach. He was crouched in front of the grate, laying the fire.

In the flickering light of the oil lamp his battered face took on a scary harshness, and his pale eyes seemed to glitter as he turned to her. Her hand trembled slightly as she handed him the matches, but if he noticed, he gave no indication as he took them and turned to the fire.

She turned to the kitchen and picked up the other lamp, then carried it with her to the door that did indeed lead to a small bathroom. Her footsteps and even her breathing seemed to echo in the silence of the house. After closing the door behind her, she stared at her reflection in the mirror over the sink.

The face that stared at her looked haunted—as well it might, she thought grimly. The large, thick-lashed hazel eyes that regarded her solemnly seemed to be saying they didn't recognize this woman. Surely this couldn't be the cautious, by-the-book woman who'd studied hard to gain entry into her chosen profession, who always looked carefully before she leaped into anything. *That* woman would not be here in her friend's isolated cabin with an escaped felon she barely knew.

And yet the other woman was there, as well, the woman who had recognized, at some impossibly deep level, that this man was worth it, that they were bound together in some as yet undefined manner.

She ran her fingers nervously through her chestnut curls, thinking irrationally about the hairdresser's appointment she would miss in the morning. And there were errands to run—her VCR to be picked up at the repair shop, clothing to be taken to the dry cleaners, a shopping trip to find a new winter coat.

It comforted her to think about those ordinary things that made up a normal life, the life that had been hers until yesterday. But now, having made a sudden detour from the familiar path of her life, she found herself in new, uncharted territory.

When she returned to the main room, the fire was blazing and Zach was nowhere to be seen. Then she heard his footsteps in the loft, and a moment later he came down the spiral staircase.

"Does your friend own a gun?" he asked.

"I doubt it. Is one really necessary?" she asked in a voice that sounded—to her, at least—close to hysteria.

He studied her in silence, then gave her a crooked grin. "Between the army and being a cop, I've carried one all my adult life. Believe it or not, when they put me in jail, that's what I missed the most—not the lack of freedom, but that little bit of extra weight."

She nodded. She *did* understand, though she didn't like what it seemed to be saying about him. And yet she thought about her father and his ever-present gun. She still had it, packed away with his personal papers she hadn't yet dealt with. She had given away his clothing and many other items—and yet she'd been unable to sell or give away his gun. It had seemed far more personal than any of those other things.

Zach wandered into the kitchen and filled a kettle with water, then turned on the stove. "Bottled gas," he commented. "He probably has that for the hot water, too, but there must be a generator because he's got some outlets and a refrigerator."

"There is," she told him, recalling that Scott had mentioned it. "It's probably back there," she said, gesturing to the door at the rear of the house.

Zach went out, and while he got the generator going, she found some instant coffee and fixed some for them, then checked the food supplies. There wasn't much—canned goods and basics like sugar and salt. She'd have to buy some things for him.

She thought about her own grocery list, tacked to her refrigerator door. At this point, she didn't know which seemed more real to her—her quiet, organized life or the confusion and danger of the moment.

Then Zach returned, and when she turned to hand him a mug of coffee, she found him staring at her in that quiet, intense way that never failed to send her thoughts spinning into erotic fantasies. She'd never been quite certain what that look meant—and she wasn't now, either.

She felt a sharp stab of longing for the safety of those other times, when she could let her mind roam through her fantasies about him knowing they couldn't possibly come true.

They sat down amidst the pillows in front of the cheerfully blazing fire that was already taking the chill off the air in the cabin. The distance between them was probably about the same as had existed in her office, but there the similarity ended. Instead, she was edging dangerously close to some of those fantasies.

"You should get some sleep and then go home," he said, his gaze fixed firmly on her. "I'll have to ask you to come back to bring me the money and some food, but then you'll be out of it."

She was too stunned and too hurt to speak immediately. He was dismissing her, pushing her out of his life. Never mind that she'd been questioning her involvement herself.

"But what will you do?" she asked. "You don't even have a car."

"I'm going to have to hole up for a while anyway," he pointed out. "After a week or so, the search will end. They won't give up, but they won't really be looking for me all that hard, either. Anyway, there's an old Jeep in a shed out back. Do you know if it runs?"

She shook her head. "I didn't even know it was there. Scott didn't mention it."

"It has a current license and inspection, and the keys are probably around somewhere."

"But what are you going to *do*, Zach? I don't see how you can possibly clear yourself when you can't show your face anywhere around here."

"The first thing I need is a disguise. I'll figure out something."

"Maybe I could help you with that," she said slowly. "When I was in college, I got involved with a drama group. We all did a bit of everything—including makeup."

"I was offering you a way out, C.Z.—not a way to get yourself into trouble."

When she said nothing, he went on. "Even now, there's nothing to connect you to me. You're still safe."

"I want to help you."

"Why?"

She stared at him, once again startled into silence. He

was asking the one question she hadn't been able to answer for herself.

"Is it because that's your profession, helping people?"

She laughed nervously. She'd asked herself that question, too. "My profession doesn't exactly extend to helping convicted criminals escape from prison."

Her ill-considered words hung in the brief silence between them, unable to be taken back, even though she wanted very much to do just that.

"I mean, I know you're innocent, but…"

"*Do* you know that?" he asked, tilting his head to one side and regarding her thoughtfully. "I never told you the whole story."

A chill swept through her, and she hurriedly set down her mug before he could see her hand trembling. His ice-blue eyes bored into her, and she knew he could see her doubts, no matter how much she tried to hide them.

"I *am* innocent," he said firmly. "If I'd wanted to kill Summers, he'd be dead. I shot to disarm him. That was the only line of defense I wanted my lawyer to pursue. He used my military and police records to prove that I'm a crack shot and that if I'd really wanted to kill Summers, I would have." He shrugged. "Unfortunately, the jury didn't buy it—and I can't blame them for that."

He said that Harvey Summers, the longtime county commissioner, had been against hiring him from the beginning. He had wanted Dave Colby, a veteran of the force, to be appointed chief. But Summers was outvoted by the other two commissioners, who were impressed with Zach's record and felt he could bring a new level of professionalism to a county that was beginning to see an increase in population and an increase in serious crime.

From the beginning, Summers had tried to make life difficult for Zach, questioning his decisions and pushing him to make arrests without sufficient evidence. Matters had come to a head when the fourteen-year-old daughter of a prominent local businessman was raped. The rapist had worn a ski mask, but the girl thought she knew who he was, a twenty-year-old ne'er-do-well with a record of minor arrests but no previous sexual assaults.

Zach had taken it slow, letting the suspect know he was under investigation as a way of preventing further trouble while he tried to build a case against him. The young man maintained his innocence and had an alibi of sorts, a friend he claimed to be with when the assault took place.

Harvey Summers had kept pressing for an arrest, even to the point of ignoring the district attorney, who agreed with Zach. The victim's father was an old friend of Summers.

"He and I got into a shouting match over the thing," Zach said, "in front of a lot of witnesses. I shouldn't have shot off my mouth, but I was frustrated over the case myself—especially since it was beginning to look like I'd been pursuing the wrong suspect.

"Summers said he was going to get me fired if it was the last thing he did, and I told him to butt out of it or it just might *be* the last thing he did."

A week later, Zach's caution proved to have been correct when another young man was brought in for questioning and confessed. And just days after that, Summers called Zach and asked him to meet him at Summers's hunting camp outside town that evening. Zach went, figuring Summers wanted to make peace. He didn't question Summers's choice of a meeting place because it was on Zach's way home.

"When I got there," Zach continued, "the place was dark and there was no sign of Summers. I figured he was just playing games—making me wait. So I got out of my Cherokee and was just standing there, waiting for him to show up, when someone took a shot at me—and barely missed me.

"At that point, I was too busy trying to save my hide to give much thought to who it might be. It was just after dark, and I couldn't see who it was. He fired again, and this time, I figured out where he was and went after him and shot him, but only after I'd warned him. I aimed for his gun arm, and that's where I got him, in the shoulder.

"Then, just as I was going to see who it was, headlights came up the road and suddenly someone was yelling, 'Police! Drop it!' It was Colby, my deputy, and Summers was the one who'd shot me."

Zach paused, sipping his coffee as he stared into the fire. "The rest you can probably guess. Summers denied he'd set up the meeting with me and that he'd shot at me. He claimed I must have known he'd be there for his regular weekly poker game. Colby backed up everything he said. He was one of the regulars at the game.

"At the trial, they had plenty of witnesses who said that I'd threatened Summers when he said he was going to get me fired, and Colby threw in some lies to add to it.

"The jury was out for a long time, but in the end, they convicted me. My attorney said my biggest problem was that I hadn't fit into the community yet. People didn't know me well, and of course they all know Summers and Colby. He tried to get a change of venue, but the judge wouldn't go for it. He's still appealing, but he doesn't expect to get anywhere."

"And you have no idea why the two of them would frame you?" C.Z. asked. She knew both men, though not well. Colby had worked for her father, too, and she could recall her dad complaining about him a few times, saying he was incompetent.

Harvey Summers was another matter altogether. Her father had liked him, as did everyone else, apparently. She could remember how kind he'd been at the time of her father's death. He'd even offered to help her clear out her father's house, though in the end, she'd done it herself, with the assistance of her father's attorney and close friend.

Zach shook his head. "Like I said, he let me know from the beginning that he disapproved of my being hired. I know he wanted Colby to get the job, but there has to be more to it than that."

"Colby *is* the chief now, isn't he?" she asked.

Zach nodded, then smiled the kind of smile that reminded her of just how dangerous this man could be. "Those two aren't going to be sleeping too well when they find out I'm on the loose."

C.Z. frowned. "It would make a lot more sense if Colby was the one who shot at you. After all, he had something to gain if you were arrested—or dead."

"Right, but the really weird thing is that I don't think Colby expected me to be there. I can't be sure, but there was something in the way he reacted when he saw it was me that told me he wasn't part of it at that point."

"And yet you said that he backed up Summers's story?"

"He did—and even added to it. Colby's incompetent. The guy couldn't catch a criminal if he had a smoking gun in his hand and was standing over the body—but there's a big difference between being incompetent and being an outright liar. He knew Summers had a gun. It was lying there where he dropped it when I shot him. But he lied about it."

"Maybe he was just being opportunistic. Harvey Summers probably told him your job could be his if he went along with the lie."

Zach nodded. "That's the obvious explanation, but I don't know. I never really got the impression Colby wanted the chief's job all that much. In his own way, I think he knew he couldn't handle it. He even said as much to me once.''

''Could Harvey have some hold over Colby that he used to blackmail him into going along with it?''

''That's what I've been thinking, but even if it's true, it doesn't answer the more important question—why Summers tried to kill me in the first place. I keep thinking there must be something Summers was worried I'd find out about. If he'd gotten Colby appointed, he could have kept it under wraps—but I was a loose cannon.''

Zach heaved a sigh. ''I don't know what it could be, and I've had a lot of time to think about it. Official corruption of some kind is the most obvious possibility, but Summers is only one of three commissioners and he can't act alone. I got to know the other two pretty well, and I can't see either of them going along with anything illegal.''

''Is Mary Williams still a commissioner?'' C.Z. asked.

Zach nodded. ''You know her?''

''Slightly. She and her family lived next door when I was little. Her husband died a few years before Dad died, and she said something at his funeral that made me think they might have been seeing each other, even though Dad never mentioned it.''

''I think they were,'' Zach said. ''I heard about it somewhere, though I don't think it had been going on for very long. She's a nice person. She came to see me in jail before the trial.''

He stared silently into the fire for a moment, then abruptly stood and turned to her. ''We both need some sleep, and then you've got to go home. It isn't likely anyone will be coming to your home to ask you questions, but you need to be prepared for that.''

He gestured toward the loft. ''You take the bed. I'll sack out on the sofa.''

She got to her feet, too, surprised at his abrupt tone. But

before she could say anything, he had gathered their mugs and carried them to the kitchen. After that, he went into the bathroom, closing the door behind him without another word to her.

He was right, of course. It was three o'clock. They were both tired. But his abrupt dismissal still rankled. Each time she felt she was getting close to him, he backed off—and he wasn't subtle about it.

Nevertheless, she knew that now was not the time for her to criticize his shortcomings. He was both a cop and a fugitive, and she guessed that the two parts of him were almost certainly at war with each other. So she climbed the spiral staircase to the loft—only to find that she, too, was at war with herself.

The big bed filled most of the space—and filled her mind with the fantasies she'd managed to set aside for a time downstairs. If only she didn't remember those moments in his hospital room so well! If only his kisses hadn't lived up to her fantasies—and then some!

"If there's an extra blanket up there, toss it down," he called from below. In truth, his tone was matter-of-fact, but what she heard was a taunt.

She opened the closet and found several neatly folded blankets on the shelf. Was he waiting for her to make the first move? Should she do that? Fantasies were so simple— and reality was so complicated. She thought it surpassingly strange that she should be feeling such hesitance considering what she'd done to get them to this place.

She took a blanket from the shelf and walked to the railing that overlooked the main room. He was standing there, his face raised to her. But in the dim, flickering light, she couldn't read his expression.

For one long moment, she didn't move. She was achingly aware of the man below her and the big bed behind her. Then she threw the blanket to him—and with that gesture, a decision had been made. She was retreating behind the barrier of the railing just as she had once stayed safely behind her desk.

SUNLIGHT FLOODED the A-frame, pouring in through the tall windows that filled most of the front wall. They had dealt with the issue of where and when she should pick up his money. They had discussed the possibility of her being questioned. They seemed to have little else to say to each other as they drank more coffee and ate the package of crackers he'd found in the cupboard.

C.Z. thought he seemed as wary as she felt. She would sneak glances at him when he wasn't looking, then avoid his gaze. She was sure he was doing the same. The silences seemed to be filled with questions not asked and with the silent clamor of needs unfulfilled. Everything seemed brittle, fragile—ready to shatter or explode.

She picked up her purse and announced that she was leaving and would return before dark, since even with Scott's map, she feared she might not be able to find the place again. He nodded and followed her to the door.

It felt as though *she* was the one escaping. She didn't know what it was she wanted from him, but whatever it was, she knew she wasn't going to get it. He'd built a wall between them, though she had to admit she'd contributed a few bricks.

She turned when she reached her car. He was standing on the small deck, his hands jammed into the pockets of his jeans as he watched her. The breeze ruffled his thick, black hair. The lower half of his battered face was shadowed by a day's growth of beard. He looked just like what he was—a tough, dangerous fugitive from the law—the kind of man her normal self would have given a very wide berth.

But instead, she found herself drawing in a sharp, quavering breath as she fought a wave of desire so powerful that, for a moment, she simply could not move. Her hand rested on the door handle as she struggled against that desire—and finally won. She climbed into the car and drove away quickly.

Chapter Three

Stop it! C.Z. ordered herself. *You're being paranoid.* Then she smiled grimly, recalling the old joke about even paranoiacs being right sometimes.

There was no police car in the lot when she returned to her condo, and there were no messages on her machine demanding that she account for herself. She'd seen only one police car during her journey home from the cabin—not the swarm of them she'd expected.

There had been mention of Zach's escape on the local radio news, but the announcer's laconic tones had ascribed no more importance to it than to the item that followed, about the governor's latest battle with the state legislature.

The clerk handed her her driver's license after writing down the number, then gave her a form to sign. Then he proceeded to count out more money than she'd ever seen at one time. Unable to shake her paranoia, C.Z. kept expecting the man to question her, even though transferring cash across the country was their business.

With the bulging envelope weighing down her purse more than it should, C.Z. forced herself to walk to her car without looking around to see if anyone was watching her. Then she set off to do her shopping.

When she arrived at her condo, she closed the door behind her and sighed with relief. No police. No questions.

No one following her. She was safe, after all—just as Zach had said.

Then the phone rang, driving out the image of him standing on the deck of the cabin. She debated letting the machine pick it up, then hurried to the kitchen to grab it. It was Jack Sanford, her boss. Not exactly the police, but not a call she wanted, either.

"Hollis escaped from the hospital last night," he informed her.

"Yes. I just heard about it on the radio." Could he have been asked to call her?

"Did you see him yesterday?"

C.Z. confirmed that she had. "He was really worried about going back to the prison. He told me they were planning to discharge all of them today."

"I can't say I blame him for escaping, under the circumstances," Jack said. "I just thought you'd better be prepared to answer some questions when they find out you visited him. He didn't hint at any plans to escape, did he?"

"No, of course not. But I guess I'm not really surprised," she added hastily. "He's very determined to clear his name and he struck me as being very resourceful. He was with the Army's Special Forces, you know, and I think they're trained for all sorts of things."

"Do you think he's innocent?" Jack asked curiously.

C.Z. hesitated. If she said yes and he passed that on to anyone, it could cast suspicion on her. But she could not bring herself to lie any more than she already had.

"I don't know, but based on what I've read in his file and what he told me, I think there's a very good chance that he is."

It wasn't exactly a ringing defense of Zach, but it *was* honest. She'd replayed his story endlessly, and still she wasn't completely sure.

"Well, if he is, then I wish him luck. It happens sometimes. The jury system's far from perfect. I only interviewed him that one time, but he impressed me as being the classic cop type, not a killer—and very bright, besides. At times, I wasn't sure just who was conducting the interview. I'll see you on Tuesday, then. If anyone questions you and you need my help, I'll be home all weekend.''

C.Z. thanked him and hung up, thinking about what he'd said—especially his last comment. It was one of the things that troubled her about Zach. According to him, he'd never taken a single course in psychology, and yet he seemed to have an instinctive understanding of human motivations and weaknesses. And she couldn't help wondering if he had put that understanding to good use when it came to her.

He'd said at one point that she'd helped him because helping people was her business. Had he counted on that—plus her attraction to him? Was she kidding herself when she thought he was attracted to her?

Suddenly, she was very glad she'd gotten into her car and left when every fiber of her being was screaming out at her to go back to him. But it was only a temporary reprieve. The battle between a body that wanted him and a mind that told her he was dangerous was far from over.

She put away her groceries, separating the things she would be taking to the cabin, then went upstairs to pack a bag. She would be spending two days—and two nights—with him. Surely in that time, she could come to some conclusions.

She had already loaded the car when she started to run back for her father's gun. She hesitated, wondering if she should. She was uneasy about him having a gun. If they somehow found Zach, she didn't want to be responsible for anyone being harmed.

Then she thought about what he'd said, that giving up his gun was worse than being confined to a cell. She didn't understand that on an intellectual level, but she *did* understand it on a deeper level because of her father. She went inside and got a kitchen stool, then carried it upstairs to the trapdoor that led to her attic storage space.

Standing at the top of the ladder, she grabbed the pull chain that switched on the single light bulb. Then she winced. Her storage space was a mess, a case of out of sight, out of mind plus a dose of pack-rat mentality. The small space was nearly filled with boxes of notes and mementos from college, clothes she should have discarded long ago and four sealed boxes of her father's belongings—boxes that had been packed for her by his attorney after he'd gotten the financial records he needed to settle the estate.

She could no longer recall which box contained the gun, though she remembered well her reluctance to sell it as the attorney had suggested. Instead, she'd stuffed it into a box he'd already packed. The shock of her father's sudden death in the midst of her grueling graduate program had resulted in C.Z.'s failure to be her usual organized self.

The first box she opened contained only files, so she resealed it and turned to the next one, wondering guiltily how many times she'd promised herself she was going to come up here and go through the boxes to see if there was anything worth saving. But perhaps that time hadn't yet come. Seeing her father's bold but neat handwriting brought tears to her eyes. She had neglected him during what had turned out to be the last year of his life. But at the time, she'd thought she would be able to make it up to him when her graduate work was finished.

Naturally, the gun was in the last box, together with a heavy box of ammunition and the gun-cleaning kit. The gun was still in the holster attached to the shoulder harness her father had worn since he'd been promoted from uniform to detective.

She picked it up, thinking about the accident that had

cost him his life and wishing he could be here now to advise her. Of course, if he *were* here now, Zach would have stayed with the NYPD or gone somewhere else, and none of this would have happened.

She slung the harness across her shoulder, picked up the box of ammunition and the cleaning kit and made her way down the ladder, her thoughts on her father.

He'd said very little about Zach that day he'd walked her out to the car after breakfast, but she remembered thinking he'd seemed to like him a lot. Still, would he agree with what Zach had done—even if he was innocent?

C.Z. knew that among the complex reasons she'd decided to help Zach was that her father had liked him—and the two of them were much alike. She'd neglected her father for the last year of his life—was this her way of making up for that?

She grimaced. It was the kind of question only a psychologist would ask, but she suspected there just might be some truth there.

Lost in thought, she started for the front door, stopping only when she realized that she was, as it were, armed to the teeth. She put the gun into a plastic bag, then smiled and greeted a neighbor as she walked out with her deadly cargo.

As she drove to the cabin, each mile seemed to be filling her with an eagerness to be with him again. It was obvious that she simply could not be rational where Zach was concerned. He had turned her world upside down and inside out and had drawn her into another place altogether, a strange world of danger and eroticism where she scarcely recognized herself.

She was less than five miles from the turnoff to the cabin when she saw the police car. Her eagerness to see Zach vanished beneath an onslaught of icy fear. The car was sitting at an intersection, and when she drove past, it pulled out behind her. She thought about the clothing she'd bought for Zach, about the thousands of dollars in her purse—and about the gun in the plastic bag.

If they stopped her, could they search her car? Didn't they have to have a reason? She was angry with herself for being so frightened. The only emotion she'd ever felt toward the police was reassurance, a sense they were doing their job, and she was therefore being protected.

But now it was different. She wondered how anyone could contemplate a criminal act when the result was the terror she was feeling now. Were they wondering what she was doing on this deserted road only used by a few locals? Might they even now be calling in her license number? Could she already be on some list of possible suspects who had aided Zach in his escape?

The cabin was not in Ondago County, where both her father and Zach had been chief, but was just over the line in a neighboring county. Still, she was fairly certain the insignia she'd seen on the car was the one she remembered from her father's car.

Fear prickled her spine, and her hands were sweating as she gripped the wheel. Her gaze shifted constantly from the rearview mirror to the speedometer and back again. At any moment, she expected to hear a siren or see flashing lights.

Daughter of Former Police Chief Aids Convict's Escape. She could see the headline now—perhaps with a subhead about a lovelorn psychologist falling for a handsome ex-police chief.

Ahead of her was the curve and beyond it the turnoff to the cabin. She wanted nothing more than to run to the safety of Zach's arms—which was totally absurd, since his arms were anything but safe. And yet, such was the power of his presence that she truly believed she would be safe with him.

She passed the turnoff and continued along the winding

mountain road, trying to remember what lay ahead. There had to be at least five more miles before she would reach the small village of Neff's Mills. Any intersecting roads before that were likely to be gravel or dirt roads leading to hunting cabins or vacation homes.

She could pull into a gas station in Neff's Mills—assuming there was one. Probably there was. Not even the smallest village was without a combination gas station and convenience store. But what if the police car pulled in, too? Wouldn't they be very suspicious of any strangers in the area right now? And she *was* a stranger, even if she'd once lived here.

She drove on, trying out in her mind various excuses for the men's clothing and the money—ignoring the gun because she couldn't think of any explanation for that. She was pretty sure that carrying a handgun in her car was illegal.

Then there were lights ahead, and she was coming down a long hill into a tiny village. She reached the single traffic light as it turned red. She waited, praying the police car would turn onto the intersecting road. But when the light changed, it continued to follow her.

Then she saw a brightly lit gas station a half-block ahead and put on her turn signal before she could talk herself out of it. She would have to take her chances. Being a stranger shouldn't arouse too much curiosity. In recent years, many people from the city had begun to build weekend homes up here, and it was a holiday weekend.

For one exhilarating moment, she thought the cruiser would continue on its way, but then she saw its signal begin to wink. So terrified she could scarcely draw a breath, C.Z. pulled up to the self-service gas pumps. The cruiser pulled up near the entrance to the convenience store.

The single officer inside got out as she got out to go to the pump. She could see the insignia clearly now, and it *was* an Ondago County car. She didn't recognize the young officer, but she knew he might recognize *her*. All her father's men had attended his funeral, and she knew that, being cops, they had long memories.

They exchanged brief glances and then he went into the store. C.Z.'s hands were shaking so badly she nearly spilled gas all over herself. The tank was nearly half-full, and she worried the cop might see that from the display inside and wonder why she'd stopped. She stopped trying to tell herself how irrational she was being.

The officer was still inside, talking to the clerk, when she replaced the gas cap and got out her purse. *Don't ignore him,* she warned herself as she started across the lot to the store. *Maybe you should even flirt a bit. It worked with the guard at the hospital.*

Both men turned toward her as she pushed open the door. She managed to fix what she hoped was a pleasant but neutral expression on her face, though she felt the movement of every tiny muscle. Her legs were trembling, but somehow she managed to walk to the counter.

The clerk glanced at the device that showed the amount she owed. The officer stepped back to make room for her at the counter. She could feel his eyes on her, and she thought about her father telling her how easy it was to spot someone who was trying to hide something.

She handed the clerk her money. Her gaze dropped to the counter—and she froze. Staring at her was a large black and white photograph of Zach!

It was a head shot, professionally posed and an excellent likeness. Above it, in bold print, was the word 'Wanted,' and below it a warning that he should be considered armed and dangerous, together with a phone number.

Her hand had frozen in place, and the clerk was giving her her change. Her mouth had gone dry, and she could see the tremors in her hand as she fumbled to put away her change. Some coins clattered to the floor, and before she could bend to retrieve them, the officer got them for her. She managed to smile and murmur thanks.

She became convinced he was going to follow her out to her car, so instead of leaving, she made her way over to the refrigerated cases that lined one wall. Behind her, the two men resumed their conversation.

"He'd have to be nuts to come back here," the clerk said.

"Yeah, but you never know," the officer replied.

"You must have known him pretty well," the clerk remarked.

"Sure. He hired me just a couple of months before it happened. Hard to figure. I really liked the guy. Most of the others did, too—except for Colby. We all figure he went back to the city, but Chief Colby is convinced he's around here somewhere."

"What did Colby have against him—before it happened, I mean?"

Unfortunately, the clerk's question went unanswered as a group of young men came in, laughing and talking loudly. C.Z. took a bottle of fruit juice from the case and went to the counter to pay for it, stealing another glance at Zach's photo in the process. It really was an excellent likeness. Probably he'd had it taken for publicity purposes when he was named chief. Even in black and white, his remarkable eyes stood out.

She pushed through the door and started across the lot, fearful the officer would follow her. She risked a backward glance as she reached her car. He was pouring himself a cup of coffee from the machine opposite the counter.

She sighed with relief as she slid into the car, then started it and rolled toward the street. As she began to turn the wheel, she realized he might notice if she went back the way she'd come. So she turned in the other direction, and after several more turns through back streets, she was on her way to the cabin, her gaze once again shifting constantly from the road to the rearview mirror.

WHEN SHE REACHED the cabin, there were no lights showing, and she traded her fear of exposure for the fear that Zach had vanished. But how could he? Where could he go?

Cautiously, she opened the car door, leaving the engine and lights on. As she stepped out, a shadowy figure emerged from the darkness at the side of the A-frame. A scream had started to well up in her when he called out.

"It's me. Just being careful. I saw your lights as soon as you drove up to the other cabin."

C.Z. sagged against the car door, no longer trusting her legs to support her. Zach reached past her to switch off the engine and the lights, then went around to open the trunk. Her fear turned rapidly to annoyance. Couldn't he see how terrified she was?

"Food!" He proclaimed as he lifted the first of the bags from the trunk. "The cupboards are bare here."

She walked toward him, fighting her anger. It was *her* fault, after all. He had told her to get out. She had no right to expect his sympathy.

He reached into the trunk for a second bag, then stopped as his gaze swept over her. He set down both bags. "Something happened."

She nodded, not trusting herself to speak. He hesitated, then reached out to her, a slow, tentative movement, as though he feared she would reject him. And she almost did. In her mind's eye, she was seeing that flyer at the convenience store, and the words "armed and dangerous."

"Charlie," he said softly, taking her hand, and then, when she didn't resist, drawing her carefully into his arms, treating her as though she were made of glass, which wasn't far from the way she felt at the moment.

He felt so good—so solid and reassuring and safe. She didn't understand how she could be feeling this, but within seconds, she wasn't even trying to understand it. Instead, she was back to those moments in his hospital room when a raging hunger had very nearly burned away all reason.

"The groceries can wait," he said, releasing her and then taking her hand to lead her inside.

She wasn't exactly sure what he meant, though her body seemed to know. He led her to the cushions in front of the fireplace, then lit some kindling and turned on a lamp, as well.

"Your friend has good taste in cognac. Do you want some?"

She nodded, still not sure what he intended and what she wanted.

He brought two large snifters, then sat beside her. "Tell me."

Only when it was clear that what he wanted was an explanation did she realize she wasn't yet ready to take that final step into intimacy. Did he know that—or hadn't he even been thinking about it?

So she told him what had happened, the words pouring out in a great rush, interrupted by a coughing spasm as she drank too much cognac too quickly. He patted her on the back gently.

"Cognac is meant to be sipped, not gulped. Do you want some water?"

She shook her head. "I know that. I just…wasn't thinking. I'll never wonder again how people can come to have such irrational fears."

"Welcome to the wonderful world of paranoia," he replied dryly. "But in this case, it's a healthy response."

She stared at him over the rim of the snifter. "Who's the psychologist here?"

He chuckled. "Okay, I'll admit that I once bought some

textbooks and studied them on my own. I didn't have the time or patience to take courses. But you weren't being irrational. If that officer had had more experience, he'd probably have questioned you. He would have noticed your behavior. On the other hand, you might have concealed it better than you thought.''

His gaze remained fixed on her steadily. "In a way, I'm glad it happened. I don't know what you've decided, but at least now you understand what it will be like if you...stay involved with me.''

It was that brief hesitation she heard far more than his words. It told her the uncertainty wasn't hers alone. He wanted her help, but it troubled him, too.

"You *need* my help, Zach—now more than ever with Colby so sure you're here.''

He studied her for a moment in silence and she saw not his face scant inches from hers but that flyer again and those words. It felt surreal. How could she, who'd never even gotten a speeding ticket, be here with a man who was wanted by the police?

"There *is* one more way you can help me," he said slowly, "and then I want you to go home and stay there.''

"What's that?" she asked, ignoring his final words. Despite what had happened, she knew she wasn't going to walk away from him. She couldn't. Life with him would certainly be dangerous—but life without him was unthinkable. The certainty of that shocked her, yet there it was.

"You mentioned you'd worked in theatre and you might be able to help me disguise myself. If you can do that, it would mean I can move around—at least to some extent.''

He rubbed a hand across his stubbly cheek. "When my beard comes in, it'll be gray—all gray. I grew one once a couple of years ago, when I was up here at my place recovering from a gunshot wound. That should help with the disguise, but it won't be enough.''

C.Z. nodded. "It will help," she agreed. "But it's your eyes, Zach. Even in the black and white photo, that's what people will notice first."

He laughed. "Yeah, my biggest asset. The guys in the precinct used to call me Ice Eyes. They work pretty well against suspects."

"And with women, too," she said, then immediately regretted it.

He smiled at her. "That, too. So what about them? Could I get some plain contact lenses to change them?"

"Yes, but I won't be able to get them for you. They have to be fitted to your eyes."

He nodded. "Then I'll get them in the city. I need to go down there anyway, to get some new ID."

She gave him a blank look, and he explained. "All it takes is money and you can get whatever you want, driver's license, Social Security card, credit cards. But first I need to work on my face. I should have a decent beard by the end of next week, and the cut will have healed well enough by then, too."

She studied him. "If I get you a gray wig to go with the beard, that and the contact lenses should do it."

"Where can you get a wig?"

"There's a store in Poughkeepsie that supplies the drama groups at Vassar College. I went there for my undergraduate work. And the store's open on Sundays, so I can go tomorrow."

"You're not getting out, are you?"

"No, I'm not." *But don't ask me why,* she pleaded silently. *I'm not ready to talk about that.*

Perhaps he wasn't, either, because he stood and said he would bring in the groceries. She sat, staring into the fire and sipping cognac. Was she in love with him? Was that possible? She didn't know, and she decided it was time to stop trying to find reasons for this madness. She would help him to the extent she could—which would be very little, since she had a job several hours away—and then, if he managed to prove his innocence, she would see what developed.

There were many stories about people thrown together by circumstance who developed intense relationships only to have them fall apart when they resumed their normal lives. It was a primitive bonding born of mutual dependence and need, perfectly understandable to any psychologist.

She began to feel much better, and when Zach brought in the groceries, she volunteered to fix dinner for them. She was unpacking the bags when she saw him take the gun out of the plastic bag. He examined it with a sound of satisfaction.

"It's the same model I had," he pronounced.

C.Z. stared at the gun, her thoughts veering to her father. What would he say if he knew she was doing this? He'd had enormous respect for the law, but he'd also said on more than one occasion that the law wasn't always just.

Zach glanced at her as she tried to blink away the tears that had suddenly filled her eyes. She managed to smile. "Sorry. It's my dad's. You'd think by now I'd be over his death. Most of the time, I am. But it was just so sudden and so…pointless."

He nodded. "Yeah, I heard about it when I came up the following weekend. I don't hunt myself, but from what I knew of him, he was a careful man. Hunting accidents are sort of the rural version of drive-by shootings."

"He *was* careful—careful about where he hunted and about wearing the right clothes. He knew more than most people what can happen because he'd investigated a number of hunting accidents. The men who were with him never saw the hunter who shot him. They said he must have been using a really high-powered rifle. And everyone said the killer was probably some idiot from the city, out to shoot anything that moved, even if it walked upright and was wearing fluorescent orange. There had been a similar shooting the previous year, but Dad caught the guy.

"What bothers me most is that I'd spent so little time with him. I was so selfish. I had my life in Rochester and then college and grad school, and so many times when he wanted me to come visit him, I had a reason I couldn't come. He came to see me, though, and he called me every week."

She was standing on one side of the island counter while he sat on a stool on the other side. He reached out to take her hand. "I don't think he'd want you to be carrying around a load of guilt, C.Z. Let it go."

She nodded. "You're right. He wouldn't." She withdrew her hand and returned to her dinner preparations, then asked him why he'd decided to leave the NYPD to come up here.

"Believe it or not, I started to think about it after your father's death. Before I could decide, they appointed Strasser. Then, when I found out he had to retire on disability, I made up my mind.

"The work was getting to me. I was in homicide, one horrible mess after another, day after day. I looked at the older guys and saw that half of them had been through a couple of marriages and were on their way to alcoholism— and the other half had become so cynical they couldn't enjoy their off-duty hours. I'd been shot at four times and hit once, and I wondered how much longer my luck would hold out.

"Your dad came over sometimes when I was up here. He'd talk about his work, and it sounded to me like the kind of work I'd wanted when I decided to become a cop. He tried to talk me into taking a deputy's position when one came up, but I wasn't ready to make the move and the pay wasn't good enough."

"After you took the job, were you happy?" she asked curiously.

"Yeah, I liked it a lot—except for Summers, that is. And Colby, although he wasn't any worse than a few I'd worked with in the city. I liked living up here, but I knew it was going to take a long time to fit in.

"The only real friend I made was Sam Gittings, the lawyer who ended up defending me. We went fishing together and played some chess. I've been trying to decide whether to ask him for some help. He knows I'm innocent and he's still trying to prove it. But I'd be putting him into a bad situation if I made contact with him."

"I know Sam—or at least I did. We grew up in the same neighborhood. His father was dad's attorney and friend." She didn't add that she'd gone out with Sam a few times when she was visiting her father in the summers.

"Maybe I could talk to him," she went on. "That way, I could find out if he's learned anything. And if I don't tell him where you are, he can't get into trouble."

"That's cutting it pretty fine," Zach said. "Even if you don't tell him where I am, it'll be obvious that you know—and he should report that."

"But *would* he report it?"

Zach shook his head. "No, I don't think he would. He was pretty upset about my conviction."

"Plus he knows me, and that would make it more difficult for him to turn me in. Zach, the problem is that you need the help of someone who knows the community, who can make a guess about why Harvey Summers would try to kill you. He was against your being hired in the first place, so it isn't likely to be something that happened after you took the job."

Zach nodded. "Whatever it is, it goes back a ways—and it also must involve Colby. Or maybe not. Maybe Summers has another hold over Colby."

"I have an old friend I know I can trust. She's a teacher in the high school, and her father's a good friend of Harvey Summers's. In fact, I think they're distantly related. Her name's Stacey Robbins."

"I know who she is. She had me in to talk to her class about drugs."

"I think that what we're looking for are skeletons in closets—most likely Harvey Summers's closet. And if there are any there, I can guarantee you there are people who know about them. There've been a lot of new people move into the area in recent years, but the old-timers all know each other well. It's a close-knit, closed circle."

Zach chuckled as he set aside the gun he'd started to clean. "This is beginning to remind me of a conversation we had before, that morning at the diner, when we were arguing about how to catch the drunk who killed those kids in the school bus."

"Are you willing to admit that I was right?" she asked archly.

"Yeah, I am. I knew you were right then, too. I just wanted to get a rise out of you because you were sitting there so calm and cool, while I..." His voice trailed off as their eyes met.

"While I was anything but calm and cool," he went on. "I wanted to call you after that, but it seemed kind of complicated. I was in the city and you were up in New Haven, and then there was your father. I knew he liked me, and I thought maybe he even wanted to get us together, but..." He shrugged.

"Circumstances," she said.

"Yeah," he agreed. "Circumstances—and we still have that problem."

"DO YOU THINK maybe you could trim it a bit?"

C.Z. smiled and shook her head. "It's fine just as it is—

or it will be when your beard grows in.''

"I look like some damned middle-aged hippie—like a Deadhead.'' He pulled off the wig and looked at it as though it were some particularly loathsome animal.

"Exactly! That's the whole idea,'' she explained. "What you want is a disguise that not only changes your looks but also changes the way people think about you. I went to Goodwill and got you some old clothes, too.''

"Hmm,'' he said, regarding her thoughtfully. "Maybe you've got a point. It's kind of like when I was working street crimes and disguised myself as a homeless person.''

"That's it,'' she said, nodding, amused to see that he could consider the idea only when he thought of it in cop terms.

He grimaced. "Just as long as I can still take showers. I don't have to smell bad, too, do I?''

C.Z. laughed. "No, I don't think that will be necessary. You're an artist friend of Scott's who's borrowing his cabin while he's in Europe. It's a disguise that could hold up even if the cops show up here at some point.''

"The only problem is that I can't draw.''

"You won't have to. There are some half-finished canvases of Scott's in the closet up in the loft—probably things he was planning to discard. We'll prop one of them up on the easel. I bought some paints and brushes, too, since Scott didn't leave anything here. And I can teach you enough to sound knowledgeable—especially to someone who doesn't know anything about art.''

He nodded, then asked in a carefully neutral tone, "Uh, what's your relationship with this Scott?''

C.Z. barely managed to conceal a smile. It was the first reference he'd made to the possibility of a man in her life, and he was clearly doing his best to make it sound like a casual inquiry. *Careful* seemed to be the operative word for them. They were both skirting the issue of their relationship, but she suspected it was on his mind as much as it was on hers.

"Scott and I have been friends since grad school. We met through the drama group. He designed the sets." She paused for a beat, unable to resist tormenting him a bit. "Scott's gay."

"Oh." His eyes met hers only briefly, but there was no mistaking his relief.

"There isn't anyone...in my life," she said, unable to bring herself to say "anyone *else*."

"Mine, either," he said after a brief pause. "There was someone in the city, but it ended after I moved up here."

Those declarations were followed by silence. Once more to the brink, she thought, amused and frustrated. It seemed that neither of them could get beyond the barriers they'd created.

Zach had turned his attention to the clothing she'd bought for his disguise. When she saw him examine the clothes with obvious distaste, she laughed. "Hippie artists do not buy their clothes at Brooks Brothers or Land's End."

"They're too big," he grumbled as he looked at the labels.

"No, they're not. You haven't seen *this* yet."

She picked up a shopping bag and drew out its contents. "This is body padding, so you can be a middle-aged, slightly overweight hippie."

"You didn't get carried away or anything, did you?" he asked dryly.

"Just wait until we put it all together. You won't recognize yourself."

"That's what I'm afraid of."

"Of course, you'll have to *act* the part, too," she went on.

"Meaning?" he asked, arching a dark brow.

"Meaning you have to practice not sounding like a cop. Take the edge out of your voice, relax your posture."

"Maybe it would be easier to disguise me as one of those weekend militia types."

"Perhaps so, but that could draw unwanted attention. You want to seem laid-back and nonthreatening—the opposite of what you are."

The words came out without thought. She was focusing on the role he would have to play, and then it was too late to take them back.

"It's pretty hard to act laid-back when you're the object of a manhunt," he observed with a grim smile. "And as for my being threatening…"

"I didn't mean that, exactly," she told him.

"Yes, you did. You still aren't sure about me, are you?"

His tone was neutral, but his ice-blue gaze was intent, and she met it with considerable difficulty.

"If I felt threatened by you, I wouldn't be here."

"But you're still not sure I'm telling the truth, are you?"

"I'm a psychologist, Zach, and we're never really sure about *anything*."

He reached out suddenly and placed his hands on her shoulders. She felt the strength of his grip and the heat of the contact—and the stirrings of the hunger she'd been keeping at bay.

"It happened exactly the way I told you, C.Z. It's really important to me that you believe me."

"I want to believe you, Zach, and I think I do. But none of it makes any sense. I've met Harvey Summers. I like him—and I know Dad liked him, too."

He took his hands away and nodded. "I know. *Everyone* likes old Harvey. But the fact is that he tried to kill me."

"WHY DID HOLLIS ask to see you, Dr. Morrison?"

"I believe that information is confidential, Detective,"

C.Z. said, meeting the cold gray eyes of the man sitting across from her desk.

He leaned forward in a manner clearly intended to intimidate her. "I could get a court order to waive confidentiality, Doctor. Courts have granted that before in felony cases—and escape from prison is a felony."

C.Z. didn't know if that was true or not, though she suspected it might be. She hadn't been able to discuss the matter with Jack Sanford, her boss, because the detectives had been waiting for her when she arrived at the prison.

She studied the top of her desk, aware of the two men's gazes on her. Finally, she shrugged. "That won't be necessary. He didn't tell me anything that could help you in any way."

"*We'll* be the judge of that, Doctor," the other man said. He was older, probably close to retirement. Both of them were investigators with the state police.

"Mr. Hollis asked to see me to express his concern about coming back here. He was certain there would be another attempt on his life—particularly now, with the sick-in. I told him that the warden had ordered a lockdown and assured him that I would speak to the warden on his behalf."

She kept her tone cool and professional, even though images of Zach filled her mind and his brief, parting kiss was still on her lips. She'd left him only hours ago, waking before dawn to make the long trip.

The kiss had been unexpected, unplanned—and all too brief, as though he'd instantly regretted his impulsive behavior. They'd talked about so much—everything, really. Everything but their feelings for each other, that is.

"In fact," she went on, "I'd already spoken to the warden, and when I told Mr. Hollis the warden said moving him would accomplish little, he agreed with me. I told him the warden planned to move the others as soon as possible, though.''

''According to the guard on duty at the hospital when you went to visit Hollis, you were carrying an attaché case in addition to your purse. Why was that?''

C.Z. sent up a silent prayer of thanks that she had prepared for this question. But even so, icy fingers were playing along her spine. She gestured to the attaché case, which she'd set on her desk.

''I carried it in because my recorder was in it, together with several books I'd gotten for him, books I thought might offer him some...comfort. Open it if you like. It's all still there. He didn't want the books.''

''You recorded your conversation with him?'' the older detective asked as he took the device out of her attaché case.

She nodded. ''I generally do. He was aware of that.''

The man rewound the tape and pressed the play button. The first voice was her own, giving the time and date and her name and Zach's. Although she'd listened to it several times on her way from the cabin, hearing Zach's voice still had the same effect.

While the two detectives listened intently, C.Z.'s mind went to the time of the recording, which, of course, wasn't the date and time she'd indicated. They had recorded the conversation last night at the cabin, sitting before the fire and trying to ignore what both of them were feeling.

She watched the faces of the two men as Zach said that sooner or later, someone would probably succeed in killing him no matter what the warden did. Their expressions gave little away, but she thought the older one, at least, seemed to be showing some sympathy for Zach.

When the recording ended, the younger one glanced through the pop psych books she'd stopped at home to collect. The recording had been Zach's idea, but the books were hers. Partners in crime.

The two men finally left her office, seemingly satisfied. But C.Z. barely had time to breathe a sigh of relief before Jack Sanford put his head through the door they'd left ajar. His expression was grim.

"What's wrong?" she asked as he came in and sagged into the chair across from her.

"The program has been terminated as of now."

"But we have *contracts*," she protested for Jack's benefit. "How can they do that?"

"Oh, they'll honor the contract. We'll both be paid for the next six months. But there won't be any program. The warden convinced the people in Albany that we weren't making any headway. Can you believe it?"

She could. It had been obvious to her almost from the beginning that neither the warden nor the staff counselors had wanted them there. Still, she'd thought the program would be allowed to run its course.

"He used the fact that all the men involved in the fight were part of the program," Jack went on angrily. "Never mind the fact that they were chosen because they were *known* to be violent."

"I'm really sorry," she told Jack sincerely. She *was* sorry—for him. This project had meant a lot to him. He'd had hopes that it could become a model program to be replicated at other prisons.

She was, however, anything but sorry for herself. And she was also well aware of the irony that the state would be paying her salary while she aided and abetted an escaped felon. Zach would probably say it was justice of a sort and perhaps it was.

They talked for a while about the project, commiserating over the obtuseness of the warden and the rigidity of a prison structure that thwarted any attempts to improve things.

"Well," said Jack as he got up, "I guess it's back to private practice for me. What about you? I'll help in any way I can."

"Thanks, Jack, but since the state is going to pay me for doing nothing, I think that's just what I'll do. I never really took a break after grad school, anyway."

"Good idea." He nodded. "Enjoy yourself."

Enjoying herself wasn't in the cards right now—though her plans were not without their pleasures. She wondered what Jack would think when it all came out.

Or would there be anything to come out? What if they couldn't prove Zach's innocence? The task before them seemed daunting to her, though Zach seemed so confident.

Shutting down the project required little effort on her part, though Jack would be there for a few more days. She left behind the chain link fences and the razor wire and the armed guards in their towers and didn't look back. Even if Zach hadn't come into her life, she would welcome the end to this job. Perhaps that had made the decision to help him a bit easier.

She drove home to her condo, fighting the urge to continue to the cabin. She had suggested coming back at midweek, but Zach had argued against it—particularly if the police showed any signs of suspecting her. And now that they had questioned her, she knew it was too dangerous.

Chapter Four

C.Z. pulled into the parking lot of the restaurant, then turned off the engine and sat there, watching the traffic. No one else pulled in—or even appeared to slow down. Maybe she was being paranoid, pushed into that state by a nagging conscience.

In the two days following her meeting with the detectives, she'd become increasingly certain she was being followed. Twice, she'd seen a black Bronco parked in the visitors' lot at her condo complex. Under ordinary circumstances, she paid no attention to vehicles parked there, but both times, the Bronco had been parked in the one spot that had an unobstructed view of her front door, an inconvenient spot at the far end of the visitors' lot. And on one occasion, she'd seen the same vehicle, or one like it, behind her in traffic.

As she was about to get out of the car, a boxy black vehicle that looked very much like the one she'd seen before passed by on the highway, slowing down then speeding up.

How many vehicles like it could there be? Probably dozens. Sport utility vehicles were very popular. Besides, she couldn't really be certain that this one was the same as the one at the condo. She'd known it was a Bronco only because she'd seen the name on it.

She hesitated, then decided to wait in her car to see if the truck came back. She was a bit early for her dinner date with her friend Stacey. Stacey had chosen a restaurant midway between their homes, and C.Z. hadn't been certain how to get there.

As she was about to go into the restaurant, the truck passed by again, this time moving fast, too fast for her to get a look at the license plate. But it was definitely a Bronco, and it was now headed in the opposite direction.

Stacey pulled into the lot in her cherry red Miata just as C.Z. got out of her car, and as the two women embraced, the black Bronco slipped from her mind.

Stacey Robbins had been C.Z.'s best friend during their childhood, and while those bonds had loosened somewhat after C.Z. moved away, they'd never been broken. In recent years, the two women had seen each other only on rare occasions, but their phone bills attested to a friendship that had continued despite the distance.

"So how does it feel to be gainfully unemployed?" Stacey asked after they were seated. C.Z. had already told her about the loss of her job.

"It feels quite nice, frankly. The prison was a rough place."

"I can't imagine why," Stacey stated dryly. "Wonderful atmosphere. Fascinating people. I never understood why you took the job in the first place."

C.Z. sighed. "I think it had something to do with my feelings of guilt over my father. I guess I thought that working in the law enforcement field would be a sort of tribute to him."

"My guess is that he would have wanted you to do what you liked best."

"You're right," C.Z. admitted. "Maybe I'll get into family practice."

"Good, because I've just learned about something that might interest you."

"Oh?"

"Ondago Family Services, a nonprofit group, is going to be looking for a psychologist. They have several, and one of them is leaving in another couple of months. She's pregnant and she plans to take a few years off after her baby is born. They're a good agency. I think you'd like them."

Over dinner, Stacey told her more about the agency and its work. She was familiar with them because as a teacher and a member of her school's student assistance program, she regularly referred kids and their families to the agency. It sounded to C.Z. like the kind of job she wanted, and if Zach cleared his name and stayed on...

Wishful thinking, she told herself. As far as Zach Hollis was concerned, she couldn't let herself think beyond the moment. The truth was, despite their changed circumstances, Zach continued to exist solely in the realm of fantasy. It was definitely safer that way, if more than a little frustrating.

She wanted very much to tell Stacey about Zach, to unburden herself of this secret life she was now living, but she couldn't do it. It wasn't until their dessert arrived that Zach's name entered the conversation—and then it was Stacey who brought it up.

"They've got his picture everywhere," Stacey told her. "Chief Colby seems to think he's somewhere in the area." She sighed. "You know, I still can't believe he tried to kill Harvey Summers—and neither can a lot of other people."

"Apparently, twelve jurors thought so," C.Z. observed neutrally.

"That's not really true. I talked to one of them afterward, and they didn't really want to convict him. But they just couldn't buy Zach's story that Harvey had tried to kill *him*.

Do *you* think he did it?'' Stacey already knew C.Z. was
Zach's psychologist in prison.

''No, I don't. He told me he was innocent, and I believe
him. But I don't understand why Harvey Summers would
shoot at him, either.''

''You see? That's just it. If it had been anyone else, I'm
sure the jury would have believed Zach—but Harvey? It
makes no sense.''

''Could there be something in Harvey's background that
he was afraid Zach would find out?'' C.Z. asked.

''Like what? The man's lived his whole life in Ondago
County and he's been in public life for years. No one's
ever said an unkind word about him that I know of.'' Stacey paused and frowned.

''Still, it wouldn't be the first time someone we all
thought we knew well turned out to have a dark side. Remember Mike Taylor?''

C.Z. did. He was a quiet, pleasant man, well-liked in the
community. Only after he killed his mother did everyone
learn about his dark fits of rage. It was the talk of the town
right before she had moved away.

''And afterward, several people admitted to having
known about his violent tendencies, but they'd kept their
mouths shut because they didn't want to believe anything
bad about him.''

C.Z. nodded, wondering if Harvey Summers could have
his dark side, as well—and how she could find it.

SHE STARED in disbelief at the faint, dusty footprints on the
hallway carpeting. The first print was directly beneath the
trapdoor that led to her attic storage area, then the trail
vanished in the direction of the stairs. When she bent to
look closer, she also saw the faint impression left by her
kitchen step stool.

They were large prints, definitely those of a man's shoe,

and an image of that black Bronco quickly came to mind. She stared at the trapdoor. She had left such prints when she'd gone up there to get her father's gun for Zach. The attic floor was dusty.

Someone had broken into her home. C.Z. questioned her assumption that she was being followed by the police. Surely if they'd suspected she was harboring Zach, they would have gotten a search warrant and confronted her.

But who else could it be—and why would they go up to the attic? After making a thorough check of all her possessions, she became convinced that whoever had been here was no ordinary burglar. Nothing was missing—not even her brand-new laptop computer. Surely no burglar would have missed that. Nor would they have left without her stereo system and her grandmother's silver tea service.

She checked the small room downstairs that she used as a home office and found everything in order—no indication that anyone had touched her personal papers.

Finally, she got the step stool and climbed to the attic. In the light that poured in through a louvered window, she could see more footprints, a lot of them, though at least some of them were undoubtedly her own.

She surveyed the boxes, trying to determine if anything was missing or had been moved. It was impossible to tell. She'd moved things around when she'd been up here searching for her father's gun. But no boxes had been opened, except for the ones that contained her father's things, and she'd opened them herself.

She considered calling the police—but what was the point? Nothing was missing, and as far as she could tell, nothing had been disturbed in any way.

Could it have been the police—searching to be sure she wasn't hiding Zach? That was certainly the most obvious explanation and would even explain their going up to the attic. But she couldn't believe the police would engage in an illegal search.

And if it wasn't the police, then who could it be, and what were they after?

The question remained on her mind as she went through her day. She went out for a while, driving around aimlessly to see if she was being followed. But there was no sign of the black Bronco, or of any other vehicle tailing her. Finally, she returned home, confused and uneasy and wishing she could see Zach.

It startled her to realize just how much she missed him, how quickly he'd become such a powerful presence in her life. That had never happened to her before. Cautious by nature, she'd never allowed any man to alter the course of her life—until Zach Hollis came along.

She thought about those boxes in the attic that contained her father's things, and suddenly it seemed like a good time to undertake a chore she'd been putting off for too long. In all likelihood, she'd be moving again soon. It made no sense to drag them with her to another home.

So she brought the boxes down to her office and began to sort through them. The first two boxes contained only old financial records, so she set them aside to carry to the trash bins. A third box also held financial records, but contained a surprise, as well—all the letters she'd written to her father from the time of her parents' divorce until the end of grad school.

Tears spilled from her eyes as she reread them and relived moments long forgotten that had once been important enough to set down in great detail. Although she'd always known her father loved her, she'd never have guessed he could be the sentimental type who would save all his daughter's letters. And yet he had, not only the letters but cards, as well.

The old, familiar pain gripped her, tormenting her with

the knowledge of the time they hadn't had together. She'd promised him she would come for a long visit after she finished school, but by then, he was gone.

Finally, she set the letters aside and turned to the final box. She was surprised to discover that it held police records—official forms, ugly photographs of dead bodies, incomprehensible autopsy reports, many pages of notes in her father's bold handwriting.

The dates on them indicated they were all old cases, and all of them appeared to be unsolved. She recognized several of the names and remembered her father mentioning them.

She guessed he must have made copies of the records and had probably continued to work on them on his own, long after they would have been officially filed away. She knew her father and knew these unsolved crimes must have offended his sense of justice and his pride in his work. Zach, she suspected, was probably just like him. It wouldn't surprise her to find out he, too, had been looking into these cases.

Lost in a reverie about her father, C.Z. was slow to make the connection—and when she did, she stared at the files in shock. Was it possible? Could there be something in one of these files that threatened Harvey Summers? Could he have been the intruder?

Not yet ready to believe that, she nonetheless began to read the files. Then suddenly, she stopped. If the intruder had been after a file, it would no longer be here. He would have taken it. She had no way of knowing what was missing, but it was possible Zach would.

THE A-FRAME was locked and empty. C.Z. pounded on the door, then peered through the windows. With each passing second, she became more convinced that Zach had gone. The warmth inside her that had been growing with each passing mile became a cold, empty space.

Then her thoughts made an abrupt turn and she was sure he'd been captured. Somehow, the police had found out about the cabin—or they'd found him because they were searching all cabins in the area.

She sat on the steps and ignored the autumn beauty all around her as that empty space grew larger. Her world was spinning out of control. She'd helped a convicted felon to escape, then helped him hide from the police. She no longer had a job. The job Stacey had mentioned sounded perfect for her, and yet her involvement with Zach could cost her that, as well.

By all rights, she should be glad he was gone and out of her life. If there was ever a case of the wrong man and the wrong time, this was it. And yet...

"What happened?"

Startled at the sound of that very familiar voice, C.Z. turned to find Zach coming toward her from the side of the A-frame. His ice-blue gaze pierced that cold, empty spot inside her and sent shock waves through her. How could he have such an effect on her? How had this man managed to take possession of her very soul?

The stubble on his face was slowly becoming a beard, and it was gray, just as he'd said, contrasting sharply with his thick black hair. It gave him a raffish look that added to his already powerful appeal, even though she'd never really liked beards and certainly didn't like that unshaven look so popular with rock and film stars.

"What do you mean?" she asked belatedly, thinking somehow he knew about the intruder.

He stopped a few feet away at the bottom of the stairs that led to the deck. "Why aren't you at work?"

She told him about her meeting with the detectives, then explained about the warden's cancellation of the project. As she talked, he sat on the step below her, and it felt to her as though her body were melting into his.

"So you think they believed you?" he asked when she'd finished.

"I thought so at the time, but then I found out someone was following me." She told him about the Bronco then hurried on to let him know that she'd been very careful when she came here.

She thought she detected an underlying frustration. Lost in her worries, she'd failed to understand how difficult this must be for him. He'd exchanged one prison for another, and she knew that passivity was not his strong suit. Zach Hollis was a man of action, not one given to quiet contemplation.

As if to prove that, he got up and began to pace back and forth in front of the cabin. He moved with an athletic grace, light on his feet despite his size. She'd never met a man who so clearly exemplified maleness and all it meant.

"Now I'm not so sure it *was* the police who were following me," she said.

He stopped his pacing and stared at her. "What do you mean?"

She told him about the intruder, about how she'd discovered the dusty footprints. "Would the police do something like that, break into my home to search for you?"

He shook his head. "*I* might have, under certain circumstances, but they wouldn't. They could have gotten a search warrant. Every cop knows who the friendly judges are—the ones they can go to if they don't really have probable cause. I've bypassed that a few times, just to save myself the trouble, but I don't think they'd do that."

He ran a hand through his already disheveled hair. "But you said that nothing was missing, so who else could it be?"

She hesitated. She had begun to have serious doubts about her theory. There were many holes in it.

"Something *might* be missing. I'm not sure."

He had resumed his pacing but stopped again, his dark brows knitted into an impatient frown. She hurried on, certain he would think she was being foolish.

"Like I told you, he was in the attic. I have some of my own things up there, but I also have some boxes of Dad's stuff that I just never got around to dealing with. Most of it I'd never even seen because his attorney packed it for me, but I'd put his gun in one of the boxes and I had to open all of them to get it for you.

"I didn't bother to reseal them, and I decided it was time to deal with them. Most of it was just old financial records." She paused, thinking about those letters and cards, feeling again that familiar pang of guilt over her neglect of her father.

"But in one box, I found a stack of police files. They look like the records of old cases Dad must have been working on in his spare time, crimes that had never been solved."

Zach nodded. "We all have those—ones we just can't let go. I remember he and I talked about that once." He frowned. "Are you saying you think someone was after *them?*"

His tone sounded incredulous, which was just what she'd expected. "I don't know," she replied. "At the time, I thought maybe…"

Her voice trailed off as she realized how absurd her theory was. If it wasn't, surely he would have made the same connection.

"Maybe what?" he demanded impatiently.

"Nothing. I don't know what I thought. It's just that I can't help wondering if Harvey Summers tried to kill you because he was afraid you might find out something— something from his past."

"And you thought it might have something to do with

those unsolved cases?'' he asked slowly, his tone less sharp as he paused at the foot of the steps and stared at her.

She shrugged. ''At the time, it sounded like a good theory. I'd just had dinner with Stacey and we were talking about you, and about Harvey Summers. She said they convicted you because no one could believe Harvey would have tried to kill you. But then she reminded me of a case that happened a long time ago involving a man who was well-liked in the community, too, but who killed his mother. Later, it came out that he'd always had a violent streak. A lot of people had known it, but they hadn't wanted to believe it.''

She stopped abruptly, aware she was trying to justify something she'd already rejected. Zach frowned but said nothing as he turned away from her and resumed his pacing. She laughed.

''I know. You don't have to tell me. I promise not to try to play detective again. It's just that I discovered the intruder right after I'd had dinner with Stacey, and—''

''I'm not criticizing you,'' he interrupted as he spun to face her. Then he grinned. ''You have my full permission to play detective anytime you want.''

He stood there, his hands jammed into the pockets of his jeans. ''So okay, Detective Morrison, let's talk this one through. Let's suppose that Summers *does* have something to hide. That part of the theory is as good as any I can come up with. And let's further suppose that by now Summers has found out there's a connection between the two of us. Colby might have heard about that, since the state investigators interviewed you.

''Colby also knows I'd been nosing into some old unsolved cases—probably the same ones your father was looking into. And he would have known your father was looking into them.''

He paused and she nodded, not certain whether he was humoring her or beginning to believe her theory.

"But here's where it gets difficult," Zach went on. "If it was Colby—or even Summers himself—who broke into your place, it had to be because they thought there was something incriminating in those files. But even if they've guessed you're helping me, why would they risk breaking into your place to get files I've already seen?"

"Maybe they thought Dad had added something—his own speculations?"

"Right. That would be the only reason."

A silence hung between them as Zach watched her closely. She frowned, certain he was waiting for her to say something.

"Did you get the license of the truck that was following you?" he asked.

"No."

"You said it was a Bronco, right?"

She nodded.

"What color?"

"Black" she said.

"I'll be damned!" Zach swore softly. "That idiot even used his own vehicle."

"Who?"

"Colby. He owns a black Bronco."

She gasped. "Then we must be right."

"Uh-huh. But what's in those files?"

"Well, we can find out—I brought them with me. I read them all, but I couldn't see anything that could point to Harvey Summers in any of them. And then I realized that it wouldn't be there anyway. He would have taken it."

"Right. So what we're looking for is what *isn't* there."

"That's why I brought them. I wouldn't know what's missing, but I thought you might."

Zach was standing at the foot of the steps. He leaned

forward and brushed his lips against her cheek. "You're a great detective."

She managed to laugh, but she couldn't ignore the shock waves that went through her. And they weren't the result of the brotherly peck on the cheek. What sent those ripples through her was the look in his eyes, a silent acknowledgment that he wanted much more, and that he knew she did, too.

ZACH WAS SEATED on a hassock, pulling files from the box and glancing briefly through them before setting them aside. She was fixing them a meal, standing at the counter that separated the kitchen space from the rest of the room.

He had paused in his search through the files and was reading one of them. She thought again about her father and how he might well have been playing matchmaker that day she'd met Zach. It pleased her to think her father might even now be playing such a role by helping them find a way to prove Zach's innocence.

He set aside the file and continued sorting through the rest of them. She was about to ask him if he'd discovered what might be missing when he abruptly got up and went outside. She saw him standing on the deck, his hands jammed into his pockets as he stared into space.

"Do you know yet what's missing?" she asked when he came inside and sniffed appreciatively at the chicken casserole she'd taken from the microwave—a quick and easy recipe that was amazingly good.

"I'm still thinking about it," he replied nonchalantly. He gestured to the row of cookbooks on top of the refrigerator. "I got desperate enough for reading material in the past couple of days to read those cookbooks, and you know what? Cooking isn't all that difficult."

She laughed. "Are you telling me that you reached the

age of thirty-six without knowing that? What have you been eating all this time?''

"You forget that until recently, I lived in the city where you can get anything at any time. Plus, until Dad retired a year and a half ago and they moved to Florida, Mom used to come over regularly and leave things for me."

He must have seen her expression, because he put up a hand. "I know, I know. Spoiled rotten and all that. But part of it's the kind of life a cop leads—especially in homicide. The hours aren't exactly regular and... Well, you already know all about that."

She nodded. "That had a lot to do with my mother deciding to leave my father—too many ruined dinners, too many lonely evenings and weekends."

"It's not an easy life," he agreed.

His words hung there between them as they sat down to eat. C.Z. didn't know if he was issuing some kind of warning about what involvement with him would mean. Probably he was only making a general observation. But still, it *was* a warning, and one she would take seriously if only she could see past their current predicament.

"Did your father ever talk to you about those cases?" he asked, gesturing to the files in the box.

"I think he might have mentioned a few of them from time to time. Why?"

"Do you recall if he mentioned any of them right before he died?"

"No. But to be honest, I probably wouldn't remember if he had. I was writing my dissertation at the time, and I was too wrapped up in that."

"Well, it's obvious he was working on them right up to the end. I found notes he'd made about a couple of them, things that weren't in the files at the department. In one case, it looked like he was developing an interesting lead."

"But nothing that would suggest Harvey Summers's involvement."

He shook his head, then remained silent as they ate. She tried several conversation gambits, but his responses were minimal so she finally lapsed into silence, assuming that he was still trying to figure out what was missing.

His brooding silence continued as he helped her clean up after dinner, and when they had finished, he suggested they climb up the hill behind the cabin, saying that she'd like the view.

The difficulty of the climb prevented any conversation, but the view, when they finally reached the top, was worth the effort. The sun was poised just above the horizon, and the forest stretched in all directions, the trees ruddy in the glow of the dying sun with stands of evergreens providing a dark contrast.

C.Z. sank onto the hard-packed dirt, aware of Zach's gaze upon her but even more aware of his continued silence. *How well do you have to know someone before you can distinguish between different kinds of silence?* she wondered. His seemed to have a distinctly brooding quality that was beginning to make her nervous.

She turned to him as he lowered himself beside her, and he met her gaze only briefly before looking away. There was something in his eyes, an uneasiness, she thought. When he said nothing, she asked if he'd been able to determine what cases might be missing.

"Yeah. There's one that definitely should have been there."

"What's that?" she asked, annoyed that she seemed to be forced to drag the information from him. She wasn't really expecting to know anything about the missing case. Her father had only occasionally mentioned various cases, and she'd been too distracted by her studies to pay that much attention.

"The case we argued about the day I met you," he replied.

She turned to stare at him. Of course! She should have thought of that. It was the worst tragedy her father had ever worked on, and one that had continued to trouble him deeply.

"The school bus accident," Zach said, apparently misreading her shocked expression.

"Yes. I was just surprised that I didn't think of that myself."

She was silent, thinking of the possible implications. "Do you think Harvey Summers could have been involved—maybe with a cover-up? Or maybe he caused it?" She was horrified, but beneath the horror, her mind was busy. "It would make sense in a way, wouldn't it?" she asked. "I mean, it was the type of thing that could have been him." She stopped, trying to put her thoughts into words.

"What I mean is, we know he couldn't have committed just *any* crime. It would almost have to be something accidental, a mistake."

"It wasn't accidental," Zach stated harshly. "The bus driver was sure the driver of the truck was drunk. Maybe *you* see drunk driving accidents as being just that, but *I* don't."

She was struck by how closely Zach's words mirrored those spoken by her father about the incident.

"I didn't mean that," she told him. "I'm not trying to absolve drunk drivers of responsibility for their actions."

"But a lot of people do," he replied. "So in that sense, you're right."

She nodded. "Dad told me that. He said it was likely someone knew who was driving that pickup, but they wouldn't come forward because they considered it to be just a tragic accident."

"Yeah, except he also walked away from it instead of staying to help get those kids out."

C.Z. swallowed hard. She knew all the details. No one could forget something like that. The bus driver had swerved to avoid a collision with a pickup that was weaving all over the narrow road. He'd lost control, and the bus had rolled down an embankment, then caught fire. Eight children had died, and others were badly injured. It had made the national news.

"But the truck," she said. "Didn't the bus driver get a good look at it? Dad would have known if Harvey Summers had such a truck."

"All the driver saw was an older model dark pickup and two men who were nothing more than shadows from where he was. Your father got a printout from Motor Vehicles of all older model pickups registered to people in the area and checked them all out. A lot of them didn't exactly have ironclad alibis, but he didn't have enough evidence to charge any of them."

"I remember his saying once that he was convinced it had to be someone from the area."

"Right. I agree. No one just passing through would have any reason to use that road. Ordinarily, the bus driver wouldn't have used it, either. But the kids had been on a field trip to the city and they got caught in a traffic jam and were running late. He was worried that their parents would be upset, so he took a shortcut."

C.Z. thought about the anguish that driver must be living with. She knew he'd acted heroically to get as many kids out as he could, but still...

"Was Harvey Summers on that list?" she asked.

Zach shook his head. "No, I'd remember it if he was."

"So then it couldn't have been him."

"I don't know. I agree it doesn't seem likely, but it's still possible. That case obsessed me probably as much as it did your father. I guess in a way I wanted to solve it for him, too.

"What I began to wonder was whether or not the truck might have been unregistered. There are hunting camps and cabins all over the area, and I know a lot of men keep old trucks and Jeeps just to run around in the woods. They don't take them out on the highway.

"I tried to get a list from Motor Vehicles of old pickups that hadn't been reregistered, but by that time, the records had been purged from the computers. So, in my spare time, I was starting to visit the camps and cabins in the area to see if I could find one like it."

"So you're saying that Harvey could have had an unregistered truck that he kept at his cabin?"

"He could have. I hadn't checked his place. But Colby knew I was nosing around."

"Still, if Harvey did have such a truck, why would he have been driving it on the road? Is his cabin in that area?"

"Not exactly. It's not far from my place, just off Route 427. But I've been thinking about where he lives in relation to his hunting camp. If he was going to take an unregistered vehicle onto the road, he might have used that road to avoid being caught. It would have been out of his way, but he could be pretty sure he wouldn't run into any cops on it."

"Does he have a drinking problem?"

"Not that I'm aware of, but I know that he and his buddies spend a lot of time at his camp, and I assume they do some drinking. But I know he's never been arrested for drunk driving, because your father got a printout of all drunk driving arrests in the area, to cross-check them with the pickup registrations. Still, that doesn't necessarily mean he hasn't driven drunk."

"But surely Dad would have known about any time he was stopped even if he wasn't arrested."

"Maybe not. Your dad was pretty much by the book,

and if one of his men let Harvey go, he probably wouldn't have told him about it.''

''At Dad's funeral, Harvey made it sound as though they were really good friends, and if that's so, then Dad would have known if Harvey had an old pickup at his camp.''

''Summers is one of those people who makes it sound as though he's *everyone's* good friend—except for me, that is. Besides, your dad belonged to a hunting camp, and as far as I know, he spent his free time there. I went there with him once.''

C.Z. stared at him. She was beginning to realize he'd known her father better than she'd thought. In all likelihood, he'd spent far more time with him than she had in his final years.

''So what can we do?'' she asked, pushing those guilty thoughts away.

''The first thing we need to do is to find out if Summers has an old pickup at his camp. Or more likely, if he had one. If it was him, I'm damned sure he would have gotten rid of it after the accident.''

''Did the pickup actually hit the bus?'' she asked. It was one detail she couldn't remember.

Zach nodded. ''The truck clipped the bus at an angle as the bus was swerving. The driver's memory wasn't all that clear, but he thought there should be some damage to the fender on the driver's side.''

The sun was by now no more than a glow along the horizon, and C.Z. stood up, saying they'd better climb down the hill before it got dark.

By the time they reached the A-frame, Zach had once again lapsed into that strange, brooding silence, and when she met his gaze, she saw again that troubled look. He went to light a fire against the growing chill of the evening while she went to the kitchen to make them some coffee.

Zach's brooding stirred up uneasy thoughts in her, as

well, as though something was troubling her that hadn't yet surfaced. She dismissed it as being merely a reaction to his mood, but as she carried the coffee to him, it struck her.

Even if their speculation was right, why would Colby— or anyone else—want to steal that file from her father's things? The only reason they would take such a chance would be if they thought her father was coming too close to the truth and might have left incriminating information behind.

She handed Zach a mug, then set her own on the hearth, her mind working uneasily. And then, suddenly, she gasped. Zach turned to her sharply, and her words began to tumble out.

"Colby must have broken in and taken that file because he knew or suspected there was something in there—something in Dad's notes. That means they guessed that Dad might be getting close to the truth, and..."

She faltered, unable to go on. She had only to stare into Zach's eyes to know what had been troubling him. Still, she had to say it aloud.

"Harvey Summers killed my father."

Chapter Five

Having spoken the words, C.Z. could not believe them—and yet she did. What other explanation could there be for the missing file? Chills skittered through her.

Zach stared at her in silence, then spoke in a quiet, reasoned voice. "We're leaping to a lot of conclusions, C.Z. We don't have anything concrete. One thing a detective learns early on is that you can't make conclusions without good, solid evidence."

She was certain he, too, had reached just that conclusion some time ago and was playing devil's advocate. "But how else can you explain the missing file? Why else would someone risk breaking into my house to steal it?"

"We don't know that it *was* stolen. Maybe it was never there in the first place. And if it *was* there and it *did* contain something that would have incriminated Summers, why wouldn't he have taken it before, right after your father's death?"

But as she listened to him, as she wanted to believe him, a memory stirred. "Harvey came to Dad's house that evening, after I'd gotten there. He said he came to offer his condolences, and he also offered to help me pack Dad's things. In fact, he repeated that offer at the funeral. He said he knew it would be hard for me to deal with."

She clenched her fists as anger swarmed over her. "I

thought he was being so kind. I might even have accepted his offer if Dad's attorney hadn't already said he would help me.''

"Maybe that's all it was, kindness. Harvey Summers has built a reputation on his kindness and generosity. He's always helping people.''

She glared at him. "Do you hear yourself, Zach? You're defending a man who tried to kill you and then sent you to prison?''

"I'm only repeating what anyone would tell you about him,'' Zach replied in a neutral tone.

"You aren't anyone,'' she retorted hotly. "You *know* what he is.''

"No, I don't—at least not yet. Other than the fact that he's a liar, that is.''

"A big-time liar! There's a difference between telling a few little, harmless lies and lying to send someone to prison. Not to mention trying to kill someone.''

"I know that. Maybe I'm not putting it right. What I'm saying is that we just can't afford to leap to conclusions at this point.''

"You're not making any sense! You want me to believe that he tried to kill you, but you aren't willing to believe that he actually did kill my father!''

"That's because I know he tried to kill me. I was there. But I don't know that he killed your father.''

"And you're afraid I'll confront him,'' she said, calming down enough to begin to understand.

"Yes. We can't afford to do that, C.Z.—not yet.''

She nodded. Her anger was mixing unpleasantly with a sense of hopelessness. How could they ever prove anything?

"The thing is,'' Zach said quietly, "if we're right about him killing your father, then the proof must be out there somewhere. He had to have some reason to think your father was getting close to it.''

She sank down in front of the fire and picked up her mug. She understood what he was saying. ''But Dad had ways of getting evidence that we don't have,'' she pointed out bleakly. ''After all, he wasn't running from the law. He *was* the law.''

Zach lowered himself beside her. ''That's true, but he had to be careful, too. He couldn't afford to let people know he suspected Summers until he had the evidence to back up his suspicions. Not only is Summers well-liked, but he was your father's boss.''

''Still, Dad made a mistake somewhere,'' she said bitterly. ''Harvey obviously found out.''

''Right, assuming that your father was in fact after him. But Summers would have known that he was still working the case. No doubt he asked for an update from time to time—a perfectly legitimate thing for him to have done. And then there was Colby, who would have been able to keep a close eye on it.''

''Colby,'' she echoed, having nearly forgotten him. ''Do you think Colby was the other man there the night of the school bus accident?''

''It's certainly possible, even likely. The two of them have been friends all their lives. Everyone—including me—assumed that's why Summers wanted Colby to have the chief's job. But if you look at it from the perspective of our suspicions, having Colby as chief would have put an end to any investigation of the crash.

''And it also explains why Summers wouldn't have wanted an outsider for chief. Anyone local would never suspect Harvey Summers, but an objective outsider could be dangerous. He even said that was his chief objection to me, that I was an outsider.''

He paused and sipped his coffee. ''You know, I remember telling the commissioners I was still carrying a few cases that I'd never solved and probably wasn't going to solve but still couldn't let go. It was true, and I said it as a way of explaining my dedication, but if we're right, that would only have fueled Summers's fears even more.''

"I don't know why it makes such a difference to me," she said plaintively, her thoughts spiralling to her father. "Dad is gone and nothing will bring him back. It shouldn't really matter whether he died in an accident or was…murdered.''

She choked back a sob, and Zach reached out to take her hand. "It *does* matter. It matters because the desire for revenge is part of our nature. You just don't want to accept that.''

"You're right," she admitted. "I've often told clients not to waste their time seeking vengeance—to get on with their lives.''

"Sometimes you just can't get on with your life until you've gotten that vengeance. I've seen that a lot over the years. I've even gotten letters from families telling me that only after I'd arrested someone could they begin to grieve for the person they lost, let alone get on with their lives.''

She used her free hand to brush away her tears. "I guess I never really understood that before. Dad used to say that he loved police work because he believed in justice. I always thought that maybe he was just a bit too self-righteous.''

"He probably was. I am, too. But someone has to be the designated avenger.''

She smiled, thinking Zach was helping her understand her father in a way she never had before.

He was still holding her hand, and his thumb began to trace slow circles against her sensitive palm. When she glanced at him, he was staring into the fire, and she thought

he was probably completely unaware of what he was doing—or the effect it was having on her.

Not for the first time, she found herself caught between
wanting to make love with this man and wanting to let her
feelings grow more slowly. For the moment, at least, it
seemed that her innate caution had gained the upper hand
over desire. But it was, she knew, a very delicate balance
that could be upset by something as simple as a glance or
a casual touch.

THE NIGHT was cold, but instead of going inside, C.Z. drew
the blanket around her more tightly, then daubed at her
tears with a corner.

Delayed reaction, she told herself, but understanding it
didn't help. Neither did Zach's explanation. Yes, she
wanted vengeance—but she also felt as though a wound
that had almost healed had been torn open. It hadn't been
easy for her to accept that her father had been the victim
of some hunter's stupidity, but facing the possibility that
he'd been murdered was far worse.

How could they go about proving Harvey Summers's
involvement? She had been relying on Zach to come up
with a plan. After all, he was the detective. But she was in
a better position to gain information than he was. Even in
disguise, he could not afford to become too noticeable,
while she could quite easily move around, asking questions,
prising information out of various people.

She was just beginning to consider how she might go
about that when she heard a sound behind her and Zach
appeared on the deck. He had offered her the bed in the
loft, but she'd insisted on using the sofa downstairs. The
conversation had been fraught with tension because they
both knew there was a third choice, the one they both
wanted but refused to voice.

"It's cold out here," he said. "Come back inside."

His voice was soft and filled with understanding, and she was struck by how very gentle he could be and how appealing that gentleness was, coming as it did from a man like him.

She followed him inside, but kept the blanket wrapped around herself, since she was wearing nothing beneath it but an oversize T-shirt.

"I was actually hoping you wouldn't make the connection," he said as he tossed another log onto the fire. "At least not until later. We could have this all wrong, Charlie."

"I know," she said, smiling at his use of the nickname. "But I think we're right."

"I do, too," he admitted, glancing at her as he squatted in front of the fire. "But proving any of it isn't going to be easy."

She told him about the job with Ondago Family Services. "That would make it easy for me to be here and maybe look up some old friends. In fact, Stacey invited me to come stay with her for a while."

"That's fine, except that you'll have to be very careful. If we're right, this is a man who's killed once and tried to kill a second time to protect his secret. We have to assume he's already made a connection between us."

"If we don't take some chances, we'll never get at the truth," she pointed out.

He stood up and jammed his hands into the pockets of his jeans. She tried to avoid staring at his bare chest with its sprinkling of dark hairs, but her eyes followed the thin, dark line that disappeared into the waistband of the jeans. She clutched the blanket still tighter.

"Taking chances is my business—not yours."

"Not anymore," she insisted. "If he killed Dad—"

"That's why I hoped you wouldn't make the connection," he interrupted harshly.

"Well, I did, and now I have to know. Getting information out of people without revealing my thoughts is part of my work, Zach, and I'm very good at it.''

''That's a whole lot easier to do when you're not emotionally involved,'' he observed.

Their eyes met, and she knew he was reading her thoughts. She had been emotionally involved even before she realized Harvey Summers might have killed her father.

The cabin was lit only by the shifting glow of the fire. The only sounds were the soft hissing and cracklings as the fresh logs succumbed to the flames. C.Z. grew very warm inside the blanket, but she knew it wasn't the result of the fire's heat.

''There's an irony here somewhere,'' he said into the tense silence. ''Back at the hospital, we were both ready to forget where we were and take a chance. But now…''

He paused, and she was about to ask him why that had changed for him. But before she could form the words, he'd closed the small space between them. His fingers grazed her cheek softly, and then his lips were on hers.

His kiss seemed all the more potent because he wasn't otherwise touching her. Instead, his lips and tongue teased and tormented and promised, then withdrew only to begin tracing a moist, hot trail along the curve of her jaw and across her throat. A sigh escaped from her lips, and her grip on the blanket loosened.

The folds of the blanket bunched between them, and Zach tore it away, his impatience contrasting sharply with the slow meanderings of his lips.

But then he seemed to regain his self-control as he drew her carefully into his arms. Taut nipples brushed against the hardness of his chest through the thin barrier of her T-shirt. She moved closer, fitting herself to him, sliding her arms around him, feeling the smooth muscles beneath her fingertips.

There were good reasons this should not be happening,

but they no longer seemed important to her. Or perhaps a part of her illogically believed it wouldn't happen because it hadn't happened before. But they were no longer at the prison or at the hospital. They were alone in a cabin miles from anywhere and anyone, with a blazing fire casting a ruddy glow that softened the hard edges of reality.

His hands slid down to press her more firmly against him, and she felt the force of his desire being answered by her own throbbing need. Before she could even think it, her lips were forming the word.

"Yes," she whispered huskily. "Yes."

His only response was a deep groan as he slid his hands beneath the T-shirt and pulled it quickly over her head. She arched backward, clutching at the taut muscles of his arms as his lips traveled with agonizing slowness across her throat and along the soft swell of her breasts, lingering, teasing—until he finally captured one aching bud and then the other as he ground his hips against hers.

Instinctively, she fought against the wildness that was taking her over, but the battle was lost almost before it began. With a sigh, she surrendered to the flames of passion that were consuming her. Every fiber of her being cried out for his touch as he eased her onto the rug before the hearth, then stood over her as he stripped off his jeans.

In the flickering light of the fire, she saw him as dark and dangerous and so essentially male that it took her breath away. Before, she could never have imagined herself wanting such a man, but now she knew she could want no other. His pale eyes glowed with an electric intensity as he stared at her. The stubble on his cheeks and some of the hairs on his chest gleamed silver. He seemed so alien to her, strange and wondrous and as different from herself as it was possible to be.

She reached out to him, and he came to her arms, all hardness and roughness but still gentle, his passion contained, coiled within him by sheer force of will. She could feel him shuddering beneath her touch.

Bodies entwined, they sought to learn each other, quickly embarking on a journey of discovery as desire screamed silently through them both. With lips and fingers, they explored each other and laid claim to each other and yielded their secrets.

His beard had not yet grown long enough to be soft, and it scraped against her skin as he kissed her, moving with deliberate, taunting slowness along the length of her body, a body she yielded to him willingly, eagerly.

It was a wild coming together, the ultimate joining of male hardness and female softness in a frenzy of need that drove them both all too quickly over the edge into pure, mindless ecstasy, then sent them spiraling down slowly, softly, as the ancient rhythms of love gave way to pleasant, rippling aftershocks.

"ZACH! Someone's out there!" C.Z. whispered urgently as she moved from the warmth of his arms to the cold reality of their situation in a heartbeat. It couldn't be happening— they couldn't take him away from her now!

He slid naked from the bed, but without any great urgency. "It's that damned bear again. I forgot to bring in the trash can."

"Are you sure it isn't—"

"They wouldn't come at night," he said, but she noticed he had picked up her father's gun.

He disappeared down the stairs from the loft and was swallowed by the darkness. Despite his assurances, her heart was threatening to leap into her throat. She could hear him below her, opening a cabinet in the kitchen. What on earth was he doing?

She got out of bed and went to the railing just in time to see him open the door and step onto the deck. Instead of the gun, he had what looked like a couple of pans in his hands. A moment later, she heard him shout and then heard a metallic crash as though he was beating the pans together.

The door opened and he was inside. He glanced up and saw her. "That should get rid of him for the night," he said as he walked to the kitchen. "But just to be sure, I'll bring the can inside."

C.Z. returned to the bed, willing her fear to go away. But it refused to go. It could have been the police—if not at night, then sometime in daylight. How could she have let herself believe they were two ordinary lovers enjoying an interlude in a romantic,. isolated cabin?

Zach came up the stairs and put the gun in the drawer of the nightstand. When they'd come up here earlier, it had been on the top of the nightstand, but the moment he saw her staring at it, he'd put it away.

He sat on the edge of the bed. "They won't come at night, Charlie."

"But they *will* come," she persisted. "Stacey said they were searching all the cabins in the area."

"That's going to take some time, and they'll probably start with the ones closer to town. There aren't enough men on the force to get to them all quickly."

He ran a hand over his stubbly cheeks. "By the time they get here—if they get here at all—my disguise should be ready."

She said nothing, but she was wondering how a disguise—even a good one—could hold up against the scrutiny of men who knew him.

He slid in beside her and drew her into his arms. "I want you again," he murmured against her ear. "I can't stop wanting you."

"WHERE ARE WE GOING?" she asked nervously. How could he risk going out with her in broad daylight?

"Just down to the other cabin. He has a garage, and we can keep your car there. There's no place to hide it up here."

"Oh." She hadn't given any thought to that.

"Then, after we hide the car, we'll take the Jeep and go over to my place through the woods. I need to get some things."

"Zach!" she cried. "You can't go over there!"

"They won't be watching it every minute. In fact, they're probably not watching it at all. They won't be expecting me to go there. And as long as I'm in that area, I'm going to see if I can get to Summers's camp through the woods. I want to see if he's keeping an old truck there."

She started her car. "But surely he wouldn't have kept the same truck."

"No, but I'd still like to see if he has one."

C.Z. didn't see how that would prove anything and she couldn't imagine he needed anything from his own place so badly he should risk going there. But she didn't protest because she understood what was really behind this. He needed to do something, and for now, this was all he could do.

She pulled up in front of the small, detached garage, and Zach asked her to open the trunk. When she did, he took out the lug wrench and started toward the garage door.

"What are you going to do?"

"Pry the door open. I checked it the other day, and it's locked. But it's a perfect hiding place for your car because there aren't any windows."

Trespassing and breaking and entering, C.Z. thought as Zach forced the door lock. It really bothered her that she could be so blasé about committing a crime. And she wondered how many other laws they would break before this was over.

Zach turned to her, and she realized her misgivings must

be obvious because he cupped her shoulders with his hands and stared hard at her.

"This may not be the last law we'll have to break before this is over," he said somberly. "You can still bail out, you know. I wouldn't blame you for that."

She shook her head, grateful he'd said it, even though it pointed out the fragile nature of their relationship.

"Have we made a mistake?" he asked in that same quietly serious tone. "What happened last night was *my* fault, Charlie. I just lost control."

"What happened last night—and this morning—was mutual, Zach. I wanted you, and I still do."

He dropped his arms and looked away from her. "I, uh, I'm not very good with words sometimes, but it was more than sex. It's just that I have nothing to offer you—except more trouble, that is."

She smiled, thinking how very strange it was to see this normally confident man so uncomfortable. Perhaps *he* thought he wasn't good with words, but *she* thought he was being very eloquent.

She touched his cheek, drawing his face to her. "I don't expect you to offer me anything, Zach. And it isn't just sex for me, either."

He nodded, then searched her face for a moment before gesturing to her car. "Let's get it into the garage."

A short time later, they set off into the woods in the old Jeep. C.Z. cast him a covert glance as he drove slowly on a barely discernible track that led along the base of the hill behind the A-frame. As she stared at his hands on the wheel, memories of his lovemaking inundated her, and she smiled. Zach Hollis was the most eloquent man she'd ever known—in his own way. She thought about telling him that, but decided it wasn't necessary. She remembered very well the look in his eyes after they'd made love, a look that said he knew he'd turned her world upside down and inside out.

They made their way slowly through the woods, sometimes on narrow, deeply rutted roads and sometimes lurching through the dense undergrowth. Finally, she asked how he could possibly know where they were going.

"I'm just heading northwest," he replied without turning to her. "Sooner or later, we should come to an old road I remember that will take us nearly to my place."

She decided she would have to trust that he knew what he was doing. Her sense of direction was so poor she regularly lost her car in shopping mall garages.

Sometime later, they crested a small hill, and Zach exclaimed with satisfaction when they saw a road. It was nothing more than a narrow, deeply rutted dirt path, but compared with what they'd been driving on, it looked like an interstate highway to her. She commented on the footprints that were visible in places. It was hard for her to believe they could run into anyone out here, but still she was uneasy.

"It's probably Davy Crockett," Zach said in an unconcerned tone. "I've run into him a few times. But I don't think we need to worry about him even if we do run across him."

When she heard the name, she assumed he was joking, but it seemed that he wasn't. "Davy Crockett?"

He nodded. "Didn't your father ever mention him? He's kind of a local legend. No one knows what his real name is, so they call him Davy Crockett because he's always wearing this old buckskin jacket with fringe and he carries a rifle that looks like it belongs in a museum. He's got a shack out here somewhere, but I don't think anyone knows where it is."

She frowned. "I think I *do* remember Dad mentioning

him. But why did you say we wouldn't have to worry even if he sees us?''

Zach turned to her and grinned. ''He isn't much for talking. In fact, I'm not really sure that he *can* talk. He might be mute.''

''How does he live?'' she asked, curious.

''Off the land. He comes into town once in a while for supplies, so he must have some money stashed away. According to Colby, he showed up about ten years ago. Periodically, the folks from the county's Adult Services Unit get riled up and insist that the police do something about him for his own protection. But he seems to be doing okay and he's not bothering anyone. Your father was chief the first time they wanted to find him, and he refused to go after him, so I just followed that precedent.

''I'd run across him before I became chief, but after I took the job, I told him I was now the chief and told him where I lived, just in case he ever needed anything.

''He just grunted, so I couldn't be sure he understood, but a couple of days later, I came home to find an old bucket filled with wild strawberries sitting on my doorstep. I'd never had them before, and they were really great. I guessed he must have left them, so I put the bucket on the doorstep filled with cans of soup and tuna. It sat there for about a week and then vanished.''

''He was reaching out to you, Zach. That's a good sign.''

''Yeah, except that I'm not there for him anymore. Colby told me that your father had some sort of arrangement with him while he was chief. Apparently, he made it to keep the social services people off his back. He'd meet him once a month somewhere, just to see if he was okay. But I thought my arrangement would work out just as well. Your dad lived in town, and Davy wouldn't come there, but since I lived in a more remote location, I figured just letting him know where he could find me was enough. I hope he's okay.''

A few moments later, Zach brought the Jeep to a halt, then turned off the engine. ''This is as close to my place as I want to go with the Jeep. It's only about a mile or so. You wait here. Give me an hour, and if I don't show up, just follow this trail until it comes to a paved road. Then turn right, and that will take you into Neff's Mills. You can find your way back to the A-frame from there, right?''

His tone was casual and matter-of-fact, but it still sent a chill through her, reminding her of the danger of what they were doing. ''I'm coming with you,'' she told him.

''Somehow, I knew you'd say that, but at least I tried. Life must sure have been a whole lot simpler when women let men tell them what to do.''

She grimaced. ''Ah, the good old days, when men were men and women knew their place.''

He grinned. ''You have to admit that it has its appeal.''

''To men, maybe.''

''Right. That's what I meant. Okay, well, it will help to have you along. You can carry some stuff.''

They got out of the Jeep and she followed him into the woods. ''Pay attention to where we're going in case you have to find your way back alone,'' he told her.

''I hate to say this, but the only way I could ever find my way back is if I keep the Jeep in sight. Besides, I thought you said this wouldn't be dangerous.''

''I don't think it is. I just believe in being prepared for all contingencies.''

They walked for a few minutes, then he stopped and turned, facing the way they'd come. She turned, too, frowning a question at him.

''See that big tree with the dead limb?''

She nodded, not understanding his point.

''Remember it. It wasn't obvious when we passed it, but

when you're coming in the other direction, you can see it easily. You do the same thing whenever you come to an intersecting path, because the intersection could look different coming from the opposite direction—especially if they don't meet at right angles.''

She studied the scene carefully before they continued. ''Was this part of your military training?''

He nodded. ''Most of it is pretty simple, really—the kind of thing anyone learns if they spend any time in the woods. But it was all new to a city kid.''

They stopped regularly and turned. She was amazed at how simple it was, or at least how simple it seemed. Each time she faced the way they'd come, she could find something to use as a landmark—a brilliantly colored maple, a jutting rock, a clump of birch. She got so caught up in the game she very nearly forgot its purpose.

Then she saw the house through the trees, only a few hundred yards ahead of them. ''Is that your house?'' she asked in surprise.

His amused expression told her he was aware of her shock. ''Yes. I bought it about ten years ago, before real estate prices up here started to climb. I used an inheritance from my grandmother—just in case you're starting to think about corrupt cops.''

She hadn't been thinking that, but she *was* surprised. It scarcely looked like a weekend cabin, which is how he'd described it. For one thing, it was larger than she'd expected. And it boasted a starkly modern design, all glass and hard angles and weathered cedar.

''At least it's still mine,'' he said, stopping to stare at it. ''My legal fees took everything else. You wait here while I check to make sure that no one's around front.''

He moved quickly through the trees and around the side of the house, and while she waited, she studied his home. She was curious about the interior. Seeing the house made her reexamine her thoughts about him. Somehow, she'd been expecting a small, Spartan sort of place, the home of a man who gave little thought to decor. It unnerved her to realize she still didn't know him well.

He reappeared quickly and beckoned for her to join him. She left the woods and started toward him as he lowered himself to the ground and crawled beneath the deck after removing a crosshatched wood panel. The large deck stood about four feet off the ground, and the space beneath was enclosed.

By the time she reached him, he was wriggling out with a key in his hand. "Trust Colby not to get it right," he said with grim satisfaction. "He put a padlock on the front door, but he didn't bother with the kitchen door. We can get in that way."

They went up the steps to the deck. Long, sliding glass doors led out to the deck in its center, but at one end, there was a regular door. Zach used the key to open it and they stepped inside.

The kitchen was rather small but very well organized, designed to make maximum use of space. While Zach began to collect the things he wanted, she wandered through the house, keeping an eye out the front windows in case anyone showed up. The driveway was visible for only a short distance as it wound its way through the woods and down the hill to the road.

The house was handsomely furnished, with a lot of leather and good art on the walls and a scattering of Oriental rugs covering parts of the polished wood floors. There were a few good antique pieces she assumed must be family heirlooms.

C.Z. felt slightly disoriented. This was definitely not what she'd expected. It seemed that even now, he could still surprise her.

The master suite was on a level of its own, and she

climbed up to find Zach pulling clothing from the big walk-in closet. A large duffel bag already stuffed to capacity sat on the floor, and he was carefully fitting more items into a hanging bag.

One wall of the bedroom had sliding glass doors that opened to a small deck overhung by trees. She walked to the opposite wall, where a set of windows faced the front of the house.

"This is a beautiful house, Zach," she said sincerely.

"Thanks. Take a look at the bathroom. That's the only place I made any changes."

She walked to a door that stood slightly ajar and peered in. He came up behind her and slid his arms around her waist. "After our sessions at the prison, I used to go back to my crummy cell and imagine the two of us here. Unfortunately, I'm still only halfway there. You're here, but we can't stay long enough to use it, and the hot water's shut off, anyway."

She smiled. So he'd had his own fantasies. She liked thinking about that. And she liked thinking about the two of them in the big spa tub set against windows that faced the deep woods.

"We'll get here," he said confidently, drawing her against him. "With candlelight and champagne to celebrate."

She wanted to believe him, but not even his confidence could lighten the burden of her fears. For all their speculation, they were no closer to proving his innocence than they had been when he'd escaped from prison. Instead, it felt as though they were treading water, staying out of trouble but getting nowhere.

Suddenly, Zach stiffened and let her go. She followed him to the windows, but he stopped her. "There's a cruiser out there. I don't think he's likely to come in. He'll probably just check to see if there's any sign of a break-in."

His voice was calm, but her heart was thudding painfully in her chest. So much for their fantasies. It was back to ugly reality.

"If he does come in, you get into the closet and stay in the back, behind the clothes. I'll hide somewhere else, and if he really starts to search, I'll let him find me. Then, after we're gone, you go back to the Jeep."

She nodded, unable to speak as a hard lump filled her throat. He picked up the bags he'd packed and stowed them in the closet, then went to the window to take a cautious peek outside. There was a rattling sound at the front door. C.Z. jumped and could not quite prevent a small sound of alarm from escaping her lips.

"He's just checking the padlock," Zach said in a whisper, then added, "now he's walking around the outside."

He started toward the bedroom door. "You stay here. I'm going to keep an eye on him. If you hear anything, get into the closet and stay there."

Alone in the room, she paced, trying to calm her fears. Even if they evaded their would-be captors this time, how many more confrontations would there be? She wanted to believe Zach could keep them safe, but even he could make a mistake.

Still, as she waited out the minutes, fearing at any time she would hear shouts and lose him, she vowed that if he was captured, she wouldn't stop searching for a way to clear his name—and to avenge her father's death.

The deep silence in the house was oppressive, even though it meant they were still safe. Then Zach was in the room, arriving so silently that she started and cried out when she saw him. He hurried past her to the window, and even before he announced it, she heard a car door slam and an engine start up. They were safe.

"Was it Colby?" she asked.

"No. I didn't recognize him. He must be a new hire. I

have only a few more things to get from the basement, and then we'll get out of here.''

C.Z. DIDN'T QUITE let go of her fears until they were in the Jeep and bumping into the woods. Not until they'd gone some distance did she realize they weren't headed to Scott's place.

"Where are we going?" she asked, though she thought she knew.

"Over to Summers's camp."

"Zach, even if we find an old truck there, it won't prove anything," she protested.

"Maybe not, but I still want to check on it."

"You *like* danger, don't you? That's why you like being a cop. You're addicted to it."

He slanted a quick glance at her. "Stop playing shrink, C.Z. There's less danger going to Summers's place than there was in visiting my house. Besides, we'll do the same thing there, leave the Jeep in the woods and walk in. You can stay with the Jeep this time."

C.Z. bit off a sharp reply—she wasn't exactly playing at being a shrink since she *was* one. As they continued along an old trail, they remained silent. Several times, she could feel his gaze on her, but she still said nothing.

She could feel a gulf opening between them. He had seemingly brushed off the danger they'd faced and didn't seem to understand how she could be worried. And this from a man who only hours ago had been a tender and considerate lover.

Finally, he stopped the Jeep and turned off the engine. "His camp is just on the other side of that hill," he said, pointing to the left. "I won't be gone long."

She hesitated as he started to walk into the woods, then opened her door and got out. He stopped and turned toward her.

"There's no reason for you to come with me."

"Maybe not," she admitted. "But I am."

He jammed his hands into his pockets in characteristic fashion. "Look, I'm sorry. Forget what I said. I know you can't stop being what you are any more than I can stop being what I am."

He ran a hand through his thick black hair. "If we were living normal lives right now and going out to dinner and getting to know each other the way most people do, it'd be different."

She wasn't exactly certain what he meant by that statement, but she thought he was right. She also wondered if things would have gone beyond a few dates. There would still be that powerful physical attraction, of course, but...

"You're right," she said, deciding to leave it at that. There was certainly no point in speculating about what a normal life would be like for them.

When they reached the top of the hill, she saw the cabin in a hollow. It looked much like what she'd expected Zach's home to be like, old and slightly ramshackle, covered with dark green shingles and featuring a large stone chimney that looked much sturdier than the rest of the place.

Behind the cabin were two outbuildings, one of which was little more than a lean-to filled with wood. The other one was about the size of a single-car garage, though she couldn't tell from this side if that's what it was.

They also had a clear view of the land in front of the cabin, and there was no vehicle in sight. Shutters covered the windows, which indicated that no one was likely to be there. Still, they made their way cautiously down the hill, staying within the cover of the thick underbrush until they reached the larger of the outbuildings.

"Wait here a minute, just till I see if there's anything in here," Zach ordered.

He started around the side of the building farthest from the cabin while she waited behind it. After only a few minutes, he called out to her and she hurried to join him as he stood before an old wooden garage door without windows.

"Damn! It's probably locked," he said in frustration as he went to try to open it.

To their surprise, however, the door rolled up noisily. C.Z. turned to cast a quick look at the cabin, fearing someone might be in there. When she turned back, Zach was staring at the battered old truck that sat on the dirt floor of the garage. He walked alongside it to the front and peered at the windshield.

"Interesting," he said as he came back to her.

"What do you mean?" She couldn't see anything interesting about it. It was red. The truck they were seeking was black.

He gestured to the license plate. "It expired three years ago, and so did the inspection."

"So?" She couldn't see the importance of that, since it obviously wasn't intended for road use.

"The school bus crash happened a little over three years ago."

"Oh." Now she understood. If they were right about Harvey Summers having been the driver of the truck, then he would have gotten rid of it and acquired a replacement about that time.

"But what could he have done with the other truck?" she asked. "He wouldn't have taken it to a junkyard."

"He probably did what a lot of locals do—abandoned it in the woods. I've come across a couple of old wrecks out there."

"Do you think we could find it?" she asked eagerly, staring at the woods around them. "How much land does he own?"

"A lot, I think, but he wouldn't be dumb enough to leave it on his own land." He pulled the garage door down.

"We'll never find it," she said unhappily, thinking about the huge expanse of forest.

"He must have bought it from someone around here. Our best hope is to find out who the seller was."

"But how?"

"That I don't know—yet. Come here. I want to show you something."

She followed him to the front of the cabin, then discovered that the something he wanted to show her was what had happened the night he shot Harvey Summers. She stood quietly while he went through it, showing her where he'd been and where Harvey had been. His voice betrayed no emotion, which gave a surreal quality to the performance. She didn't understand why he was doing it. Could he think she still had doubts about his truthfulness?

"What I've never understood," he said, "is why he or Colby didn't just kill me and claim self-defense. If they got away with the lies they told, they could have gotten away with that, too.

"It seems to me that maybe Colby did just happen to come along at that moment, like he said. I didn't see his truck when I came up the road, so he couldn't have been here already."

"But if Colby wasn't in on it, then why would he have gone along with it—unless Harvey has some hold over him?" she offered.

"Exactly. That's why it seems likely he was the other man the bus driver saw. I don't like Colby much. He's dumb as a stump and he's as lazy as they come, but it's still hard for me to see him being involved in something like that—so he has to be protecting his butt."

"But he might also have realized that by framing you, he'd get to become chief," she pointed out.

"Yeah, but I don't think he really wanted to be chief. He's just smart enough to know he's not smart enough, and he said more than once he hates all the paperwork that goes with the job."

C.Z. sighed. "It's complicated, isn't it? Nothing about this is straightforward. Everyone thinks Harvey Summers is a saint, and on the surface, at least, Colby has no reason to lie. I can remember Dad complaining about how stupid Colby was, but he also said that he's goodhearted."

Zach nodded. "He is. He does a lot of community work, coaching Little League and the like."

"Two pillars of the community," she murmured. "How can we ever bring them down?"

Chapter Six

"I understand you met Zach Hollis in prison. I defended him, you know."

C.Z. was grateful Sam Gittings couldn't see her face. They were sitting side by side on the playground swings, the very same playground where he'd tormented her with bugs and even a garter snake once, though at least he'd been reprimanded for that.

"Yes, I met him, but it was before he went to prison. Dad introduced us a couple of years ago when we ran into Zach at the diner."

She peered across the grassy field to the fair, where people were milling about, hoping that Stacey would summon her to the booth where she'd been working. She didn't want to think about Zach right now, let alone talk about him.

Zach had gone to the city this morning to get the rest of what he needed for his disguise. She had driven him to Poughkeepsie to get the train and she could still see him in her mind's eye, walking away from her without a backward glance. She was terrified for him—and once again angry, as well, because he seemed so unconcerned. Was he just very good at hiding his fear, or was he truly unafraid? Not only was he out in public with a disguise that might not work, but he was also going into a neighborhood filled with criminal types.

"So what do you think?" Sam asked.

She turned briefly to face her childhood friend. "I think he's innocent, if that's what you mean."

Sam nodded. She noticed he still had that same serious demeanor he'd acquired once his bug and snake days had passed. Solid, serious and reliable—that was Sam Gittings. She knew he'd had a crush on her and wondered why she'd never felt anything more than a sort of absentminded affection for him. Too much history, she supposed. Or too little danger, she added silently as she thought about Zach.

"But what I don't understand," she went on, "is why Harvey Summers would frame him."

"That's the million-dollar question. I've known Harvey all my life. Everyone has. It doesn't make any sense."

She stifled a pang of disappointment. It was foolish to hope that Sam would have anything to offer, and yet she had. But if Sam, who'd lived here all his life, couldn't offer a reason...

"Stacey says that Colby believes he's somewhere in the area."

"Yeah. He's questioned me. I think he half believes that I'm hiding Zach somewhere or helping him somehow."

"Would you do that?" she asked. "Help him, I mean?"

"That's a tough one. I don't know. It'd be risky, but I *know* he wasn't trying to kill Harvey." He paused and stared toward the crowd. "Speaking of Harvey..."

C.Z. turned and saw the county commissioner heading toward them. She glanced around, hoping he might be planning to join someone else, but they were the only two people on the playground.

"You can't be one of his favorite people," C.Z. said as Harvey continued toward them. "Especially since you defended Zach and tried to make him out to be a liar."

"Oh, we get along fine, just like always. He even called me after the trial, just to make sure I understood that there were no hard feelings. He said he knew I was just doing my job.''

C.Z. studied the man walking toward them, the man who, among other things, might well have murdered her father. What she saw was exactly what everyone else saw—a pleasant, middle-aged man of average height, beginning to show a potbelly, with a thick thatch of white hair and an open, friendly face.

"Well, well, Ms. Morrison, C.Z., isn't it? I thought that was you over here."

C.Z. forced herself to smile. "How are you, Mr. Summers?"

"Just a little nervous, to tell you the truth," Summers said with a self-deprecating smile. "I find myself looking over my shoulder and avoiding dark places."

"Oh? You mean because of Zach Hollis?" she asked innocently, hoping that he *was* telling the truth. In fact, she hoped that he was truly terrified.

Summers nodded. "Chief Colby seems to think he's somewhere in the area."

Sam snorted derisively. "What I think is that he's long gone. His folks have some money and I'm sure they've helped him disappear."

"I don't know about that," Summers replied. "Hollis always struck me as the kind of man who'd never give up." He paused. "What brings you back here, C.Z.?"

His tone was pleasant, and try as hard as she did, C.Z. couldn't hear any underlying edge to his voice.

"I'm visiting an old friend, Stacey Robbins. But I'm thinking about moving back to the area. I'm job hunting at the moment."

"Ah, I see. You're a psychologist, aren't you? I believe you were in graduate school the last time I saw you."

"Yes, that's right. I was working at Walkill Prison, but the program was canceled."

"Walkill?" Summers echoed with seemingly genuine surprise. "Did you run into Hollis there?"

"Yes, I saw him a few times, including just before he escaped. But I'd met him before that. Dad introduced us a couple of years ago."

"I see." Summers nodded. "A sad situation. It's no secret that I voted against hiring him, but still…" His voice trailed off and he shook his head sadly, then smiled at her.

"Well, if there's any way I can help you, please don't hesitate to come see me. I'm sure your daddy would be very happy to know you're thinking of coming back here."

You could help me quite a lot by telling the truth, C.Z. said to herself as she returned his smile and thanked him. Then she watched as he moved away to greet a family coming their way. She sighed inwardly. It was so difficult to believe that this man could be guilty of one heinous crime, let alone three.

As a trained psychologist, C.Z. thought she had very powerful antennae where lying was concerned, but she had to admit that those antennae were failing her this time. He *had* to be lying—at least where Zach was concerned—and yet she found it very difficult not to believe him.

"C.Z.! What a surprise!"

"Oh, hello, Mrs. Williams."

"Please call me Mary. After all, we're both grown up now. What brings you back to us?"

As C.Z. explained why she was here, her mind raced. Mary Williams was a county commissioner and now, thanks to Zach, she knew Mary had also had a relationship with her father. C.Z. had always liked her, but now she saw the possibility of gaining some information, as well. If Mary had been close to her father, it was always possible that he'd mentioned to her his continuing investigation into the school bus tragedy.

C.Z. didn't know how close Mary was to Harvey Summers, but at least they'd had a long professional relationship. And she recalled, as well, that Zach had said Mary had visited him in jail before his trial. So when Mary suggested they have dinner together soon, C.Z. leaped at the opportunity.

"I'll be back next week. We could get together then," she offered.

C.Z. PULLED INTO the station about twenty minutes before Zach's train from the city was due to arrive. She'd told Stacey that she had to return home but would be back in two days. Stacey was delighted to offer her home to C.Z. whenever she needed a place to stay, which was both a blessing and a curse, as far as C.Z. was concerned. The good side to it was that it meant she could nose around as much as she wanted without anyone wondering about her spending so much time in the area. But the bad side was that she wouldn't be able to see Zach as often, though with both Stacey and her husband gone during the day, that might not pose too much of a problem.

She sat in her car in the nearly deserted station and thought about her encounter with Harvey Summers. In fact, she'd thought of little else. She knew that sociopaths and psychopaths could often present charming facades, but Harvey Summers couldn't possibly fit into that category. This was a man who'd lived his entire life among the same people and most of his adult life in a very public manner. He simply could not be other than what he seemed to be—and yet she knew that he was.

What frightened her most about Harvey Summers was that he made her doubt Zach. In the absence of any proof that Summers was involved in the school bus tragedy or in her father's death, it all came down to his attempt to kill Zach. Every other suspicion they had about him arose from that incident.

She knew many people had tried to rationalize that incident as some sort of tragic mistake, but that was only to ease their minds. They didn't want to believe Harvey had tried to kill Zach, but neither could they accept that their police chief could be guilty of attempted murder.

C.Z. had nearly fallen into that trap after her meeting with Summers. But unlike the others, she'd forced herself to look more deeply into that evening, and there was just no way it could have been a mistake on either of their parts.

The arrival of the train put an end to her uncomfortable thoughts but brought back her fears for Zach. She seemed to career wildly between a certainty that he could handle any situation and a fear that he would be caught. Just as she was once again wavering in her certainty of his innocence, she thought unhappily.

Given the lateness of the hour, she was surprised to see so many people getting off the train. She scanned the five cars nervously, searching for him and wondering what she'd do if he failed to appear.

When she finally spotted him, she wasn't at first completely certain that it *was* him. Despite the fact that she knew he was wearing his disguise, she had held in her mind the image of the man she knew.

He wasn't wearing the same clothes. Somewhere, he'd acquired black pants and an old sheepskin-lined suede vest with embroidery, as well as a pair of black ankle-high boots. He was carrying a large, well-worn duffel bag and wore a pair of wire-rimmed glasses.

She watched him in total astonishment as he made his way down the platform toward her. He was walking differently, a slow, shambling sort of gait rather than his long, athletic stride. She detected a slight limp.

Instead of being amazed at his ability to transform himself, C.Z. felt the icy fingers of fear skitter along her spine.

Given her thoughts of a moment ago, she didn't want to see this proof of his ability to transform himself.

Instead of going to the passenger door, he came around to her side and bent to peer in at her. She very nearly recoiled as she stared into a face that bore no trace at all of Zach Hollis. Most of his face was covered by gray beard, which was growing thicker by the day, but even in the dim light, she could see that his striking eyes had disappeared, too. Behind the lightly tinted glasses they appeared to be a muddy brown or gray.

Before she could get the window down, he had gone around to the passenger door and she leaned over to unlock it for him. When he slid into the car, she was still staring openmouthed at him. He grinned, but even that seemed different, thanks to the beard. He put out a hand.

"Travis Bentley. Pleased to make your acquaintance, ma'am. Scott's talked a lot about you."

Her hands went out automatically to be grasped by his, engulfed by a hand that seemed larger, though she realized that wasn't possible and had to be the result of his looking larger with all the padding and the heavy vest.

"Travis Bentley?" she echoed in disbelief, only now realizing that she was also hearing traces of a Texas accent.

He reached into an inside pocket in the vest and drew out a worn leather wallet, holding it up so she could see the driver's license. "License, Social Security card and a couple of credit cards that I can't use," he said, dropping the accent.

"Who is he—Travis Bentley?"

Zach shrugged. "No idea. Maybe he doesn't exist or maybe he's dead. My source doesn't like questions—especially from cops."

"The clothes," she said, "and the accent. You were even walking differently."

"I spent some time hanging out in the Village and in

SoHo, then picked up some clothes in a secondhand shop after I'd figured out how I should look. The accent's easy. My partner for a couple of years was originally from Texas.''

"You're scary," she said sincerely.

"Scary? I'm trying to look harmless.''

"What's scary is how well you've succeeded.''

His eyes searched her face solemnly. "I thought you'd be pleased.''

"I am, but—" She stopped, not knowing how to explain her irrational fear. She turned on the engine and backed out of the parking space.

"What is it, C.Z.? Something happened.''

She told him about her day, about seeing Sam Gittings and Mary Williams and finally about her encounter with Harvey Summers. He remained silent until she had finished.

"So *that's* it—Summers," he said quietly. "And now you're having doubts about me again.''

"No! That's not true. I—"

"I'm not blaming you, Charlie," he said gently. "I know you still have some doubts. If our situations were reversed, I'd have some doubts, too. We haven't had time yet to build trust.''

C.Z. WAS a sound sleeper, and by the time her brain woke up enough to tell her that the loud pounding noise wasn't part of a dream, Zach was already out of bed and halfway dressed. Even then, she watched him put clothes on over the padding and reach for the wig before the terrible truth dawned on her.

"Is it the police?" she asked, praying that wasn't the case.

Zach nodded as he adjusted the wig in front of the dresser mirror, then expertly popped in the contact lenses, followed by the glasses.

Terror kept her paralyzed, sitting in the bed with the blankets clutched in both hands. Below, the pounding started again, and Zach turned to her briefly as he reached the top of the stairs.

"I doubt they'll come up here, but get under the bed."

She climbed clumsily from the bed and lowered herself to the floor, then remembered her clothing. But it was nowhere to be seen—at least until she began to ease herself under the bed. Then she found it, rolled in a ball and stuffed far underneath the bed.

"Just a minute!" Zach called out, and then she heard him moving around, first in the kitchen, and then in the bathroom. She realized he was getting rid of any traces of her there, as well, and her fear turned briefly to wonder that he could function so smoothly. Had he been mentally rehearsing for this while she had been busy denying it would happen at all?

Then he opened the door and slipped easily into his Texas accent. She held her breath as the officers—a couple of them, she guessed—began to question him.

There was dust under the bed, and she had to fight an urge to sneeze. Her heart was pounding as loud as their knocking had been. One of them must have asked to use the bathroom because she heard Zach tell him where it was, then continue talking to the other man, casual conversation about the area and the house.

She could not believe that she was up here, safely hidden under the bed but terror-stricken, while below her, Zach was chatting amiably with two men who knew him and were searching for him. It was surreal.

The toilet flushed and then all three of them moved outside and their voices trailed away. Seconds dragged past. She finally sneezed, controlling it as best she could. More time passed. She couldn't hear them, but she knew they must still be out there. She would have heard their car start up.

With each passing moment, she became more and more afraid that they had recognized him, or at least that they were becoming suspicious. It seemed impossible to her that a man as distinctive as Zach Hollis could disguise himself well enough to fool those who knew him, and she felt that same uneasiness she'd felt when she'd seen him at the train station.

Then, at last, she heard a car starting and the front door opening and closing, followed by Zach's footsteps as he came up the stairs. Before she could begin to crawl out from under the bed, he had crouched beside it and was reaching for her. She sneezed again, then pulled herself into a sitting position, naked and surrounded by her clothing.

The stranger who was her lover bent down to kiss her, his lips and tongue a tease and a promise that did little to soothe her frazzled nerves.

"That wasn't my idea of a way to wake up in the morning," he said dryly as he drew her to her feet and then into his arms.

She shivered, partly from the cool morning air and partly from a strange mixture of fear and desire and vulnerability. She was naked and he was fully clothed and in his disguise. He looked and felt like a stranger.

"Get back into bed until I get the place warmed up," he ordered, then kissed her again and went downstairs.

She huddled dazedly beneath the blankets, all her tangled emotions beginning to resolve themselves into disbelief. How could he be so calm, even joking about his near capture? In her mind, she could still hear his slow drawl as he talked to the officers.

I'll never understand him, she thought dismally. *And if I can't understand him, how can I trust him?*

When he returned and began to strip off his disguise and

his clothing, she stared at him, wanting to see some sign that he was at least slightly nervous. But his movements were completely natural and unhurried.

He slid beneath the covers and drew her against him, but she resisted, even though the hard, muscled body pressing against hers was wonderfully familiar. He let her go, then raised himself up on one elbow and stared at her.

"They're gone, Charlie. The disguise worked."

"I know that," she told him, staring into eyes that were once more ice-blue. "What I don't understand is how you can be so nonchalant about it."

He stared at her for a moment, then abruptly sat up in bed and ran his fingers through his hair, which had been flattened by the wig. "I'm *not* being nonchalant," he insisted with a slight edge to his voice. "I know how dangerous it was. But it worked, and that's all that matters. Would you rather see me go to pieces?"

"Under the circumstances, that might be more appropriate," she replied in a tone not unlike his own.

"Appropriate," he echoed. "Look, I *was* scared—all right? When you're in my business, you learn how to control that fear. If I hadn't controlled it, they would have seen it, and then they'd have been suspicious. And it wasn't just *me* I was worried about, either. If they'd gotten suspicious, they would have insisted on searching the place and they might have found *you.*"

"Did you know them?" she asked to change the subject.

He nodded. "One of them. The other is a new hire."

He was silent for a few moments, then turned to her. "Like Yogi Berra said, this is déjà vu all over again. One of the reasons it ended with Kelly, the woman I was involved with before, is that she thought I was cold. Afterward, I began to think maybe she was right, and that's when I decided to leave the city and come up here. But I guess it didn't do much good. I can't change who I am. But I don't want that to ruin things for us. When this is over, I want us to have a chance.''

"So do I, Zach," she said softly. "And I never said you were cold. It's just that you're so different from any other man I've known.''

"Is this where we both start talking about our pasts?" he asked with a grin.

"No. I think I'd rather stay in the present," she replied with a smile, even though she'd never been one to live completely in the moment.

"Good," he murmured as his mouth covered hers.

They made love slowly and deliciously, lingering in each moment even as they both felt the ever-stronger drumbeat of passion. She let go of all her doubts and fears and yielded herself to him even as she made her own demands, delighting in her power over this man, liking the way he made no attempt to hide that fact.

Whatever else Zach Hollis might be, he certainly wasn't cold.

"WHAT WILL YOU be doing while I'm gone?" she asked, trying to hide her nervousness.

"I'm going into the woods to see if I can find that truck. But I don't have any great hopes for success. And I think I'll start hanging out a bit at the Antlers.''

"What's that?" Her uneasiness ratcheted still more.

"It's a bar out on Route 17. A lot of local guys who are into hunting and fishing hang out there—mostly ones who can't afford to join a camp. Some of Summers's men hang out there. The place is so damned dark and smoke-filled that I could probably walk in without my disguise and not be recognized.''

"What do you mean, Summers's men?" she questioned, confused.

"His trash haulers. That's his business. Being county

commissioner is, theoretically, at least, only a part-time job.''

"Oh. I didn't realize that.'' She frowned, suddenly remembering something. "Was William Davis one of his men—before he went to prison?''

Zach frowned, too. "Davis? You mean that little rat-faced con? Why?''

"I never told you," she said. "I'd nearly forgotten about him because the warden told me right before you said you were going to escape.''

"The warden told you what?'' Zach asked impatiently.

"That he'd heard Davis was behind the attack on you. He's from Ondago County. I remember wondering about it at the time, but I knew he would already have been in prison by the time you became chief.''

"I didn't know that. What's he in for?''

"Manslaughter, as I recall. He killed someone in a bar fight. When you mentioned Summers's business, it rang a bell. I interviewed Davis for my group, and I seem to recall that his information sheet mentioned he was employed by a trash hauling company.''

"Whitfield Sanitation?'' Zach asked eagerly.

"That could have been it.'' She nodded. "It sounds familiar. Is that Harvey Summers's company?''

"Yeah. It's an old business. Summers inherited it from his mother's family.'' He was silent, nodding. "That makes sense. I never could figure out why those four came after me. I wrote it off to the fact that I was a cop, but there seemed to be more to it than that.''

"You think that Harvey Summers paid them?''

"It's possible. He could have set it up through Davis, if you're right about Davis having worked for him. Davis wouldn't have had the guts to take me on himself, and in any event, Summers would have told him not to get personally involved, because if Davis *was* his employee, it could come back to him.

"In fact, I have a vague recollection of one of my men— Colby, I think—mentioning a killing at the Antlers a few years back. That could have been Davis. Or maybe it was your father who told me. Homicides are rare enough around here that he could have mentioned it."

"And you're going to start hanging out there?" she asked.

"I have to go where the information is," he replied in a distracted tone, obviously lost in his thoughts.

"But you said that Summers could have killed you that night and didn't. So why would he have tried it after you were in prison?"

"A couple of possibilities. Number one, that he couldn't do it that night because Colby wouldn't have gone along with it. And number two, if he'd succeeded in getting me killed in prison, everyone would have assumed I'd been killed because I was a cop."

"Colby is beginning to sound like the key to all this," she suggested. "If we could just get him to talk…"

"He won't," Zach stated flatly, interrupting her. "He has too much to lose, especially if we're right about Summers being that drunk driver and if Colby was with him. The only way Colby would talk is to save his own skin—a deal with the D.A. And we're a long way from having enough information to go to the D.A.

"But you're right that he's the key. If he knows it's over, he'll definitely be willing to plea-bargain."

They walked down the road to the other cabin where her car was hidden in the garage. C.Z. was going home for a day and then returning to stay at Stacey's as planned. But she didn't like the idea much since now she knew what Zach would be doing.

"There's something we both need to be aware of," he

said as he opened the garage door. "We can't assume that Colby and Summers are working together at this point."

"What do you mean?"

"Summers could have a couple of lowlifes out looking for me or keeping an eye on you. Don't assume that he bought your story about your reason for being here. I think you'd better stay away for a while—stay with Stacey, I mean."

She stared at him. "You intended this all along, didn't you? Even before I told you about Davis."

His gaze slid away from hers, but he nodded. "I figured all along that Summers wouldn't give up, and what you told me about Davis proves that. It's time for you to stay out of it, C.Z. It's too risky, and there isn't a lot that I can do to protect you right now."

"You could have been honest with me," she protested.

"I'm being honest now. If I'd told you earlier, we'd just have wasted time arguing about it."

He reached for her and drew her into his arms. "I don't want to let you go, Charlie girl, believe me. You're the only good thing in my life right now. But that's why I want to keep you safe. I'll find a way to see you soon, but I want you to promise me you'll wait until you hear from me."

"But how—"

He cut off her question with a kiss. "Get out of here now," he said gruffly, "before I can't let you go."

ZACH WATCHED as her car churned up a cloud of dust and vanished around a bend in the road. She was barely out of sight, and already he missed her.

He didn't know which was worse, the risk of keeping her with him or the worrying about what she might be doing when he wasn't there. He knew she thought he was a risk-taker—and he was—but the difference between them was that he knew the risks, and he wasn't sure that she did. Still, he was convinced that she would be safer staying at Stacey's and staying away from him. Summers couldn't be sure she was in this with him, and if she didn't do anything suspicious, he'd give up on her.

He started up the road to the A-frame, plotting a course of action. Now that he knew the disguise worked, it was time to make some moves. He could feel that edge, that feeling he always had when he was pursuing a case. She was right when she'd said that he was addicted to his work. He just hoped she could learn to live with it—because he didn't think he could learn to live without her.

"THIS WILL BE your room," Stacey said. "Actually, it's my favorite, but we kept the master bedroom because it's much bigger."

"It's lovely," C.Z. said sincerely. "The whole house is wonderful, Stacey."

Stacey smiled proudly. "Thanks. But you know, we've put so much time and work into it that it's kind of a letdown, now that it's finished. Ted is half-afraid I'm going to want to move and start all over again."

When Stacey left her to get settled in, C.Z. walked to the window and stared at a huge old sycamore that shaded the window, its heavy, mottled limbs nearly touching the pane. It was a wonderful old house. She envied her friend. She'd always been torn between a love for big old houses and an equal attraction to the starkly modern.

As she stared through the branches into Stacey's garden where clumps of mums provided the only color, her thoughts turned to Zach's house—and then to Zach.

She knew he was right to want her to stay here, but she also knew that meant long, lonely nights of worrying about the chances he might be taking.

Stacey had told her that Sam Gittings had called the evening before, asking when she was returning. Her old friend had teased her that Sam still had a crush on her, and C.Z. thought that just might be the case. If only she could tell Stacey that she wasn't interested, that she was in love with Zach. She hated the need for secrecy. Somehow, part of being in love was telling everyone in your life about it, and she was being denied that pleasure.

But there was no doubt in her mind that she was indeed in love with Zach Hollis. Two days away from him had confirmed that. What had begun as a powerful physical attraction had deepened into something much bigger, stronger.

He had rough edges that could never be softened, and there was no doubt that he was addicted to danger, but he also had a strong sense of honor and integrity and a very great and private gentleness, as well.

What it all came down to, she thought, was that she *knew* Zach Hollis was the man for her. But in between this time and the future she could see them sharing lay a dark and twisted path.

She turned from the window and began to unpack, then selected a long challis skirt, silk top and lightweight wool jacket to wear for her dinner with Mary Williams. Although she naturally harbored some hopes that Mary might be a source of information that could help Zach, C.Z. was also very curious about Mary's relationship with her father.

"MARY, forgive me if I'm prying, but I understand that you and my father were…close."

Mary Williams blushed. "We were. It sounds silly to say we were dating at our age, doesn't it? I didn't think you knew, because I knew he hadn't told you. But I guess you found out from Stacey. There are no secrets in this town."

C.Z. laughed and didn't tell her that she'd guessed it herself, then had it confirmed by Zach, not Stacey. Instead, she talked about her guilt over her failure to spend time with her father.

"He understood, C.Z.—believe me. He said that you were planning to come and spend some time with him after you finished grad school. In fact, right before he was killed, he suggested that might be a good time to announce that we were going to get married."

Tears sprang to the eyes of both women and they reached out to clasp hands for a few moments, sharing the grief that hadn't gone away.

"It was just so terrible," C.Z. said. "I mean, Dad was always so careful in the woods. He'd investigated other hunting accidents, so he knew the dangers."

Mary nodded as she daubed at her eyes with a tissue. "They were hunting on the camp's lands, and it was posted. He wouldn't hunt on public game lands because he was always worried about trigger-happy nuts from the city. My husband had belonged to that same camp, you know, and they never had a problem there before."

C.Z. chose her next words very carefully. "Did anyone ever suggest that it might not have been an accident?"

Something in Mary's eyes gave her away. C.Z. knew that she, at least, *had* questioned that at some point. But could it be nothing more than a refusal to accept the truth, that it was nothing more than a random accident?

"What do you mean?" Mary asked.

C.Z. affected a shrug. "Nothing, really. It's just that it *was* unusual, as you said, and Dad certainly could have had some enemies. I mean, he could have been working on something and was maybe getting too close to the truth."

Mary let the silence drag on for a few moments, then shook her head. "If he was, I didn't know about it. And his men would certainly have looked into that possibility."

Their entrees arrived, and C.Z. reluctantly let the matter rest. But she was nearly certain there was something Mary wasn't telling her. Still, why would she do that? She'd obviously loved him, and that meant she'd want to see his murderer caught.

They talked about Mary's children, both of whom were somewhat older than C.Z., though of course she'd known them, since they'd grown up in the same neighborhood. C.Z. told her that she was considering moving back to the area and mentioned the position that would soon be vacant at Ondago Family Services, saying that Stacey had already arranged for her to meet the woman who was leaving and learn some more about them.

Mary said her sister sat on the board of the nonprofit agency and promised to speak to her on C.Z.'s behalf. C.Z. knew her sister, since she'd been her teacher in third grade. She was reminded of just what a small, insular world this was.

Zach's name didn't enter the conversation until dessert, when they were talking about how the area was growing and changing.

"I suppose you must have heard about our former police chief who's in prison for trying to kill Harvey Summers. Or I should say, he *was* in prison. He's escaped."

C.Z. nodded. "I was working at the prison while he was there, but I'd met him before that. Dad introduced us when I was here on a visit one time."

"Oh?" Mary said, obviously startled. "What do you think of him?"

"I like him," C.Z. replied. "It's hard for me to believe he could have done something like that."

Mary sighed. "Yes, I know what you mean. I liked him from the first time we interviewed him for the position, and I know that your father liked him, as well."

"But the jury obviously believed Harvey Summers and Chief Colby," C.Z. commented neutrally.

"Yes," Mary said, then lapsed into silence before suddenly asking, "Did you actually speak to him while he was in prison? Did he tell you anything?"

C.Z. was certain that she heard *something* in Mary's voice beyond just curiosity, but she wasn't sure what it was. So she said Zach had told her that, in fact, it was *Summers* who had tried to kill *him.*

"But did he give you any reason why Harvey might have done such a thing?" Mary asked in an oddly intent tone.

"No. According to him, that was the problem. He couldn't defend himself because he couldn't think why Harvey would have tried to kill him."

She waited for a few heartbeats, then asked if Mary could think of any reason.

Mary's gaze met hers briefly, then slid away as she toyed with her chocolate mousse cake. "No, I can't. Harvey was adamantly opposed to our hiring Zach in the first place, but he was outvoted. It was a very uncomfortable situation for Walt Jackson, the other commissioner, and me. We've always worked well together and we've tended to reach a consensus on such matters, but Harvey refused to make it a unanimous vote. He wanted us to consider Dave Colby, even though Dave hadn't applied for the job."

"But he has the job now," C.Z. commented.

"I think Harvey talked him into it. Frankly, neither Walt nor I believe that David is up to the job, but after the fiasco with Zach, we felt that we had to go along.

"Dave is just beside himself right now, because Harvey's convinced him that Zach must be in the area. In fact, Harvey's so frightened that he got a permit to carry a gun."

Unable to think of a way to gain any more information through indirect means, C.Z. opted for the direct approach. "Mary, is it possible that there's something in Harvey's background that he feared Zach would expose? If so, that could explain why he tried to kill Zach and then lied to get him sent to prison."

Unfortunately, their waiter chose that moment to inquire if they were ready for the bill. C.Z. had only a fleeting impression of something troubling in Mary's eyes before she nodded to the waiter. Then, when the waiter had departed, she shook her head.

"Nothing that I know of, and I've known him all my life."

Chapter Seven

"C.Z.!"

C.Z. jerked to wakefulness. Caught in that strange place between consciousness and sleep, she thought she'd heard Zach's voice, low and urgent. It didn't surprise her that she'd imagined it. A week had passed since she'd seen him, and with each passing hour she came closer to ignoring his order to stay away. Every morning, she made sure to listen to the local radio news, fearing that he'd been captured. Fortunately, both Stacey and Ted left for work early; otherwise, they might have wondered at her intense interest.

"C.Z.! Let me in!"

A startled cry escaped her lips as she sat up in bed and stared at the window. The drapes were drawn, but she'd left the window open just a bit, and they billowed in the night breeze.

Her heart pounding in her chest, she climbed from the bed and ran to the window, still half convinced that she'd imagined his voice. But when she parted the drapes, there he was, crouched on the heavy limb of the sycamore, his hands braced on either side of the window frame!

Reality clashed with her memory of him, rendering her temporarily paralyzed. He was wearing his disguise, including the body padding. It crossed her mind fleetingly that the additional bulk must have made it difficult for him to climb the tree.

Her fingers trembling, she raised the window and then fumbled with the latches on the screen before finally getting it up, as well. Then she quickly stepped back on shaky legs as he climbed over the sill and stepped into her bedroom.

"What— How—"

But Zach's only response to her half-formed questions was to push her against the bed and then tumble into it with her, his mouth covering hers even as she sank into the mattress.

"I've missed you," he growled as his hands quickly found their way beneath her nightshirt.

She shivered, partly from his rough, cool touch and partly from the heated passion of his words. "How did you—"

"Later," he murmured as he tugged the nightshirt over her head and began to rain kisses over her exposed flesh.

His beard was longer now, and softer, but it still tickled her sensitive skin, making her giggle even as desire began to thrum through her, building quickly and threatening to explode.

She tried to unbutton his shirt, and then gave up on that and reached for the waistband of his jeans. But there was still the padding to deal with, and she made a sound of frustration. In the pale moonlight that poured in through the window, she saw the flash of his smile as he levered himself off the bed.

"So you missed me, too," he said with quiet satisfaction as he stripped off his clothing and the padding.

Missed him? It went far beyond that, though she could not find the words to tell him that, certainly not at the moment, as he stood there naked before her with the moonlight bathing his body in a silvered glow and revealing the evidence of his desire.

So instead, she opened her arms to him and drew him to her and gloried in the feel of him. And in that moment before she let all thoughts vanish beneath the sensual onslaught, C.Z. knew that she was not just welcoming him back but was also welcoming back a part of herself.

Zach tried to temper his eagerness to have her. She could feel the effort he made to control himself, and that only made her want him still more. This was a Zach who was ruled by passion—a far different man from the one who faced danger so calmly and coolly.

She liked feeling the battle he was waging with himself while at the same time she enjoyed taunting him, pushing him close to the edge.

With a groan that signaled his surrender to a force beyond his control, he parted her and thrust into her and she arched to him and clung to him, and they both rode the flood tide of passion to the highest crest, then slid slowly down amidst sighs of pleasure—and of regret that it had all been too brief.

"I love you," he murmured, his lips brushing lightly against the top of her head as she nestled against his chest. "I didn't want to say that until I could be sure we have a future."

She kissed the taut, hair-roughened skin of his chest. "I know. I love you, too, Zach, even though it's too soon and too dangerous."

"It's because it's dangerous that it's happened so quickly," he said, drawing away from her and propping himself up on one elbow. "If we weren't in this situation, we'd both be doing a lot more thinking before we admitted it."

She nodded, rather surprised at his perceptiveness. When, she wondered, would she stop underestimating this man? It was the conceit of her profession, she supposed, that she should think him incapable of such thoughts.

And it was also her perception of him as a man of action, not much given to introspection. But lately, he'd had little to do but think. Perhaps he was even having trouble recognizing himself.

"I've got to make something happen," he said after a long silence. He rolled over onto his back and stared up at the ceiling.

She was momentarily confused until she realized that he wasn't talking about them but rather about their situation—*his* situation, actually, but she was too involved now to think of it that way. The man of passion had once more become a man of action, or rather, a man frustrated by inaction.

"I had dinner last night with Sam," she told him. "He talked quite a lot about you. Maybe he could help us. I know we could trust him."

He rolled onto his side and stared at her. "You had a dinner date with him?"

His tone of voice startled her. "Well, I suppose you could call it that. I told you I've known him for ages."

"But he asked you out, and you accepted."

"Yes, but—"

"That sounds like a date to me."

"Are you saying that you're jealous? Because—"

"Yeah, that's exactly what I'm saying. I tell you that I love you, and now you tell me that you're going out with Sam Gittings."

"Don't be ridiculous! I went out with him because I know he wants to help you, and I thought I'd sort of feel him out, see if he can be trusted."

"Maybe that's your reason for going out with him, but it sure wasn't his reason for asking. And we're *not* going to get him involved. It's too risky for him."

"It's a risk he might be willing to take, Zach. He really cares about you."

"I like him, too, but we're not getting him involved."

"Because you're jealous of him."

"So what? Is this some earth-shattering discovery, that I can be jealous? How do you think I feel when I hear that the woman I love is going out to dinner with some other guy while I have to sneak around to see her at all?"

"Not seeing me was *your* decision," she pointed out. "You're blowing this all out of proportion, Zach."

He was silent, but she could feel him seething with frustration. She thought back to what he'd said earlier, about making something happen. All that pent-up frustration was going to find an outlet soon—and quite probably a very dangerous one.

"I had dinner with Mary Williams, too," she said, trying to ease them away from the volatile subject of Sam Gittings. "It could have been nothing more than wishful thinking on my part, but it seemed to me that she knows something."

To her very great relief, his brooding turned quickly to a keen interest as she related her conversation with Mary.

"The problem is," she said with a sigh, "if she really does know something, she wouldn't keep it secret. Or at least I don't think she would, especially if she had any reason to suspect that Harvey Summers might have killed Dad."

Zach nodded. "You've got a point. Still, she knows him well. They've worked together for a long time, and from what I heard, her husband was one of Harvey's closest friends. I know he used to be part of Summers's poker-playing crowd."

C.Z. chewed on that bit of information for a few minutes. "Do you think that she might have told Dad something? They were pretty serious, according to Mary. They'd even talked about marriage."

"It's a stretch, but I agree that it's possible. Still, if she knew something that could have helped me, I think she would have spoken up.''

''Maybe it's a case of not being sure. She certainly wouldn't want to accuse Harvey of anything unless she was very certain about it.'' She frowned thoughtfully. ''I think it's time for me to start pushing her a bit. She knows that I've met you and I told her that I thought you were innocent. I could tell her that I'm trying to help you without admitting that I know where you are now.''

''Okay. That sounds good. If she's troubled by something she knows or has guessed, then she might be willing to talk to you. But there's something else I want to do, and I need your help.''

''Of course. What is it?''

''I've spent two nights over at the Antlers, and I picked up hints of something. It's about Willie Davis—the con who was supposedly behind the attack on me.''

''Hints about what?''

''Someone was saying that his family's been living pretty well, considering that he's in prison and his wife is a maid at one of the local nursing homes. In fact, the guy joked that they've been living better since he's been in prison than they did when he was home. He knows Willie. They worked together—for Harvey Summers.''

''So you think that Harvey paid Davis's wife for him instigating that attack on you in prison?''

''It could be. He couldn't very well have paid Davis himself, and if anyone started to ask questions, Summers could just say that he was helping out the family of an employee.''

''What do you want to do?''

''I want to get into their house and have a look around. I checked the phone book and they live out on Circleville Road. Most of the houses out there are set far apart, and there should be a mailbox with their name on it.

"The reason I need your help is that she's not likely to let me into the house, no matter what story I come up with. But if I have a woman with me, it'll be easier. With luck, no one will be home if we go during the day, but she could work different shifts."

PRIVATELY, C.Z. thought that this expedition was useless. Even if they did find proof that the Davis family was living beyond their means, it would scarcely help them. As Zach had said, the Davis woman could simply claim that Harvey Summers was helping them out.

But she was going along with it because she knew that Zach had to do something, and if it wasn't this, it might well be something far more dangerous.

When she drove out to the A-frame and picked him up, she could feel the tension in him, the growing urgency to take some sort of action, and damn the consequences. This side of him both disturbed and attracted her. But she understood his frustration at his inability to clear himself, and for that reason, she had decided to take some action of her own that she had no intention of telling him about—at least until it was done.

"I'm sorry about last night," he said suddenly, breaking a long silence as they drove along Circleville Road, studying the mailboxes.

"I was out of line," he continued. "It's just that I like Sam and he's free and I'm not, and I got jealous."

"I understand," she said, reaching over to touch his hand briefly.

"Do you?" he asked, studying her face carefully. "I don't want you to think that I'm some sort of jealous maniac. I'm not like that, Charlie. Slow down! There it is!"

She slowed down opposite a single mailbox where the name Davis had been painted on the side in bold black letters. He told her to pull over and stop. She did so, but before he got out of the car, she laid a restraining hand on his arm.

"Zach, you can't really believe that I'd think that about you. Give me some credit for knowing you better than that."

He settled back against the seat. "It isn't you, it's me. I'm spending too much time in my own head." Then he chuckled. "It's a damn good thing I managed to fall in love with a shrink, isn't it?"

She laughed, too. "One could call it serendipitous."

He turned to stare up the narrow dirt road beside the mailbox. "It looks like there are a couple of cars up there, but they might just be junkers. Let's go."

They both got out and began to walk up the road. If Mrs. Davis or any of the children happened to be home, they intended to ask to use the phone to call a garage, claiming that a warning light had come on and the engine was acting strangely.

There were two cars and a pickup parked haphazardly in the weedy front yard. One car clearly wasn't road-worthy, but it was impossible to tell about the other car and the truck.

"If Harvey is paying them, she certainly hasn't spent any of it on the house," C.Z. remarked. The front porch listed to one side and the steps sagged. Dirty white paint was peeling from the wood frame construction.

"Yeah, but look at that," Zach said as they drew nearer. "That's the same system I have, and it runs over a thousand, plus the monthly fees."

She followed his gaze to the side of the house, where a satellite dish sat amidst a clutter of ancient appliances. At that moment, a dog began to bark, and C.Z. saw it, chained to a crudely built doghouse at the side of the house. She'd never understood why people kept dogs if they didn't want them as house pets. It made no sense to her.

But she had little time to dwell on that subject because the front door opened and a woman peered out warily. She had the look of a woman grown old before her time, beaten down by poverty and hard work. And perhaps beaten as well by a worthless, drunken husband, C.Z. thought as she recalled her encounter in prison with William Davis and wondered if his wife might be happy he was there.

"Hello," Zach said, walking to the porch steps. "Our car broke down out there and I was hoping we could use your phone."

C.Z. followed him to the porch, noting the way he had slipped so easily into his un-coplike voice. The woman peered at him silently for a moment before shifting her gaze to C.Z., who smiled pleasantly. Then the woman nodded and stood aside for them to come in. C.Z. guessed that Zach had been right—she would never have let Zach into the house if he'd been alone.

The interior of the house confirmed their suspicions. There was new furniture in the living room, together with a big-screen TV, and when the woman led them to the kitchen, C.Z. saw that all the appliances were new, as well. She wondered if Davis knew how his wife was spending Summers's money and wondered, too, why Summers had paid it, since his scheme hadn't worked.

While Zach went to the phone, she smiled disarmingly at Mrs. Davis and asked if she might use the bathroom. She guessed there wouldn't be one downstairs, and if she got upstairs, she could see what else was new.

The woman nodded and told her it was upstairs, the first door on the right. Zach appeared to be carrying on a conversation with someone, though who it might be, she couldn't imagine. She hurried up the stairs and quickly used the bathroom, then tiptoed quietly down the hall. One door was closed and she didn't want to risk opening it, but in the two bedrooms, she saw new furniture and two more TV sets. There was no doubt that Mrs. Davis had gone on a recent shopping spree.

By the time she came downstairs, Zach was off the phone and waiting near the staircase for her, with the silent Mrs. Davis hovering nearby. He was admiring the big-screen TV and asking her questions about the satellite. Her responses were monosyllabic, and she wouldn't meet his eyes.

They thanked her and left, and as soon as they were out of earshot, C.Z. told him what she'd seen upstairs. Zach grunted.

"She'd better hope they keep him inside for a long time. He probably doesn't know what she spent the money on. That's a battered wife if I ever saw one." He smiled grimly. "Maybe we can do her a favor. If we nail Summers and he admits to paying Davis to get me killed in prison, that'll be enough to keep him there for a while longer."

"But we're really no closer to proving anything," C.Z. said unhappily, then asked who he'd called.

"My old number. I guessed that they hadn't reassigned it yet—and they hadn't." He reached out to take her hand. "We'll get there, Charlie. It's just going to take a while. All I need is time and some luck."

C.Z. thought that somehow, their situations had become reversed. Zach was the one who'd seemed so impatient, so determined to take some sort of risky action—while she had wanted to avoid just that. But now, he seemed content to move slowly, while she was about to take a big risk herself—one she had no intention of telling him about.

"What are you going to be doing?" she asked.

"Spending my days in the woods looking for that truck and my nights over at the Antlers drinking with some of Summers's men. From what I've heard so far, most of them have worked for him for years, and my guess is that they know something or have guessed something."

He turned and gave her a decidedly evil smile. "It turns

out that one of the regulars is Dave Colby's brother-in-law. I'd never met him before, but I remember Colby talking about him. They don't get along, and the guy's a drunk. If he knows or suspects anything, he'll talk sooner or later, especially if I'm buying.''

"I'm pretty sure that no one has been following me," she told him. "I want to come out to see you."

He shook his head. "Stay away, C.Z. It's safer that way. I'll come to see you again in a week, or sooner, if I find anything."

"You're shutting me out of this, aren't you?"

They had reached her car, and Zach drew her into his arms. "I couldn't shut you out of my life even if I wanted to," he said softly. "But I *can* do my best to keep you safe."

Then he hooked a finger beneath her chin and drew her face up, forcing her to meet his gaze. His eyes were muddy brown behind the lenses and the glasses, but their effect was just as piercing as if she were seeing his own ice-blue eyes.

"Don't start thinking about taking any chances, Charlie girl. If you come up with any ideas, run them by me first. Summers has got to be feeling nervous already with me on the loose. Nervousness turns to desperation real fast, and if he has any reason to suspect you of helping me, he might just try to kill you."

She nodded but did not say she still had trouble believing that Harvey Summers was a killer. She also did not tell him of her plan, for the very simple reason that she knew he would not approve.

Zach needed to believe he was keeping her safe. She understood that. But she could not stand idly by while he tried desperately to clear his name.

C.Z. OPENED THE TRUNK of her car in the parking lot outside the courthouse that also served as police headquarters.

She picked up the box, then paused, inundated by memories of visiting her father here. She knew that the children of police officers often got themselves into trouble just to prove something to their peers, and she wondered if she, too, might have done that, if her parents had stayed married. Instead, as a child, she'd been very proud of the fact that her father was a police officer, and she'd loved coming to the station.

Carrying the carton, she walked across the lot and through the side entrance that led to police headquarters. She recognized the officer at the desk, an older man nearing retirement now. He frowned at her, then suddenly smiled.

"You're Tom's girl! I thought you looked familiar. I remember you from the funeral." The smile drained away. "Sure do miss your dad around here."

"I miss him, too," C.Z. said, surprised to find her throat suddenly constricting. "And it's because of him that I'm here. Is Chief Colby available? I have something for him."

He picked up the phone, spoke briefly, then gestured to the hallway. "The office at the end. But I guess you remember that."

She did, and she could almost believe that she would find her father there, sitting at his big desk, surrounded by neat, orderly piles of the paperwork he hated. But of course, what she found instead was Dave Colby.

Like her father, Colby was a big man, both tall and broad. But in Colby's case, there seemed to be more fat than muscle. He was just putting on his jacket as she appeared in the doorway. His shoulder holster hung from the back of the big leather desk chair. At least, she thought dryly, he hadn't found it necessary to put that on.

"C.Z.," he said with a hearty, booming voice, even as his gaze slid quickly from her face to the box she carried into his office. She thought he seemed to tense at the sight of it.

"I hope I'm not interrupting you, Chief Colby." She smiled pleasantly. Then she gestured to the box she'd set on the edge of his desk. "I recently discovered these files and thought I should bring them back. After Dad died, we packed up his personal things and I just never got around to going through them until recently. His death had hit me really hard, and I couldn't face any reminders of him." She paused, feeling slightly ashamed of her obvious play for sympathy. But it *was* the truth, after all.

"I can understand that," Colby said quickly. "We all felt that way. Your dad was a good man and a good boss. I learned a lot from him."

Their eyes met, but his slid away quickly, though not before C.Z. could see what she could only think of as a tortured soul. It seemed to confirm what Zach had said, that Colby might have been an unwilling participant in all of this.

"What's in the box?" he asked, staring at it.

"They're police files. I looked through them, and it seems like they're all old files—cases that hadn't been solved. I assume that Dad must have been working on them. Maybe these are just copies that he kept at home for his own convenience, but I thought I'd better bring them back."

Colby walked around the desk and began to go through them. C.Z. watched him covertly, wondering if he was an example of the kind of person her father had once talked about, someone who takes one step outside the law and is then plunged into a life of deception and crime. A passenger in a truck that swerved into a school bus filled with children, perhaps drunk himself, who flees the scene and then watches helplessly as his life goes out of control.

"Yeah," he said, nodding. "It looks like that's what they

are. But these are copies. I know the original files are here. I've seen a couple of them.''

He continued to stare at the contents of the box, then said, seemingly more to himself than to her, ''Tom just wouldn't quit.''

C.Z. heard the pathos in his voice, and she was as certain as she could be that if someone had deliberately shot her father, it wasn't Colby. Still, given what must be his role in all this, she couldn't feel much sympathy for him. Legalities aside, Dave Colby's greatest problem was a lack of moral courage.

''That's the way Dad was,'' she agreed. ''I recognized some of those cases because he used to talk about them. But what really struck me as being strange was that there's a file missing.''

Colby had been riffling through the files, but at her final words, his head snapped up and he stared hard at her. His fear was palpable. ''What file?''

''The school bus crash. No case ever bothered Dad as much as that one, but it's not there. It's strange, because he mentioned to me the last time I talked to him that he thought he knew who was driving that truck that hit the bus. That was only a week before he died.''

''Hmph!'' Colby went through the files again, as though searching for what he certainly knew wasn't there.

C.Z. had been standing, but now she took a seat and strove to find exactly the right tone. ''Chief Colby, please don't misunderstand what I'm about to say. I know that all of you would have done your best to find the man who killed my father, but is it possible that it *wasn't* an accident, that whoever Dad suspected knew he was under suspicion?''

Colby dragged his gaze away from the box and stared at her. ''Are you suggesting that your father was *murdered?*''

''It's possible, isn't it?'' she asked. ''I mean, if Dad

knew something that could have put him in jail, he could have done it and just made it look like a hunting accident.''

Colby said nothing as he walked around the desk to his chair. And in those few seconds his back was turned, he managed to compose himself.

"A hunting accident's just what it was," he said sternly. "We've never had any reason to think otherwise."

Perfect, she thought, rising from her chair. It was exactly the reaction she'd hoped for. She could now take the next step. She held out her hand to the startled Colby, who took it rather belatedly.

"Thank you for your time, Chief Colby."

Then, before he could say anything else, she walked out the door and out of the building. But instead of going to her car, she walked around to the front entrance. And on the way, she saw what she hadn't noticed before: Colby's black Bronco parked in the space reserved for the police chief. It looked exactly like the vehicle she'd seen parked outside her condo.

After checking the directory posted in the lobby of the elegant old courthouse, C.Z. walked up the stairs to the second floor suite of commissioners' offices. A secretary in the outer office confirmed that Commissioner Summers was in, and after conferring with him on the phone, pointed the way to his office.

By the time she reached it, Harvey Summers was out from behind his desk, his face wreathed in smiles and his hand outstretched. She wondered if Colby had called him.

"C.Z.! What a pleasure! Have a seat. How can I help you?"

C.Z. took the proferred chair, thinking that it was no wonder this man had remained in office all these years. He was the consummate politician. The only wonder was that he hadn't parlayed all that heartiness into a higher office.

"I hope you meant what you said about being willing to

help me, Mr. Summers, because that's why I'm here,'' she said with a hopeful tone and smile.

"Of course I meant it,'' he assured her with seeming sincerity. "But please call me Harvey. Everyone else does.''

"Thank you, Harvey. What I'm here about may be a kind of delicate matter, and I could be wrong. In fact, I probably *am* wrong, but…'' She let her voice trail off uncertainly, then went on.

"I've just come from Chief Colby's office. He was very nice to me, but I don't think he intends to *do* anything.''

Once again, she paused, searching Summers's face. If he had any idea of what was to come, he was certainly hiding it well. She told him about her discovery of the files, then repeated her lie about her father's telling her that he thought he knew who was responsible for the school bus tragedy.

"It was only a week before he died, and I can't help wondering if he could have been killed by whoever it was that he suspected. But Chief Colby didn't seem to want to consider that possibility.''

"I see,'' was all Summers said as he got up from his chair and walked to the big windows that looked on the town square. After a few seconds, he turned to face her.

"Well, I'm sure you know that your father's death was thoroughly investigated. But let's just say that you're right. If he *did* suspect someone, don't you think he would have told someone about it—his men, I mean? And he must not have, or it would have come out during the investigation.''

"I thought about that, and the only reason I could think of that he might have kept it secret is that the person he suspected was someone with enough power or influence in the community that he didn't dare go public with it until he was sure.

"It was such a terrible thing, after all. And if the man

he suspected *was* the driver and knew that Dad suspected him..." She shrugged, paused and then went on.

"And there's something I didn't tell Chief Colby, because he didn't seem interested. Someone broke into my condo recently. I didn't report it to the police because nothing seemed to be missing. But later, when I went through that box of files and saw that there was no file there for the school bus crash, I began to wonder if whoever broke in might have taken it."

"But if nothing was taken, how do you know someone broke in? Was there a broken window or broken door lock?"

She shook her head. "No, it was the footprints. There were dusty footprints in the upstairs hallway carpeting. Someone had been in the attic, and that's where the box of files was."

Summers looked at his watch. "I have a meeting in a few minutes, but I'll speak to Chief Colby. I can't make any promises, C.Z., because I know the investigation into your father's death was very thorough, but I'll try."

She got up and put out her hand. "Thank you, Harvey. I really appreciate it."

She had turned to leave. His voice stopped her. "You said this break-in occurred recently. Don't you think that if someone was worried about that file, they would have come sooner?"

His question caught her off guard, but she answered easily. "Yes, I *did* think about that, but I don't have an answer—yet."

"YOU THINK your father was *murdered?*" Sam Gitting's dark eyes grew wide.

C.Z. glanced quickly around them. There were empty tables between them and the other diners, and no one appeared to have heard Sam's outburst. She leaned toward him, keeping her voice low.

"I can't be certain, Sam. Maybe I'll never know for sure, but yes, I think it's possible."

Then she went on to tell him everything—or *nearly* everything. She left out the minor detail of her role in Zach's escape and her relationship with him, and she repeated once more the lie about her father's last conversation with her.

"You see, I just didn't begin to put it all together until recently—what Dad had told me, Harvey Summers's lies about Zach Hollis, the break-in at my condo. But it makes sense, Sam. I think Summers was the drunk driver who killed those children, and I think Dad had found out something that made him suspect Summers. So Summers killed him and made it look like a hunting accident.

"Then, when Zach Hollis was hired as chief, I think Summers began to worry that he would continue the investigation, or at least start it all over again. Zach is smart and he's persistent, just like Dad was. Remember, Summers didn't want Zach to be hired. He wanted Dave Colby to get the job. Not only isn't Colby all that smart, but I think it's possible he was the passenger in that pickup. That would explain why he'd go along with Summers when he lied about Zach.

"And I'm pretty sure Colby was the one who broke into my condo and took that file. I saw a black vehicle just like his in the parking lot several times, and it followed me for a while, too."

To his credit, Sam didn't interrupt her once, and when she'd finished, he leaned back in his chair and frowned thoughtfully. Sam was the opposite of Zach, a quiet, thoughtful, deliberate man. In fact, he was much like she was, or like she had been, before Zach Hollis turned her life upside down and inside out.

For one brief moment, watching him ponder the story

she'd told him, C.Z. found herself longing for that lost self, for a time when her life had been normal. But then she saw in her mind's eye the ice-blue eyes of Zach Hollis, sparkling with a passion that could even now send a soft heat stealing through her.

"Well," said Sam after a long pause during which their dinners arrived, "as a theory, it sounds possible, except for one thing. If Summers and Colby suspected your father had left something incriminating in that file, why did they wait so long to try to get it back? Surely they'd have worried that you'd find it."

"I'm sure they *were* worried. Harvey Summers offered to help me pack up Dad's things after he died. I think they just didn't have a chance to get it then, and they probably counted on my being too upset to go through them—or on the fact that if I'd found them, I would simply have returned them to police headquarters, where Colby could easily have gotten it and destroyed it."

"Okay, I'll buy that. But why would they decide to go after it now? What made them get worried again all of a sudden?"

Now came the tricky part, she thought. She'd anticipated this question and had an answer ready—if Sam would believe it.

"My guess is that they found out I was meeting with Zach Hollis in prison as his psychologist, and they were worried that the two of us would put our heads together and come up with the truth." She paused. "I visited Zach in the hospital only hours before he escaped. He'd asked to see me because he was worried about returning to the prison. I was questioned later by the state police, but they decided that I had nothing to do with Zach's escape. However, if Colby knew all this, he might have believed otherwise."

Sam stared at her in silence. C.Z. waited, hoping he

wouldn't ask if she had, in fact, helped Zach to escape. She didn't want to lie to him, and she knew she could trust him, but Zach had pointed out some time ago that they had no right to put Sam into an ethical dilemma that could ruin his career—or get him sent to jail.

"I suppose you must realize that by talking to Colby and Summers, you could be putting yourself into danger," Sam said.

She tried not to let her relief show and wondered if he hadn't asked because he suspected he wouldn't like the answer. "Yes, I know that. But I'll be careful. It was the only thing I could think of to do, Sam—unless *you* have some ideas."

"The key to everything is proving that Summers was driving that truck. I'd like to see the police file on the school bus accident."

"Can you do that, or could I get it myself? I'm not sure how that works."

"I can get it if you retain me to look into it."

"Consider yourself retained, then. I'm sure that if Dad had discovered something that made him suspect Harvey, it won't be in there, but maybe there will be something we can use."

They finished their dinner over other conversation, but C.Z. could almost see the wheels turning in Sam's head. She knew he would want to solve this not only for her sake, but for Zach's, as well.

They left the restaurant and Sam walked her to her car, which was parked some distance from his. She'd met him there because it was she who had invited him to dinner, and he lived on the opposite side of town from Stacey's place.

"Come to my office tomorrow," Sam said as they stopped beside her car. "You can give me a small retainer and make it official that you've hired me. I'll give it back.

This one's on me. If you're right, it will not only bring justice for your father's death, but it'll also free Zach. His case has really been bothering me, especially since my appeal was denied.''

She nodded. ''I'm really grateful to you, Sam.''

He reached out and took one of her hands in both of his. ''And I'm really worried about your safety. If you're right, then Summers has already killed, and my guess is that that would make it easier to kill again.

''That's one reason I want to make this all official. I want to make it known fast that you've hired me, because that means you've told me about your suspicions. And that means that going after you would be too risky for Summers.''

She hadn't thought about that, but she saw that he was right—maybe. ''Or it could mean that you're in danger, as well.''

''I don't think so. There has to be a limit to the risks they'd take. Still, I want you to promise me that you'll be really careful, C.Z.''

He was still holding her hand, and she leaned toward him and brushed her lips against his cheek. ''I'll be careful.''

Then, just as she moved away from him, she saw, over his shoulder, a sight that made her freeze. The restaurant was located in an old inn that had a bar with a separate entrance on the side. She'd been vaguely aware of a vehicle pulling into the side lot by the bar, but she'd paid it no attention. And now she saw the driver, still standing beside the battered Jeep as he stared at them.

''What is it?'' Sam asked, turning to see what she was staring at.

''Nothing,'' she said quickly. ''For a moment, I thought I recognized him, that's all.''

The driver started across the lot, his back to them as he

walked toward the bar entrance. C.Z saw Sam watching him with a frown, but she knew he'd never recognize his friend and client.

They said good night and C.Z. got into her car. But all the way to Stacey's house, she kept envisioning that scene as Zach would have seen it—two people close together in the shadows sharing a kiss. And she remembered Zach's burst of jealousy over Sam Gittings.

Chapter Eight

She couldn't sleep. No matter which position she tried, no matter how many times she pummeled the pillow, no matter what mental exercises she tried—nothing worked. It was almost as though she'd somehow snatched his vision of her and Sam. She could see them through his eyes, with his mind.

For a time, she tried on righteous anger. How could he think she would betray him when she'd told him she loved him? What kind of person did he think she was?

But the anger wouldn't hold. He was alone, a fugitive from the law, and he was frightened even if he refused to show it. She was the one person he trusted. And even if he didn't think she was betraying their love, he would be hurt. She kept remembering what he'd said about not being able to take her out to dinner. It had seemed to her to be such an inconsequential thing, but she realized it was far from unimportant to him.

Before she was aware that she'd made the decision, she had slipped quietly out of bed and was dressing, pulling on an old pair of jeans and a sweater. Surely it would be safe to go to him at this time of night.

The big old house had two staircases, the elegant, curved front stairs and the narrow back stairs to the kitchen. She chose the latter, to keep away from Stacey and Ted's room.

She felt like a sort of reverse thief, stealing out of their house in the middle of the night.

Her car was parked at the rear of the driveway, in the wide, paved area in front of the detached double garage that had once been a carriage house. It wasn't likely they would hear her leave, but still, she kept her eyes on the upstairs front windows as she started it, then rolled quietly, without lights, down the driveway.

There were only a few cars parked on the street in this neighborhood, where most homes had long driveways and garages. She studied them as she drove past them, but she saw no one. Then, when she made the turn onto Main Street, she slowed down and watched her rearview mirror. There were no lights behind her. She didn't really expect to be followed at this hour of the night, but after her encounters with Colby and Summers, she couldn't be sure.

She'd gone to them at least in part to take the heat off Zach and to establish an independent reason for her inquiries. She wanted them to think that she represented more of a threat to them than he did at the moment, and tomorrow, when Sam went to police headquarters to request the file on the school bus tragedy, they were likely to put finding Zach on the back burner for the moment—perhaps even believe that he'd simply disappeared.

She drove along dark, quiet streets, still keeping an eye on the rearview mirror. At one point, she saw headlights several blocks behind her, so she turned onto a side street. The car passed by on Main Street. She made several turns to get back there herself. The car was nowhere in sight. She hadn't gotten a good look at it, but it definitely wasn't Colby's Bronco or a police car.

Should she tell Zach what she'd done? It would explain why she was with Sam, but it would also mean that she'd ignored Zach's request not to take any action without consulting him first. A dilemma.

She turned off Main Street onto the mountain road that led to the A-frame, still undecided. Either way, Zach wasn't going to be happy with her. Trust between them was so important now, and regardless of what she said or didn't say, he would believe she'd betrayed him.

Most of the road she was traveling was winding, but when she reached the end of a relatively long, straight stretch, she suddenly saw headlights behind her. Cold fingers of fear slithered down her spine. Why would anyone be out here at this hour of the night?

She made a sound of disgust. *She* was out here, after all. Did she think she was the only one who had a reason to be on this road?

As she drove on, she passed several gravel and dirt roads that led to homes and cabins, but still she saw the lights behind her, always the same distance behind.

At the top of the mountain, she reached the intersection with the road that led to the A-frame. For a moment, she considered going straight, away from the A-frame. But then she turned left, toward it, deciding that if the car followed her, she could always drive past the entrance.

Her brief hesitation brought the other vehicle closer, and she saw it turning in the same direction. She was frightened, thinking about the lengthy stretch of deserted road that lay ahead. What if she *was* being followed and the driver tried to ram her or force her off the road? She gripped the wheel more tightly. Beads of perspiration popped out on her brow. At any moment, she expected the vehicle to speed toward her in a blaze of bright headlights. But it stayed where it was, vanishing from view as she rounded curves, then reappearing the same distance away on the straight stretches.

She slowed down, knowing that she risked a confrontation but unable to stand the uncertainty any longer. The turnoff to the A-frame was only a few miles ahead.

For a brief moment, the headlights seemed to come closer, but then the vehicle slowed and turned onto a gravel road she'd noticed and assumed led to some cabins. C.Z. came to a stop in the middle of the road and watched as the headlights lit up the woods briefly, then vanished as the car moved deeper into the woods.

Breathing a noisy sigh of relief, C.Z. set off again, driving fast and not slowing until she reached the turnoff to the A-frame. And as she turned, she dismissed the other vehicle and concentrated instead on Zach and what she should tell him.

When she reached the first cabin, she slowed to a stop, trying to decide if she should put her car in the garage and proceed on foot. But she couldn't stay. She would have to return to Stacey's before dawn. So she drove on, still undecided about how to handle the situation.

The A-frame was dark. The old Jeep was nowhere in evidence, but she assumed it must be parked around back. By now, it was past the bar closing time, so Zach must be here, probably watching uneasily from the darkened windows until he recognized her car. Or perhaps he'd already guessed she would be coming. He knew she'd seen him.

She turned off the engine and got out, then waited a moment for her eyes to adjust as much as possible to the darkness. A chill wind blew around her. It seemed much colder than it had only a short time ago when she'd come out of Stacey's house. She didn't need a sense of direction to know that it was coming out of the north, bringing the first real hint of the winter to come.

"Zach, it's me!" she called as she started up the steps to the deck, wondering if he might already be asleep. If so, he'd apparently been able to slough off the events of earlier this evening much better than she had. Perhaps she'd been mistaken about his reaction.

She peered in through the glass, but could see nothing,

not even the glow of a fire in the fireplace. C.Z. pounded on the door, and called his name again. But no light came on inside, and in the utter stillness of the night, she could hear no movements in there.

Terrified that something had happened to him, C.Z. hurried down the steps and around the side of the little house. The Jeep was gone! She stood there for a moment, willing it to appear as she searched her mind frantically for an explanation that would leave him safe.

And she thought about how little she really knew him, how foolish she'd been to declare her love for a man who was still, in so many ways, a stranger to her. Moments in her office at the prison and hours spent in complete isolation with him here did not add up to knowledge. To truly *know* someone, you had to see them in the context of their normal life—and nothing about their lives had been normal.

She retraced her steps to the front of the A-frame, then belatedly tried the front door. It was locked. There was nothing for her to do but to return to Stacey's, then come out later, during the day. Should she tell him she'd been here tonight? Now there was yet another decision to make, when she hadn't even decided what to tell him about the reason for her being with Sam.

Instead of going to her car, she sank down on the steps. The cold wind whipped her, finding its way through her sweater. She ignored it. It was certainly no worse than the chill inside her at the moment.

Some part of her began to back away, to peer with cold objectivity at this woman who sat in front of an empty cabin contemplating a man she didn't really know but thought she loved. And this objective being was not pleased.

"C.Z., it's me!"

The disembodied voice broke through her unhappy thoughts, causing her to leap up and stare into the darkness, uncertain where it had come from—uncertain if in fact she'd even heard it.

Shadows moved amidst deeper shadows, and then he emerged, walking calmly toward her. The disguise was gone. Except for the gray beard she hadn't gotten used to, it was Zach.

"Where were you?" she asked as he came to a stop a few feet away, her voice harsher than she'd intended.

"I saw the headlights and decided to get the Jeep into the woods, even though I guessed it might be you."

Now she saw the gun—her father's gun—stuck in his waistband, and she wondered why he had it if he'd thought it was her. If it had been the police, would he have used it? She wanted to think he'd never do such a thing, but she wasn't sure.

"Why would you think it was me?" she demanded, unable to let go of her anger even though a part of her wanted to fling herself into his arms.

He stared at her in silence for a moment. "I thought you might come out here with an explanation."

Try as hard as she could, she could not determine his mood from the tone of his voice. If he disliked her talking and behaving like a psychologist, she hated even more his cop's voice.

She was just beginning to formulate a response when she heard something. He apparently did, too, because his head swiveled sharply toward the road as he held up a hand to silence her.

And then they both heard it clearly, the sound of an engine, growing steadily louder. Her heart leaped into her throat. The car that had been following her!

Zach grabbed her arm and began to run, half dragging her along with him as they fled into the woods. Behind them, the sound of the approaching vehicle filled the silence.

She started to say something, to explain about the car that had followed her, but he hushed her as he continued to pull her deeper into the woods. She didn't see the Jeep until they were nearly upon it.

He reached inside and grabbed something, then started off again. She followed him, even though she guessed that he'd intended for her to wait there. By the time he stopped at the crest of a hill, she could see that he was carrying what looked like a pair of bulky binoculars.

He motioned for her to get down, and they both crawled to the edge of the hilltop. He propped his elbows on the hard ground and peered through the binoculars, which she realized must be the infrared type that were used for night vision by the military. She'd heard about them somewhere, though she'd never seen them, and she wondered where he'd gotten them. They must have been in the duffel bag he'd filled at his house that time.

He swore softly, then lowered them. "It's not the police," he told her in a cold, dead voice. "It must be Summers's men."

"It's my fault, Zach," she said in a choked voice, then told him about the car that had followed her, then turned off.

He picked up the glasses again but said nothing. She stared into the darkness, then flinched involuntarily as a bright beam of light began to sweep the area below them. Until the light illuminated the A-frame, she hadn't realized they were directly above it.

Zach lowered the glasses, and they both watched in silence as the bright beam continued to sweep the area around the A-frame. In the silence, she could hear the faint sounds of voices, two of them, she thought.

"Not too damned smart," Zach muttered, seemingly more to himself than to her. "You'd think they were out spotting deer instead of looking for an armed and dangerous man.''

The lights swung around again, briefly illuminating her car. C.Z. let out a soft sound of surprise. ''My car! They'll know—''

''Unfortunately.''

She edged away from him, thoroughly ashamed of her great foolishness. Not only had she led them to Zach, but she'd tipped her own hand, as well.

''I'm sorry,'' she whispered, knowing how inadequate the words were.

He groped for her hand and found it, then squeezed it briefly before focusing once again on the scene below them. ''It could just as easily have been the police. One of my deputies came into the bar tonight, and I caught him looking at me one too many times.''

''But you must have made certain that no one followed you here,'' she pointed out.

''Yes, but he was definitely suspicious, and all he had to do to find out where I live was to talk to the ones who were out here that time. I was already trying to figure out how to get word to you that I'd have to move on.''

''Move on where?''

''I don't know.''

The spotlight was abruptly extinguished. She thought she could see a faint glow, but she couldn't tell what it was. ''What are they doing now?'' she asked as he continued to watch them through the night-vision glasses.

''I think they have a phone in the car and they're using it—probably calling Summers.''

''Or the police,'' she suggested grimly.

''No, they won't do that unless Summers tells them to.''

''Will he?''

''He might. He could say that he hired people to look for me because he was worried that I would go after him.

It would sound legitimate enough, and with Colby in his pocket, he could get away with it.

"On the other hand, he might want to find me himself. It'd be easier for him or one of his goons to kill me than for the police to do it. But your being here could complicate things for him."

No, she thought, *Summers now wants to get rid of me, as well.* But this wasn't the time or the place to explain her actions. She'd done enough damage for one day.

"They're breaking in," Zach said as he continued to watch the scene far below. Then he rolled over and sat up. "Time to get going. We won't be going back there."

"But if they leave—"

"They won't—not until reinforcements come. Summers will have told them to stay."

"Where are we going?"

Zach stood up and looked at her. He was nothing more than a big, dark shadow. "Into the woods."

THE SLEEP that had eluded her and gotten them into this mess still wouldn't come. She had made herself as comfortable as possible on the hard seat and closed her eyes. But instead of slipping into unconsciousness, she kept seeing them as though from a great height: two tiny people in their little Jeep, lost in an unending wilderness of deep green and scattered golds and reds and bare branches awaiting snow.

The night was cold. Not just chilly as previous nights had been, but truly cold. Zach was dressed more warmly than she was, but he had removed his jacket and turned on the heat to keep her warm. Fortunately, the battered old Jeep had a good heater.

Only now was the knowledge of her situation becoming clear to her. A casual decision not to hide her car in the neighboring cabin's garage had resulted in all her bridges having been burned. Or perhaps not. Whoever had followed her might have found it anyway, hidden or not. At the very least, Summers must have suspected her involvement with Zach or he wouldn't have had her followed.

Or maybe he hadn't really suspected that but had had her followed with the hope of finding a way to kill her before she caused him any more trouble.

She couldn't believe that she was sitting here, bumping along trails through an endless woods, thinking about all the reasons someone wanted to kill her.

She gave up trying to sleep and cast a sidelong glance at Zach as he concentrated on driving. In the dim light from the dashboard, his gray beard gleamed with silver highlights. It was strange how she persisted in seeing him without the beard when she should have grown used to it by now.

She wondered how much of the uncertainties about him that seemed to lie just beneath the surface could be attributed to that. He wasn't just one man. Instead, he was three—the Zach she had first met, the bigger, older, gray-haired artist—and the man she saw now. They were only superficial differences, of course, but still...

Apparently sensing that she was awake and watching him, Zach turned briefly to her. "Tell me about it," he said in a neutral tone.

"Tell you about what?" she asked, startled.

"Whatever it was that you did."

"How do you know I did *anything?*" She was amazed.

"If Summers had someone keeping a twenty-four-hour watch on you, you must have done something. We've stayed apart long enough that he shouldn't have been suspicious of you now."

"You know, you're the kind of cop who must be every criminal's nightmare," she replied, stalling for time as she tried to decide what to tell him.

"That's exactly what I aim to be. I thought we'd agreed that you wouldn't do anything without talking to me first."

"But we weren't getting anywhere, Zach. You know that. How many days did you think you could spend searching the woods for the truck and then hanging out in bars at night, hoping to hear something useful?"

"As many days and nights as it took. I'm a patient guy."

She snorted derisively. "Patience doesn't strike me as being one of your virtues."

"Then you don't know me very well. When I was with the NYPD, I had a reputation for patience and persistence. Remember those scenes in *Butch Cassidy and the Sundance Kid* where that posse kept following them no matter where they went? Butch or Sundance would always be saying, 'Who *are* those guys?' Well, I'm that guy."

"I love that movie," she said. "It's one of my favorites."

"Mine, too. Now tell me what you did."

She told him. Lying seemed pointless, since he already knew she'd done something. And then, after she'd recounted her conversations with Colby and with Summers, she told him about Sam.

"That's why I had dinner with him—to tell him what I'd done. I thought maybe he could help. But I didn't tell him about you, of course." When Zach said nothing, she hurried on. "You see, I thought it was something I could do without involving *you*."

"Right. You'd just set yourself up to get killed, but you'd keep me out of it." He smacked the steering wheel. "Dammit, C.Z. You let that glad-handing bastard convince you that he's harmless, even though you believe he killed your father and tried to frame me, not to mention killing those kids."

There was just enough truth to what he said to make her ashamed and defensive. "I was trying to help," she insisted, knowing it was a poor excuse. "And Sam is going to help, too," she added. "He guessed right away that Summers was worried you would sooner or later find out that he was the driver of that pickup. So he plans to go to the police and say he's representing me and get the file on the school bus crash."

"So now he's in danger, too," Zach said disgustedly.

"Maybe he won't do it now. I was supposed to go to his office this morning to give him a retainer and make it official that I've hired him to look into it."

"Except now you can't go to his office. And what do you suppose he's going to do when he discovers that you've disappeared?"

She hadn't gotten far enough to think of that. "He'll probably do it anyway."

"That and more," Zach said ominously. "At the very least, he'll let Colby know that you've talked to him, which will make it more difficult for either Summers's goons or Colby's men to kill you—maybe."

"What do you mean, maybe? First of all, they can't even find us, and—"

"I'm not the only one who knows these woods," he reminded her. "And if they find us out here, it would be pretty easy for them to cook up some scenario where I kidnapped you, then killed you in a shoot-out with them."

"Sam would never believe that," she replied, trying not to think about the chilling scene he'd conjured up.

"Then they'll just find a way to get rid of Sam and make it look like an accident. You don't understand the mentality here. You could argue that the school bus accident wasn't murder, which is what they must have told themselves. Running away was cowardly, but what the hell. They were drunk at the time and not thinking clearly. But when they killed your father, they were both set on a course that makes it easier to kill again—and again. After all, what have they got to lose now?''

C.Z. shuddered. ''I remember Dad telling me about how some people take one small step into crime and then can't get out. Of course, the school bus wasn't a small step, but it wasn't intentional, either.''

''Yeah. It's Shakespeare's tragic flaw theory.''

She threw him a startled look and he shrugged. ''You know the killer instinct is in most people—we all have a little of Macbeth in us—but fortunately nothing ever happens to trigger it. For some people, though, something happens, and then it's all downhill.'' She surprised herself by laughing. ''I can't believe that we're here, in the middle of nowhere, running for our lives—and we're talking about *Shakespeare*.''

He chuckled. ''It beats talking about how we're going to get out of this.''

''How ARE WE going to get out of this?'' she asked as she peered through the rain-blurred windows. It seemed to her that she could see some snowflakes mixed in with the rain. She had wrapped Zach's sleeping bag around her, but she shivered anyway.

She had discovered Zach had prepared for the possibility he would have to flee into the woods. Stored in the Jeep were the sleeping bag, a small tent, food and extra gas, and he'd kept the Jeep's gas tank filled. It made her feel somewhat better that he'd expected this to happen, but she still blamed herself.

Exhaustion had finally overcome the discomfort of the Jeep's hard seat, and she'd slept for several hours. She assumed he had, as well, because when she awoke, she discovered that he'd pulled off the trail and parked next to a small, swift-running stream.

''I've been thinking,'' he replied as he, too, stared out

at the rain. "We need to get to a phone so you can call Sam. If he knows you're alive and safe, it might prevent him from doing anything foolish. We also need to know if Summers has involved the police or if he's going to try to find us himself. Sam could tell us that."

"If only we had a cell phone." She sighed. There certainly weren't any phone booths out here.

"I looked into getting one, but most of this is a dead area. We're not far from a road here, and just a few miles from where this trail comes out, there's a closed gas station with a phone booth."

She turned to him in surprise. "You've *really* planned for this," she said in admiration.

He nodded. "Be prepared isn't just a Boy Scout motto. Like I told you, I figured it might come to this sooner or later. But what I hadn't counted on was having you with me."

"I'm sorry," she said, even though there'd been no condemnation in his tone.

He reached over and took her hand, squeezing it gently. "I'm not blaming you, Charlie. What you did was actually a good idea, but I would never have let you do it." He paused. "You came to see me because you thought I would be angry about seeing you with Sam, didn't you?"

"Yes," she replied uncertainly. He didn't seem angry, but she couldn't be sure. "I only kissed him because I was grateful for his help and for his concern for me."

"But you thought I'd see it differently," he finished for her. "Actually, I did, for a while. But then I realized that it was mostly because I was angry that I couldn't be with you." He chuckled. "See what you're doing to me, Dr. Morrison? I'm learning to analyze myself."

She leaned over to kiss him on the cheek. "Don't be too hard on yourself."

He turned in his seat and drew her clumsily into his arms.

Their lips met in a lingering kiss. Desire sizzled along her nerve endings, and apparently along his, as well. With a sigh of regret, he released her and swept a hand around the narrow confines of the Jeep.

"Even if we weren't both well past the age of making out in the back seat, it wouldn't be possible."

Their shared laughter served in some perverse way to both dampen their passion and to heighten it. Desire became a low hum beneath the incessant battering of the rain.

"Is it my imagination, or is there some snow mixed in with that rain?" she asked as they both stared through the blurry windshield.

"It's not your imagination. I heard the forecast yesterday and there's a good chance this will turn to snow tonight. It's going to get even colder, which brings us to our next problem."

"What's that?"

"Apart from the fact that snow will make it easier for them to track us, there's the matter of getting you some warmer clothing and a sleeping bag. We'll need more food, too."

"How can we do that?"

"We could try to find something by breaking into some cabins, but there might not be anything. Or we can go to the source. How do you feel about a little burglary?"

"Where?"

"You know that new strip mall on Route 117? There's an outdoor supply store there. I doubt if they have alarms. Most businesses up here don't. We can break into it tonight."

She grimaced. "Maybe we should just steal a car and get away from here."

"That won't do us any good. We need to find that truck, and I think I might know where we could get some help."

"We don't even know for sure the truck is out here," she pointed out.

"I think it is—and if I'm right, then I know who might know where it is. I should have thought about him sooner."

"Davy Crockett!" she cried, remembering the recluse. "But how can we find him?"

"I've been thinking about that, too. I know where he used to meet your dad each month, and I know which road he takes when he walks into town. Plus I know that he got to my place. So that narrows it down a bit. After you call Sam, we'll start to look for him, then go to the store tonight."

"But even if he knows where the truck is, it won't help unless he actually saw Harvey Summers dump it there. And if he saw that, surely he would have spoken up."

"No, he wouldn't have. It isn't likely he even knew about the school bus accident. He doesn't live in the world we know. If we find the truck, it may be possible to trace it back to Summers somehow. Someone had to have sold it to him."

C.Z. said nothing. It sounded like an incredibly long shot to her. It was extremely frustrating to know that they'd found the truth but were unable to prove any of it. She told him that, and he nodded.

"It's the most frustrating part of any cop's job—and it's why some of them resort to planting evidence. Sometimes the law demands too much."

"Did *you* ever do that?" she asked, sensing something in his tone.

He shook his head. "But there was one case I worked where I was pretty sure that my partner planted some evidence, and I didn't call him on it because I knew the guy was guilty. That was another sign to me that it was time to get out. So I came up here and then I got into something even worse." He gave her a grim smile, then turned the key in the ignition.

"Let's get to that phone booth."

"SAM, IT'S C.Z."

"Where are you?" he asked in an urgent tone that told her he was very worried.

"At a phone booth."

"Zach's with you, isn't he?" he asked. "No, forget I asked. I don't want to know. The police are looking for you. They say that you've been helping him. I heard about it on the morning news. They say Zach's been staying at a cabin in the area and that they followed you there, but the two of you got away into the woods.

"As soon as I heard that, I went over to police head-quarters and asked for the file on the school bus accident. I wanted them to know that you'd hired me."

"Did they give it to you?"

"Yes. If Colby had been there, I might have been in trouble, because I don't have any proof that you hired me. But he wasn't there. There's a lot of confusion and I took advantage of that."

"What do you mean?" she asked, her gaze straying from the road, where a few cars passed by, to the closed gas station. Zach was waiting in the Jeep, which he'd parked behind the station. The rain had turned to ice, and it made a soft ticking sound as it struck the glass booth.

"There are a couple of cops I know pretty well, and I think they're getting suspicious that something strange is going on. Cops are always suspicious, though, and that won't stop them from hunting you down."

"What's made them suspicious?" she asked.

"One of them told me that a lot of the guys have always had their doubts about Summers's story that Zach tried to kill him. And now that they know a former chief's daughter is involved with him and I'm suddenly showing up asking for an old file and claiming I'm representing you, they're beginning to smell something fishy. They tried to find out why I'm interested in the school bus business, but I wouldn't tell them.''

"Have you read the file?''

''Yeah, and there's one thing I found kind of interesting. It's a long shot, but—''

"What is it?'' she asked, gripping the receiver tightly. She'd never expected there could be anything of value in that file. If there was, surely Zach would have seen it.

''Your father got a list from motor vehicles of all dark-colored pickups registered to people in the area at the time of the accident. There were check marks beside all of them, indicating that he'd talked to the owners and eliminated them as suspects. But one of them caught my eye, so I went through the write-up he did on it.

"Stanley Williams had a pickup that fit the description. The printout your father got showed that the registration had expired. Stan told your father that he'd sold it for junk two months earlier, but I didn't find any record of your father's having checked that out. I know he and Stan were longtime friends, so that's probably why.''

''Mary's husband,'' C.Z. said, her mind spinning wildly. He'd died not long after that.

''Right. What got my attention is that Stan was also good friends with Harvey Summers. He was one of the regulars at the poker games out at Summers's camp right up until he died. Like I said, it's a long shot, but what if he sold or gave that truck to Summers to keep out at the camp? That's what you were thinking could have happened.''

"But why would he have lied about it?'' C.Z. said. She remembered Stan Williams quite well from her childhood, when they'd been neighbors. He'd been a kindly man and active in many community organizations.

"Well, technically, he *didn't* lie, or at least he might have justified it that way to himself. He could have sold it for junk to Harvey, who then used it in the woods."

"But he would have known why Dad was questioning him, and he must have suspected that Harvey could have been driving it that night. I can't believe he'd lie to Dad about it. Why would he want to protect Harvey?"

"Well, here we get into confidentiality. All I can tell you is that I handled Stan's estate when he died, and he knew he was going to die nearly a year ahead. He had lung cancer. You'll just have to trust me that there could have been a reason."

"I thought that Mary Williams knew something," C.Z. said, as much to herself as to Sam.

"I could try talking to Mary myself," Sam said, "but I don't think she'll talk to me. She's never quite forgiven me for representing her former sister-in-law in a very messy divorce. But I know how she felt about your father, and if she realizes that Summers might have killed him—or had him killed—I think she'd talk to you."

He heaved a sigh. "But I don't see how you can risk coming into town. Maybe you should call her."

"I'll figure out something," C.Z. said determinedly. "Thanks, Sam. I'd better go now."

"I guess this is a pretty dumb question under the circumstances, but there's something going on between you and Zach, isn't there?"

"Yes. I'm sorry I've lied to you, Sam, but we didn't want to get you involved. I shouldn't have come to you at all, but I thought it wouldn't cause you any ethical problems to look into Dad's death. Now I'm worried that you could be in danger."

"There's not much chance of that, now that the police know I've started looking into his death." He paused. "He's a lucky man."

"Let's hope so," she replied before hanging up. But the luck she was thinking of was very different from what Sam was talking about.

A car sped past on the nearby road as she opened the door of the booth. She kept her face turned, and then, when it had passed, she ran toward the back of the gas station. The raw wind flung tiny ice pellets at her, but she scarcely noticed them.

"Sam found something!" she announced as soon as she had climbed into the Jeep. "I think it could be the break we've been waiting for!"

She related the conversation to Zach, and he swore softly as he frowned in thought. "I missed that," he said disgustedly. "The name Stan Williams didn't mean anything to me. I never met him because he died a couple of years before I became chief. And I just assumed your father had satisfied himself it couldn't have been anyone on that list."

"Well, if it's any consolation, Dad failed, too. He apparently just took Stan's word and didn't check to see if the truck had really been junked. But it's still hard for me to believe that Stan would have lied to Dad."

Zach was silent for a time, then he started the engine and drove cautiously toward the road. Their luck held. They didn't come upon any other vehicles before they had once again plunged into the forest. He brought the Jeep to a halt.

"Do you want to try to talk to Mary Williams?"

"Of course, but how can I?"

"She lives in a new condo development at the edge of town. I think I could get to it—or close to it—through the woods. It isn't that far from my place."

"Then let's go there tonight. If I tell her my suspicions that Harvey killed Dad, I think she'll want to help."

"Maybe. Don't forget that she's got her own reputation to think of. If she knows something now, she knew it then, or at least suspected it. And she didn't come forward, either. Do you remember what Stan's business was?"

"Of course. He had a garage. His son, Steve, has it now. Why?"

"Right. I know Steve. That's where I got my work done, too. And it's also where Harvey Summers gets all his garbage trucks serviced. I imagine that's a pretty big chunk of his business."

"Oh!"

Chapter Nine

C.Z. felt like the proverbial thief in the night as she hid in the shadows outside Mary Williams's condo. Mary wasn't home, and she didn't know how long to wait. Zach was hiding in the woods behind the complex, and their Jeep was parked even farther into the woods.

Fortunately, he'd known which condo was Mary's because she'd had him over to advise her on security after another condo in the complex had been burglarized. It was a stroke of luck that hers was one of the ones in the back rather than in the better-lit front section.

Two strokes of luck now, she thought, wondering grimly if they could dare to hope for any more. They certainly needed it.

After Sam's information about the truck that had belonged to Mary's husband, Zach was champing at the bit, eager to force Mary to tell them what she knew. They'd argued for some time about his accompanying her to talk to Mary.

Zach had pointed out that *he* was the one who was skilled at interrogation. She had argued for going alone, fearful of his heavy-handed tactics. Mary might like him and know him better than she knew C.Z., but C.Z. finally convinced him that *she* was the one best suited to the task.

Her reasoning, which Zach finally accepted, albeit grudgingly, was that there was a powerful bond between her and Mary because of her father, and whatever reasons Mary might have for having kept her silence, it was C.Z.'s plea for justice for her father that was most likely to move her.

But her reasoning was predicated on the fact that Mary *did* know something, and that was far from certain. Still, as Zach had pointed out, even if all she had were suspicions, their story might well be enough to turn those suspicions into fact.

She glanced at her watch. She'd been here for nearly an hour, crouched in the shadow of the wall around Mary's patio. It was nearly ten o'clock, and she was getting colder by the minute. The wall sheltered her from the biting wind and most of the snow that was beginning to settle on the grass, but still, she knew she couldn't stay much longer.

A bubble of black humor welled up in her. Talk about a thief in the night! When they left here, they were planning to burglarize the outdoor supply shop to get her some warm clothing and a sleeping bag. She'd debated asking Mary for some clothing. They were about the same size. But in the end, she decided against it. If they were caught, the clothing might be able to be traced back to Mary, and she didn't want that. If they were captured, wearing stolen clothing would be the least of her worries.

She heard a car in front of the condo. She waited anxious moments, straining to hear a door being opened. Then she did hear one, but she also heard voices, a man and a woman. It was too distant for her to know if the woman was Mary, but if she had someone with her...

It hadn't occurred to her that Mary might have a new man in her life. If she did, would that mean that she'd be less likely to help? She hoped not, trying to quell an irrational annoyance with the woman. How could she have gotten over it when C.Z.'s grief felt so raw and unhealed? But then, Mary couldn't know yet that he'd been murdered.

Her thoughts were focused on Harvey Summers's smiling face when suddenly a light went on in the condo next door. She could hear the two voices much more clearly.

It was time to go. Mary might even be out of town. C.Z. got up stiffly and started toward the gate in the wall, staying in the shadows as best she could. Then, when she had nearly reached the gate, she heard, to her horror, the sound of the sliding door opening.

Immediately, a tiny bundle of fur hurtled itself toward her, yapping wildly. A Yorkie, she thought, though she couldn't see it clearly. She ran for the gate, and the little dog ran toward her, still barking hysterically. Just as she slipped through the gate, floodlights came on and she heard the man's voice.

She dashed beyond the range of the lights, over the narrow strip of grass and into the woods, then flung herself onto the ground. The man came to the gate and peered into the darkness. C.Z. felt icy sweat prickle her skin as she lay there shivering, praying that he wouldn't get a flashlight and come looking for her.

The dog was still barking, and she envisioned the man opening the gate and sending it out to find her. But instead, after what seemed like several lifetimes, he turned back and she heard him trying to calm the dog.

The floodlights remained on, though, and C.Z. waited, uncertain if he'd gone inside—and, if he had, whether or not he'd come back with a flashlight to make a more thorough search.

Then suddenly, just when she began to believe she might be safe, something heavy fell on her. A scream started to escape from her throat, but all that came out was a small squeak as a big hand clamped itself firmly over her mouth.

She was already struggling to free herself by the time she realized it was Zach, and even then, seconds passed before terror could give way to relief.

"What happened?" he whispered, his lips close to her ear and his beard tickling her cheek and neck.

"Mary wasn't home. I was waiting for her and then the neighbors came home and let out their dog. I don't know if he saw me or not, but I think he might have. The dog certainly did."

He chuckled, a low sound that soothed her more than it probably should have. "I heard it. That's why I came. It sounds like one of those ferocious mobile mops."

She laughed, too. It was a good description.

"Let's get out of here," Zach said, propping himself on his elbows over her. "That is, unless you'd like to stay a while and..."

Even in the darkness, she could see the gleam in his eyes. Desire surged through, amazing her with its sudden appearance and its power. But she pushed him away and got up, glancing at the condos.

"He might have called the police."

"Right," he replied dryly. "Thanks for reminding me. For a moment there, my brain wasn't working too well."

He stood up, too, and she stared at him pointedly. "Your brain is working fine. It just moved south a bit, that's all."

They made their way to the Jeep, stopping periodically to glance behind them in case Mary's neighbor had called the police and they were searching the woods. But there were no sounds and no lights. If he'd called, they hadn't arrived yet.

"We'll try again tomorrow night," Zach said as he started the Jeep and then eased it forward slowly over the bumpy ground toward one of the trails.

"What if she's out of town?" C.Z. asked, thinking that Zach wasn't the only one who wanted desperately to get on with it.

"You can call the commissioners' offices tomorrow and

find out. They might recognize my voice, but they won't know yours.''

For the next hour, they drove through the woods, sometimes on barely identifiable trails and other times on rugged terrain where they moved at no more than a walking pace. Light snow continued to fall, and here in the woods, it had already coated the ground. This concerned Zach, because it meant they could be tracked more easily, but there was little they could do about it other than to keep moving.

C.Z. marveled aloud at his knowledge of the woods—especially given the fact that he wasn't a native. He told her that he'd made it his business to learn what he could when he took the chief's job.

"Besides," he added, "I have a stack of topographical maps back there, and most of these old roads and trails are on them."

After a while, he left a trail, and a few minutes later, they emerged at the end of a residential street filled with new homes. C.Z. had no idea where they were, but Zach explained that it was a new development at the southwest corner of town. That meant nothing to her, either, but she murmured knowledgeably. This was her hometown, but it was clear that he was the one who knew it better.

They drove for several blocks along dark, quiet streets. New construction was all around them, and the occupied houses were mostly dark. It was past midnight.

She was just beginning to figure out that the southwest corner of town wasn't the right direction for the outdoor supply store when they left the development behind and Zach turned onto another road.

"The municipal garage?" she asked, having seen the sign.

He nodded. "With luck, we'll be able to get some gas."

Ahead of them was a big building, and Zach pulled quickly to one side, then jumped out, leaving the engine idling. "Wait here until I check to be sure no one's around. If you hear anything, get out of here and into the woods, then wait for me."

She tried not to envision herself being chased by the police as she sat there waiting for him. When he was with her, she felt safe—or as safe as two fugitives could be— but alone, as she was now, she was all too aware of her vulnerability. And she could still not quite believe that she'd gotten herself into this situation.

Zach returned just as she was beginning to think he'd been gone too long. He grinned and held up a key.

"What's that?" she asked.

"The key to the gas pumps. It's still kept in the same place. It wouldn't have occurred to Colby that I'd know where it was and might use it."

He drove the Jeep around to the pump and filled the tank, then filled the two large cans he was keeping in the back. Then he picked up the clipboard attached to the pump and wrote something before climbing into the driver's seat.

"You told them we took gas?" she asked, thinking he'd been unable to resist taunting Colby.

He shook his head. "The garage super is supposed to check the clipboard against the pump each day. I don't know if he actually does, but I just recorded it as being gas for the chief's car. Unless Colby shows up to get gas to-morrow, they aren't likely to notice."

She smiled, appreciating the irony. "Are you keeping track of all the laws we're breaking?"

He nodded with a grim smile. "Stealing gas is way down on the list."

"THIS REALLY FEELS WRONG," she said, her back to him as she scanned the lot and the highway behind it.

"Don't worry. I'll see that they get reimbursed for everything we take. I'd leave money now, but if I do, then Colby will know for sure that it was us.''

She turned to watch him as he applied masking tape to a portion of the glass door near the doorknob. Then he tapped the glass inside the square of tape. It shattered, but with very little sound. He reached through the hole and quickly opened the door, then pulled her inside. Four stores away was an all-night convenience store, but she was sure no one from there could have heard them.

Zach switched on a small flashlight and scanned the interior of the store, then gestured to the rear. ''The clothing's back there.''

In less than five minutes, they were outside, their arms full as they ran to the Jeep, which was parked in the shadows at the end of the strip mall. She had warm clothing, a sleeping bag, and they'd acquired a stove and more easy-to-prepare foods.

Zach started the Jeep, then glanced at his watch. ''Let's go get a shower. The cleaning crew will be gone by now.''

''What? Where?'' She'd been feeling grimy, but she'd been trying to ignore it.

''At the high school.''

''You're going to break in there, too?''

''We probably won't need to break in. Except for the big main doors, the place has lousy locks. I warned them to replace them, but my guess is that they haven't.''

He was right, as it turned out. Gaining entry to the boiler room door required only one of her credit cards and Zach's skill. She decided there was probably nothing more dangerous than a cop bent on a life of crime.

They hurried through silent, darkened hallways to the locker rooms. Zach pushed open the door to the boys' locker room and then turned and bowed slightly. ''If madam will follow me...''

"You know, I think you're actually *enjoying* this," she observed as they began to undress.

"I intend to enjoy *this* part of it, anyway," he replied with a wicked grin. "In our situation, you take your pleasures where you can find them."

She breathed in the familiar odor of strong disinfectant combined with the sweat of untold numbers of would-be athletes that was well-known to every former student. It felt deliciously wrong to be here with him, the kind of wrongness that served only to increase a desire that needed no help at all.

They found a bar of soap in one of the big stalls and stepped beneath the hot, stinging spray. Zach lathered his hands, then passed the soap to her, and they began to wash themselves and then each other.

Soap-slicked hands glided over sensitive skin. Small sounds of pleasure echoed off the tiled walls. And then they slid to the hard floor, their bodies entangled as they sought for a time to forget everything but the pleasure they could find with each other. The water poured over them and steam surrounded them as they found that perfect oneness and clung to it desperately, then reluctantly let it go amidst quivering aftershocks.

Zach drew her to her feet and then into his arms again as he chuckled softly. "I feel like I've just lived out the fantasy of every kid who ever stepped in here."

She smiled. "Maybe boys think about that, but girls are too busy thinking about their own inadequacies."

"That couldn't have been your problem," he observed as his gaze swept over her.

"Oh, yes, it was. I didn't have a waist and I didn't have breasts. All I had were hips. It was terrible."

"You have them now," he replied huskily as his hands cupped her breasts, then settled into the hollows of her waist.

"I was a late bloomer. At some point, I must have decided that since I wasn't going to have a body, I'd better have a brain."

"Not my type at all, then," he said, shaking his head as he reached out to turn off the water. "In those days, my brain was zipped into my pants like every other boy's."

They stepped out of the stall, trailing water across the floor to the row of sinks, where they turned on the hand dryers, then adjusted the nozzles and wriggled around to dry themselves.

"This isn't working," she said. "There might be blow dryers in the girls' locker room."

"Good thought." He nodded. "I always wanted to see the inside of the girls' locker room."

Carrying their clothes, they walked across the polished gym floor to the other locker room, then dried themselves easily with the blow dryers. After that, they dressed quickly and left the building the way they'd entered.

The light snow had continued to fall, and it was beginning to cover the paved lot. C.Z. shivered inside her new, warmer clothing. The brief time they'd managed to carve out for themselves was already becoming a distant, cherished memory.

"THERE, SEE THEM?" Zach cried excitedly, pointing through the windshield.

C.Z. squinted into the waning light, then finally saw the footprints. "But what if it's someone looking for us?"

"I don't think so," Zach said, easing the Jeep forward slowly until they were following the faint prints. "We haven't seen any tire marks, and they aren't likely to be on foot, but he is."

They had spent the day crisscrossing the area where Zach believed the man known as Davy Crockett lived, and only now, with the last of the day's dim light leaving the sky, had they found any evidence.

The temperature in the mountains was barely above freezing, so the snow had lingered, several inches deep in spots like this. And as they continued to follow the prints, more light snow began to fall—or rather, to blow around in the strong, cold wind.

"It's going to cover his tracks," C.Z. said with a sigh.

"Yeah, but it will cover ours, as well," Zach reminded her. It was an impossible situation. They wanted to be able to track the man, but they feared being tracked themselves.

Then, abruptly, the prints vanished, even though the trail was still snow-covered. "He turned off," Zach said, bringing the Jeep to a halt and staring into the woods on both sides. "Let's see which direction he took."

When they'd gotten out of the Jeep, they could see clearly that he'd turned left, but they lost his trail when he went into a thicket of tall pines and firs. The branches had caught most of the snow, and the ground was covered with a thick carpet of needles. It was very dark beneath the trees.

"What's that?"

"Shh!" Zach put a finger to her lips as they listened. Then he swore and ran toward the Jeep. "Wait here!"

She hadn't at first identified the sound, but as Zach ran to the trail, she realized it was a helicopter. They couldn't be seen beneath the trees, but the Jeep would be clearly visible on the trail.

The distinctive whump-whump of the blades grew louder as she watched anxiously for any sign of Zach and the Jeep. C.Z. shuddered. It was bad enough to know that they were being hunted on the ground, but if they were to be tracked by air, as well...

The despair that was never far from her mind sank through her again. She didn't understand how Zach could continue to be so optimistic, and yet she knew he was.

She thought it must be because he seemed to take every moment as it came, while she was always focused on the future, a future that held little promise for them. There were too many obstacles, too many chances that they could be wrong.

The sound of the helicopter was deafening. She moved beneath the thickest clump of trees and alternated between watching the pale, colorless sky and scanning the woods for any sign of Zach and the Jeep. Any sound of its engine would be drowned out by the helicopter.

She saw them both almost at the same time, the helicopter moving just above the trees and the Jeep weaving its way slowly into the thicket. It was impossible to guess whether the searchers had seen it.

Then, as Zach came to a stop a short distance away, the helicopter moved on, taking with it the pounding rhythm that she'd felt all through herself.

"I don't think they saw us," Zach said, coming toward her on foot. "If they'd seen anything at all suspicious, they'd have been back for a second look."

She thought—hoped—that made sense. "But what about our tracks? Couldn't they have seen them?"

"It's a light snow and it's blowing around a lot. From up there, their vision would be more obscured."

They waited in silence until the sound of the helicopter faded completely. Then they got into the Jeep and made their way to the trail. Zach stopped and studied their surroundings, then got out of the Jeep. She watched curiously as he took a small hatchet from the back and strode to a thick-trunked oak. He hacked at the tree until he had carved out a wedge-shaped piece of wood at shoulder height. Then he came back.

"That'll mark the spot where he left the trail," he explained. "So we can find it again tomorrow. I think he's probably somewhere close by. It isn't the kind of day when he'd be roaming too far. And I want to have another look at those maps. It's likely that he's built his cabin near a stream, so I want to see if there's one close by here.''

She listened to his quiet determination and his certainty and marveled anew. How could he be so sure that even if they did find this recluse, it would make any difference?

''In the meantime,'' Zach said, seemingly oblivious to her uncertainties, ''we've got some traveling to do. We can camp in the woods behind Mary's condo.''

She nodded, feeling a tiny blossoming of hope at the thought of Mary Williams. She'd called the commissioners' office this morning and was told that Mary was in a meeting. So they knew she wasn't out of town.

''SHE MUST BE HOME,'' Zach said as they crouched at the edge of the woods, staring at a lighted window on the second floor of Mary Williams's condo. It was just past ten o'clock. C.Z. hoped Mary wasn't going to bed already.

Then, as if in answer to her unspoken question, Mary appeared at the window, staring into the darkness. She was fully dressed, and she stood there for what seemed an abnormal length of time, given the fact that she couldn't really be seeing anything. Then she moved away, and a moment later, the light went out. Zach put words to her thoughts before C.Z. could do it.

''I think she's guessed that you tried to contact her and might be trying again. The neighbor must have told her that he thought someone was here last night.''

C.Z. hoped he was right. But she didn't tell Zach the other thought she had, that Mary might be trying to help her but really knew nothing.

Zach gave her a quick kiss. ''You're sure you can find your way back to the campsite?''

She nodded, even though she really wasn't sure at all. He'd given her a tiny but powerful flashlight, and it wasn't really far, but she knew the woods would seem very different without him at her side. He planned to use the time she'd be with Mary to get more gas.

He slipped into the darkness and she waited a moment, then emerged into the grassy area behind the condos. When she reached the gate, she remembered the yappy little dog and hesitated, peering over the gate into the yards. The outside lights at Mary's neighbor's were off, so she assumed the dog was inside. She opened the gate and hurried to Mary's patio. No lights were on there, either, but she could see a faint light through the kitchen windows—and then, just as she started across the patio, she saw a shadowy figure behind the glass doors.

"C.Z.! Hurry, before they decide to let Caesar out again." Mary's voice was a low, urgent whisper as she slid open the door and beckoned to C.Z. "I knew it must have been you last night."

Words failed C.Z. as she stepped through the door and into Mary's warm embrace. She realized that she had fallen into the mind-set of a fugitive, believing that she and Zach were alone against the world. Mary's simple, unhesitating acceptance meant far more to her than any words could have conveyed.

"When my neighbors told me that they thought someone had been out there last night, I felt certain it must be you. I'm so sorry I wasn't here. I spent the night with an old friend. It was the first anniversary of her husband's death and she didn't want to be alone."

She led C.Z. into the living room, talking all the while about her friend, a woman C.Z. vaguely remembered as a former neighbor. Then Mary made a dismissive gesture.

"Listen to me, going on like this. Are you hungry? I can fix you something."

"Coffee would be fine, if you have some," C.Z. replied in a surprisingly husky tone. She felt as though she was about to burst into tears—all the tears she'd been holding back because she didn't want Zach to blame himself for having dragged her into his problem.

Mary left her in the gracious living room and went to fix the coffee. C.Z. swiped at her eyes and looked around her. How pleasant it was to be in a home again, to feel the security of walls around her and thick carpeting beneath her feet and comforting warmth. She took off her stolen jacket guiltily, hoping that Mary wouldn't know where it had come from.

"The coffee will be ready in a few minutes," Mary announced. "And you can help me eat some of the sticky buns Emily baked and insisted I bring home. They were her husband's favorite."

She perched on the edge of a lovely wing chair and studied C.Z. unabashedly. "You look well, in spite of it all," she pronounced.

"I'm fine," C.Z. assured her, though she knew she wasn't. "We've been living in the woods, but we have everything we need."

"Chief Colby has been saying that Zach kidnapped you, but I knew that couldn't be the case. Zach wouldn't do something like that—any more than he would have tried to kill Harvey. I don't know him well, but I *do* know him well enough to know that he's a man of integrity."

"No, he didn't kidnap me," C.Z. said, then explained.

"Harvey Summers must have had some men watching me, and they followed me to the cabin. So we ran off into the woods in my friend's Jeep."

Mary arched a brow. "According to Chief Colby, one of his men spotted you headed into the mountains late at night and decided to follow you, since they knew the state police had suspected you of helping Zach escape."

C.Z. shook her head. "The men who found us weren't police. We're sure they were Summers's men."

"Well, I suppose that doesn't surprise me too much. Harvey has been beside himself ever since Zach escaped. He's telling everyone that he's sure Zach will come back and kill him this time."

C.Z. took a deep breath. "It's just the opposite, Mary. It's Harvey who wants Zach dead. And that's why I've come to see you."

She saw uncertainty and perhaps fear cloud Mary's eyes as she got up and announced that the coffee should be ready. C.Z. watched her leave the room, belatedly realizing that Mary undoubtedly thought she'd come here to try to arrange for her surrender. If she did know anything, either she hadn't put it all together or she was assuming that they hadn't.

She felt sick, thinking about what she had to ask this woman to do. If she had any information, her reputation could not escape this unscathed. That was exactly the point Zach had made when he'd been arguing that he should come with her.

Mary returned with the coffee and the buns on a large antique silver tray. Seeing the delicate china and the handsome tray reminded C.Z. of something she'd long since forgotten. Mary came from a very old and prominent family in the area. Her father had been a state senator, and her brother was a federal judge. C.Z. could recall her mother having once remarked that Mary had "married down," a shocking situation for her generation.

And what that meant now was that Mary had even more to lose than she'd first thought.

"Tell me how I can help you," Mary said. Her words were sincere, but C.Z. thought she could still see fear in her eyes.

She launched into her story, telling it as carefully as she could and watching Mary's face as she spoke. Then, when she'd told her everything except for their suspicions regarding her father's death, she paused.

"And that isn't all. Zach and I now believe that Dad's death was no accident. We think that Harvey either killed him or paid someone else to do it. We think he did it because Dad was getting too close to the truth."

There was no doubt Mary was badly shaken, but when C.Z. told her of their suspicions that her father had been murdered, Mary quickly set down the delicate cup she'd been holding. It rattled noisily against the saucer.

"But this is just a theory," she said. "You have no proof."

"Not yet, but we will. We're going to find that truck."

The one thing she hadn't told Mary was that Sam had seen her husband's name on that list of truck owners. She held back that information, hoping Mary would confirm it.

Mary nervously fingered the string of beads she was wearing. "But surely, if you're right, Harvey would have gotten rid of that truck."

"We think he abandoned it in the woods. What else could he have done with it? He couldn't have taken it to a junkyard because everyone was on the lookout for an old black pickup with damage to the front."

Mary abruptly got up and walked to the baby grand piano that occupied one corner of the living room. C.Z. watched as she picked up a framed photograph, then set it down. From where she was, it was impossible to see the picture clearly. After a moment, Mary turned toward her again.

"It's all my fault," she said in a voice that was barely above a whisper.

C.Z. was shocked. *What* was her fault? Her confusion must have shown on her face, because Mary sank into the chair, and the look she gave C.Z. was a plea for understanding.

"I'm responsible for your father's death," she said in a

choked voice. "I let myself believe it really was an accident because I just couldn't believe Harvey would do such a thing."

C.Z.'s mind spun. "You told Dad something?"

Mary nodded. "Only a few weeks before…before it happened. I'd suspected from the beginning that it might have been Harvey who was driving that truck. I told myself to keep quiet because I wasn't sure, but there was another reason to keep quiet, too."

Her story was much as they had guessed, though there were details they couldn't have known. Mary's husband had been a regular at Harvey Summers's weekly poker games at his camp. On the night of the school bus tragedy, he had come home early, while Mary was still awake.

"He said he'd left early because George Shirer left early, too, and both Harvey and Dave Colby had started to get really drunk. He said they didn't usually do that, but both of them were having family problems at the time.

"He was worried that Harvey would try to drive. He and Dave had come together in Harvey's car, so Stan took Harvey's keys. He'd left them in the ignition. He never dreamed that Harvey might drive the truck into town. It didn't have a current license. But I think that's what they did. The road where the accident happened wasn't the fastest way back to town, but they might have taken it because they were driving the truck.

"As I said, when I first heard about the accident and how they were looking for an old, dark pickup, I thought about the truck Stan had sold to Harvey, but it wasn't until much later, when Stan was dying, that he told me he was sure they'd been driving it that night. He knew it because he was still going into the garage every day, and that next morning, he left early and went out to Harvey's camp to give him back the car keys. He heard about the accident on the way out to Harvey's camp. When he got there, no one was there—and the truck was gone. So he just left the keys for Harvey's car and came back to town. Neither Harvey nor Dave ever said a word to him about it. And he never said anything to them, either.''

Mary stopped and gave C.Z. a silent plea for understanding. ''Stan knew he was dying, and he was worried about providing for me and for Steve. A new garage had opened, and he was worried about the competition. Harvey had always had all his trucks serviced at Stan's garage. It was an important account. So he kept quiet. I know that sounds terrible, when all those children died that way, but Stan kept saying that it was all a tragic mistake, that Harvey would never have deliberately done such a thing.

''Anyway, he didn't tell me all of this until just before he died—and I never told anyone until your father and I became close. Even then, I probably wouldn't have told him, but he used to talk about the case and about how much it bothered him that he hadn't found the driver.

''I found out then that Stan's truck was on a list your father had gotten, but when he'd talked to Stan, Stan said that he'd junked it, which really wasn't a lie, but wasn't exactly the truth, either. Your father believed him, of course—they were old friends. So he never checked on it.''

Mary's knuckles paled as she gripped the wooden arms of her chair tightly. ''Oh C.Z., all of this is our fault, Stan's and mine! If he hadn't taken Harvey's keys, he would never have been driving that truck on that road. And if I hadn't told your father about it, he wouldn't have died.''

C.Z. got up and went to Mary and took her hands. ''Mary, it isn't your fault, or Stan's. Stan did what he thought was right when he took Harvey's keys, and you both did what you had to do to protect your family.''

It made C.Z. uneasy to realize that she was sincere in what she said—even though the consequences of their actions had been so horrific. The truth was that she wasn't really sure she would have done anything differently herself. She wanted to think that she would have, but...

"When that thing happened between Zach and Harvey, it just never occurred to me that it could have anything to do with this," Mary went on. "I knew Harvey and Zach didn't get along and never had."

"Harvey obviously guessed that Zach would be just as persistent as Dad had been," C.Z. said as she sank to the floor beside Mary's chair.

Mary nodded. "I should have seen that. They're very much alike. And I *would* have guessed it if I'd suspected Harvey of having anything to do with your father's death. But I didn't. I've known Harvey Summers all my life, and I just can't see him as a murderer. I mean, I know he was responsible for the deaths of those children, but I suppose I made the same excuse for him that Stan made."

C.Z. nodded. "I understand. It's hard for me to believe it, too. But seemingly good people can make one mistake and then somehow justify more to cover it up. I guess it's human nature to protect yourself any way you can."

Mary nodded. "Just as Stan and I did," she said sadly. "I told myself—and I'm sure Stan did, as well—that telling what we knew wouldn't bring those children back, so it didn't make any difference. But your father pointed out to me what it could mean to the families to know that the man who was responsible had been brought to justice. I know most of those families, and I should have thought about that."

She got up slowly. "I think we could both use some more coffee."

When she returned, C.Z. could see a new determination in her, and she felt relieved. In a way, the hardest part hadn't yet been discussed. Would Mary be willing to tell what she knew?

"What can I do now?" Mary asked. "I can't very well

go to Chief Colby, since I'm sure he was with Harvey that night, and he obviously lied about what happened between Harvey and Zach.'' She paused, frowning.

"Dave Colby has a lot to answer for, but I'd bet that he had nothing to do with your father's death. He liked your father a lot—really admired him.''

"No, I think Colby's innocent of that, and Zach isn't even sure he knew ahead of time that Harvey planned to kill him. In all likelihood, he didn't, and he might even have saved Zach's life by refusing to go along with it.

"But I'd also guess it was through Colby that Harvey found out what Dad knew, so even if he wasn't involved in Dad's death, he still must have been suspicious.''

"So what do we do now?'' Mary asked.

"I think the best thing for you to do at this point is to go to Sam Gittings. He knows all about it.'' She explained her meeting with Sam and what he had done.

"Sam will know what to do, which may be nothing at this point. Zach and I need to find that truck, and he seems to believe we will. But I wonder if even that will be enough. Even if we do find the truck and we can prove it was the one that caused the accident, how can we prove it was the same truck Stan sold to Harvey?''

"I can help with that, too,'' Mary said after a pause. "Years ago, when the truck was still new, I was driving it one day when I went to the store. Instead of putting the groceries into the back, I put them on the passenger seat and the floor.

"On my way home, a dog ran out in front of me and I had to brake hard. The bags fell over and somehow the top came loose on a bottle of bleach. I didn't even notice until I got home, but some of it had trickled down under the floor mat and bleached the rug. It wasn't obvious because the mat covered it, but it would still be there.''

"Another piece of luck!'' C.Z. grinned, then went on to

explain how it seemed that after despairing of ever getting the proof they needed, suddenly things appeared to be going their way.

"You've seen that list your father had, haven't you?" Mary asked. "You knew that Stan's name was on it."

"Yes," C.Z. admitted. "And I thought you knew something, but I wanted you to tell me yourself. I know how difficult this will be for you, Mary, and I appreciate it. We both do," she added.

Mary smiled sadly. "Believe it or not, it won't be that difficult. Even before I knew that Harvey had murdered your father, carrying this secret around was a heavy burden."

"We still can't be sure of that," C.Z. reminded her. "And we might never know—unless Harvey admits it. You should talk to Sam about whether there's anything you can be charged with. I don't think there is, but he's the one who would know. Will it be difficult for you to talk to him? He said there are some hard feelings between you two because of your brother's divorce."

Mary waved a hand dismissively. "Oh, I was angry with him for a time, but that's all in the past. I just never found a way to let him know that. I've always liked Sam."

She looked at C.Z. consideringly. "I've been hearing rumors that you and Sam have been seen together, and I remember that you dated him years ago. Is there anything between you two? Because Sam and Zach are good friends and—"

"There's nothing more than friendship," C.Z. said quickly. "In fact, that's how I came to be at the cabin where Zach was staying, when Harvey's men found us." She explained about Zach's disguise and about his seeing them together.

Mary's smile grew, and it held no sadness this time. "So

it's you and Zach. That doesn't surprise me. Your father would be very pleased.''

C.Z. nodded. "Yes, I think he would, too." She glanced at her watch. She'd been here longer than she'd intended and she feared that Zach might be worried about her.

"I have to go now. Zach will be waiting for me."

"But where are you two staying?"

"In the woods, but we're fine."

"It's so cold out," Mary protested. "Why don't you stay here tonight? You could leave before daylight."

"No, I can't do that, but thank you." She kissed Mary on the cheek. "And thank you for all you're going to do. I'll be in touch with you or Sam as soon as we find that truck."

Mary seemed to be about to say something, but held back at the last moment. C.Z. knew what she was thinking. What if they couldn't find the truck? Without it, all they had were guesses and suspicions, even with Mary's story.

Chapter Ten

C.Z. found her way to the campsite, even though she was preoccupied with the good news she would have for Zach. But when she reached it, he wasn't there!

Her elation shifted abruptly to fear. What if he'd been captured when he returned to the municipal garage for gas? She'd expressed that concern to him, but he'd been certain that his earlier theft wouldn't be discovered.

Terrified and cold, C.Z. crawled into the tiny tent and wrapped the sleeping bag around her, all the while listening for the Jeep.

One hour dragged by and then another—and still no Zach. When she wasn't worried about him, she kept thinking about the warm bed Mary had offered her. Then she would chastise herself for thinking about her comfort when Zach might be in trouble. And as still more time passed, she became convinced that their luck had run out as quickly as it had begun.

But there was another, deeper fear that hovered at the edges of her mind. What if Summers or his men had found Zach? They didn't want him to be captured—they wanted him dead.

She wasn't aware of having dozed off until she awoke suddenly, roused from her stupor by the faint sound of an engine. And then she feared it might not be Zach. Her gaze went to her father's gun, lying in its holster next to their meager food supplies. Zach had his gun, having gotten it when they went to his house.

She got up and peered through the small plastic window but could see nothing. The sound of the engine was growing steadily louder, but it seemed to be coming from the opposite direction from what she'd expected. That increased her fear that it wasn't Zach.

She picked up the gun, wondering if she could use it even to save herself, then unzipped the tent flap and crept out. As soon as she peered around the side of the tent, she could see the lights, still some distance away in the woods.

Wild, totally irrational thoughts bounced through her brain. Mary had called Harvey Summers, or Summers's men had been watching Mary's house. They'd already captured Zach and had forced him to tell them where she was.

At some level, she knew none of this was possible, but fear had destroyed her common sense. Gun in hand, she crept into the woods, then flattened herself on the ground to wait.

The lights grew brighter, although they weren't aimed at her hiding place. She tried to see beyond them but couldn't. Then the lights went out and the engine was turned off and the darkness and silence were total—and terrifying. She heard the sound of a door being opened and then closed, but she could see nothing. Minutes passed. The gun was cold and heavy in her hand.

"C.Z.! Are you out there?"

She couldn't answer at first. When she tried to call out to him, all that came out was a squeak. He called again, a sharp edge to his voice that she recognized as fear. She understood that, all right. She struggled to her feet. "I'm here."

"Where?" A flashlight beam swung around, then caught

her in its glare. She ran to him, totally forgetting the gun in her hand.

Zach saw it and grabbed it from her before he drew her into his arms. "What happened?" he demanded harshly.

"Nothing," she admitted, only now realizing how foolish she'd been. "I came back and you weren't here, and I fell asleep. Then I woke up and heard someone coming and…" She paused for breath. "I don't know what I thought."

He continued to hold her, running one hand soothingly down her spine. But she could feel her father's gun in his other hand and the hard bulge of his shoulder holster beneath his jacket, and it took a great effort on her part to push away her fear.

"I'm sorry about all this, love," he said quietly. "Sometimes I forget just how hard this is for you."

She stretched and kissed him. "That's because I've been very good at hiding it. I don't want you to feel responsible."

"I do anyway, so you can stop pretending," he said with a smile she could feel rather than see. "Come on. Let's get warm."

"What took you so long?" she asked as they crawled into the tent.

He didn't answer until they had shed their jackets and boots and zipped the two sleeping bags together, then crawled into them.

"One of the guys pulled in to get gas just as I was leaving," he explained, drawing her close. "We had ourselves a merry chase for a while, until I finally got into the woods and he tried to follow me. The cruiser got stuck, and I'm not sure that he didn't do it deliberately."

"You mean he deliberately let you get away? Did you see who it was?"

"No, but only an idiot would have tried to take a car

where he did. It took me quite a while to get back here because I deliberately led him away from this area. I wanted to be sure they wouldn't start searching here the first thing in the morning. Did you talk to Mary?''

C.Z. smiled. "After what you went through, I'm glad to have some good news."

As she told him about Mary's revelations, C.Z. could feel him growing tense with excitement. Several times, he seemed about to interrupt her, but he managed to remain silent until she had finished. Then he heaved a deep sigh, causing her head to bob up and down on his chest.

"It's probably a good thing I wasn't there," he admitted. "If I had been, I might have had trouble deciding whether to kiss her or strangle her."

"She was only protecting herself and her family," C.Z. insisted. "In her situation, I might have done the same thing. And don't forget, she never made the connection between the accident and Dad's death or your fight with Harvey, although I suppose you could make a good case for the fact that she should have."

"A damned good case," he muttered.

"In her mind, she could almost excuse Harvey for the accident," C.Z. went on, ignoring him. "She's known him all her life and she just couldn't believe that he would deliberately kill someone."

"I'm getting pretty damned tired of people nominating that slimeball for sainthood."

"Zach, you don't understand small-town people. Besides, as the world outside gets crazier and crazier, I think they cling even tighter to the belief that monsters couldn't be living in their midst. Harvey's helped a lot of people. I'd be willing to bet that the men he's hired to look for us are among them. He's probably convinced them that we're evil outsiders who are out to destroy him."

He swore vehemently, then sighed again. "Yeah, you're

right. If there's one good thing that's come out of all this—besides re-meeting you, that is—it's that I do understand these people better.'' Then he laughed bitterly. ''You could even say that Harvey Summers was right when he argued against hiring me because I was an outsider who didn't understand the people here.''

She smiled. ''If you recall, we argued about that the first time we met.''

''Yeah, but don't forget, your father *did* understand them, and he still got killed.''

''I think Dad would have felt much as Mary did, that Harvey would never have deliberately killed anyone.''

''But that wouldn't have stopped him from arresting him.''

''No,'' she agreed, ''it wouldn't have.''

''We've got to find that truck—and fast. The more worried Summers gets, the more likely he is to try to get rid of it before we can find it. He's smart enough to know that without it, we've got no case against him—at least nothing that would stand up in court.''

''I was thinking about that earlier,'' she told him. ''From what Mary said, Harvey and Dave Colby must have gone back to the camp after the accident, to hide the truck. And they were still gone early the next morning, when Mary's husband went to the camp to give Harvey his keys.''

''That doesn't really help us much, though. They would have had a lot of time to hide it. The accident happened just before eleven o'clock at night, and they would have had until dawn to get rid of it and then walk back.''

''That isn't what I meant. You're forgetting something.''

''What's that?''

''They were drunk. It's true that they could have gone back to the camp and slept it off for a while before taking the truck into the woods, but I doubt that. They would have wanted to get rid of it fast. And if they were drunk, they might not even know where they took it.''

''Huh!'' Zach sat up and stared at her. She could barely see his face in the darkness. ''You're right! No matter how well they know those woods, two drunks running around out there at night would be likely to have gotten lost.''

''Well, they obviously found their way to the camp, but we don't know how long it took them. Also, I doubt they even tried to remember where they dumped the truck. The only thing that would have been on their minds was to get rid of it.''

''Good thinking,'' he said, lying down again and drawing her to him. ''Now let's stop thinking about it for a while.''

''And get some sleep.''

''That too…later.''

''THERE IT IS!''

C.Z. saw the notched tree just after he did. It was nearly noon, and they were back to the spot where they'd seen the footprints in the snow leave the road—prints they hoped belonged to the recluse.

They parked the Jeep off the road beneath a covering of pines and left its warmth to step into a chill that felt more and more like winter. Above them, the blue sky was rapidly giving way to thick, dark clouds, and already a few snow-flakes were drifting down and swirling about in the strong northwest wind.

They set out into the woods, both of them watching for any sign that their quarry had passed this way. Zach had studied the maps and said there was a small stream not more than three or four miles away. He considered that to be a likely spot for Davy Crockett to have built his cabin.

They had managed only about a mile over the rough terrain when they heard the helicopter again and hurried into denser cover. A few moments later, it passed over them, moving slowly just above the tree line. They waited in silence until the sound began to fade, then set off again.

An hour later, they struggled to the top of a hill. She was scanning the forest ahead of them, searching for the stream, when Zach suddenly grabbed her arm and pointed to the left.

"Someone's over there! I saw something moving."

"A person?" she squinted, trying to see for herself.

"No, a vehicle of some sort. I only got a quick look before it disappeared into the trees."

"How far away is it?" she asked, unable to judge distances out here.

"Probably ten miles or so, but it was moving in this direction." He handed her the binoculars. "You keep watching for it while I have a look at the map."

He removed his backpack and took out the maps, found the one he wanted and spread it out on the ground. She used the glasses to scan the area anxiously.

"I think I know where they are," he said finally, "and if they stay on that road, it could bring them pretty close to the area where I think his cabin is."

She lowered the glasses briefly and stared at him. "Do you think they could be looking for him, too?"

"That thought crossed my mind," he admitted. "Everyone knows about him, and if it occurred to me that he could be helpful, it could have occurred to them, as well."

She was back to studying the woods through the glasses. "But we don't know who 'they' are. It could be the police—or it could be Harvey's men."

"Right. If it's the police, then all they want is some help from him. But if it's Summers's men, they could want to get rid of him. If I had to guess, I'd say it's Summers's men. The police are probably searching miles from here—where they know I went into the woods last night. They won't have enough men to be searching more than one area at a time.

"Even the helicopter points to that. They'd be using it to search an area that isn't being searched on foot."

She thought it was lucky for them that Zach could second-guess their strategy. But it certainly wasn't lucky to have Harvey Summers's thugs out here.

"Come on," he said, taking the glasses from her and slinging them around his neck. "We need to find them."

"Why?" She was appalled at the thought.

"Because if we do, I can put them out of action for a while."

"Zach!"

"I mean stop them—not kill them," he said, giving her a hurt look.

"I'm sorry," she said. "I know you wouldn't kill them, but I'm just not thinking too clearly."

He wrapped an arm around her shoulders. "You're doing fine. Offhand, I can't think of anyone I'd rather be in the woods with."

"Well, I can certainly think of a few million places I'd rather be," she replied, struggling to keep up with him as they descended the hill angling off to the left. "I never thought I'd be in a situation where a nice warm bath could look like heaven."

He chuckled. "My version of heaven is a razor and some shaving cream. This beard is itchy."

"It certainly is," she said pointedly, feeling her irritated skin chafing beneath her layers of clothing.

"Just keep thinking about that nice big tub at my place. That's the goal—or the first one, anyway."

"What do you mean, the first one?" she asked a few moments later, after she'd stumbled over a tree root and he had picked her up. "The first goal is to find the truck and then get Harvey Summers behind bars."

"I'm thinking beyond that."

"Oh? Then what's the second goal?"

"To get my job back and then marry this klutzy broad I'm stuck with," he replied, grabbing her as she started to slide in a muddy spot.

She stared at him. "That is absolutely the worst marriage proposal I've ever heard!"

He shrugged. "Well, it's the best I can do right now. There aren't any flower shops or jewelry stores around at the moment." He grinned wickedly. "Of course, I could always go rob a couple of them tonight if you like—and hit a liquor store for some champagne while I'm at it."

She shook her head. "I'm going to pretend that none of this is real."

"Now *there's* a healthy attitude—especially for a shrink."

"Just remember that I haven't accepted your proposal," she warned him. "I might decide I want to get to know you under normal circumstances."

He opened his mouth to reply, then closed it again and motioned for her to be quiet. All thoughts of the future vanished abruptly as she heard what he had heard, the distant sound of an engine.

"They're on the far side of that hill. Come on. I want to find a good spot."

"For what?" she asked, hurrying once again to keep up with his longer stride.

"To practice my sharpshooting," he replied, briefly touching the rifle strapped to his shoulder.

She didn't like the sound of that, but she knew he wouldn't harm their pursuers.

The sound of the vehicle became steadily louder as they scrambled up the hill, then began to edge carefully along the top, watching. A short time later, they saw it, a large green boxy-looking vehicle, bumping along slowly over the rough road below them.

Zach began to run through the woods at the top of the hill, staying just below the crest and ahead of the men below them. As he ran, he pulled the rifle from its resting place along his back and carried it in one hand. She followed, not even trying to keep up.

Finally, he stopped and flung himself onto the ground at the top of the hill. By the time she caught up with him, he was propped up on his elbows and sighting the rifle. She dropped down beside him and watched as the vehicle came into view.

The rifle made a sharp, cracking sound and recoiled slightly. She recoiled, as well, but managed to remain silent. Below them, the vehicle suddenly lurched to one side and then stopped. Zach fired again, and she saw the front of the vehicle drop as the other front tire went flat. Whoever was inside wisely decided to stay there as Zach fired again, this time hitting the rear tire they could see from this angle.

"Let's go," he said, getting up. "I don't think they'll be dumb enough to try to come after us, but I don't want to be proved wrong."

They took off the way they'd come, staying on the far side of the hill from the road. "What if they have a radio?" she asked, knowing from what he'd told her that a cell phone wasn't likely to be any help.

"They don't. There wasn't any antenna. And even if they did, they wouldn't be using it. Summers wouldn't want anyone to know they're out here."

"Do you think he might have been there himself?"

Zach shook his head. "Not likely. He'll be trying to stay as far away from this as possible. But I'd be willing to bet they're out here looking for old Davy, just like we are. Lucky for him that we found them first."

"Shouldn't we have waited to see who they are?"

"I memorized the license plate, so I can deal with them later, but running around in the woods isn't a crime. The best we can hope for is that they can be scared into testifying against Summers."

They continued to trek through the forest, heading toward the area where Zach believed they would find Davy Crockett's cabin. She thought about how different Zach seemed since she'd told him of Mary's revelations. He was more intense and more focused, more sure of himself, though she wouldn't have said before that he was lacking self-confidence. And unfortunately, she seemed to be moving in the opposite direction.

It didn't require much thought on her part to understand the reasons behind these transformations. Zach was in his element. He had become a cop again, using all his considerable skills to elude their pursuers, track down the recluse and find the truck. And although many years had passed since his military service, he was comfortable in the woods.

She, on the other hand, was very much out of her element. She could deal well with people face to face, but she found faceless, nameless pursuers very frightening—not to mention the deprivations of living in the woods. She'd been on only one camping trip, a disaster she'd determined never to repeat. She liked her comforts.

It was late in the day when they finally found the cabin, near a little stream just as Zach had predicted. They were quite close to it before they saw it, buried as it was in the depths of a pine forest.

C.Z. had been expecting a tumbledown shack and was quite surprised to see a sturdily built log cabin, with glass in the windows and bright blue shutters that seemed incongruous in this rough, woodsy setting.

Smoke curled from the stone chimney, indicating that he must be home or not far away. She was about to ask Zach what sort of welcome they could hope to receive when he stopped near the edge of the clearing where the cabin stood.

"You wait here. From what I've heard, he's afraid of women."

"You mean he doesn't like them," she stated, thinking that would certainly explain why he chose to seclude himself in the forest.

"No, I think it's more likely that he's just shy around them. Just wait here and give me a chance to talk to him first. When I tell him who you are, he'll probably feel more comfortable. He apparently got along well with your father."

So she waited while he walked out into the small clearing, leaving behind his rifle and his handgun. Instead of going to the door, he stopped in the middle of the clearing, then sat down cross-legged on the ground, facing the door.

C.Z. smiled, impressed with his talents. He was approaching the recluse much as one might approach a semi-wild animal, taking care not to invade its territory, at the same time trying to show that his intentions were peaceful.

After several minutes, the door to the cabin opened, and she got her first look at the man people called Davy Crockett. The name seemed apt. He was tall and rangy with a craggy sort of face, and he was dressed entirely in buckskins. In fact, she thought that his clothing looked to be hand-sewn. His hair was long and of a dirty blond shade, held back in a ponytail with a leather thong.

Zach got up and extended his hand, and after a brief hesitation, the man took it. She wished she could hear their conversation, but from this distance, all she could hear was a faint murmur. At first, Zach was doing all the talking, but after a time, she could see that the recluse was saying something, as well, and gesturing into the forest to his right.

Her hopes soared. Was he telling Zach where the truck was? Neither of them had wanted to talk about what they'd do if he hadn't seen it. With the police and Harvey Summers's men looking for them, plus the fact that they couldn't hope to get any more gas at the municipal garage, time was running out.

Then she saw Zach gesture in her direction. The man's face turned toward her, and he shifted uneasily from one foot to the other, then nodded. Zach gestured again, this time indicating that she should join them. She left the thick cover of the pine woods and stepped into the clearing. Snow was beginning to fall, and the light was failing. The Jeep and their camping gear were miles away, and she wondered if Zach intended them to stay here tonight. That seemed to be imposing on the man's hospitality.

She could feel the recluse's gaze on her as she approached, and she wished that she looked more like her father. He might not believe she was who Zach said she was.

When she reached them, she smiled but didn't extend her hand. It wasn't likely that he'd take it anyway—he looked distinctly uncomfortable.

"He's seen the truck," Zach said in answer to her unspoken question. "The only problem is that it isn't where I would have expected it to be. But it's a black pickup with the front end damaged."

She thought about that. "We've been assuming that they went back to Harvey's camp and then drove it into the woods. But what if they didn't do that? Maybe they were worried that the bus driver might have recognized them and would tell the police."

"Exactly what I was thinking," Zach confirmed, throwing her an approving glance. Then he raised his face to the heavens. The snow was falling more thickly.

"We can't get to the Jeep before dark. He's invited us to stay here tonight, and then he'll go with us in the morning to show us where it is."

C.Z. turned to the silent man and thanked him warmly as he continued to stare unabashedly at her. She doubted that the invitation had been extended without some judicious arm-twisting on Zach's part.

"I look more like my mother than my father," she told him when he continued to stare at her.

"He was a good man," the recluse said in a rusty, slow voice.

"Yes, he was," she agreed, more touched than she would have expected by this strange man's simple statement. She turned to Zach.

"Did you tell him that we think Dad was murdered?"

Zach nodded. "That's why he wants to help us."

"How FAR is it to the Jeep?" she asked, standing at the window with Zach as they watched the snow fall in the last of the day's light. It wasn't falling heavily, but she didn't relish a long trek over slippery ground even if she was wearing good, sturdy boots.

"About six or seven miles. If the snow gets too bad, you can stay here and we'll go. He has a couple of pairs of snowshoes. There's an old road only about a mile from here, so we can come back for you that way."

"You mean the road those men were on?"

"No, another one. But it's probably the road they used to get out on foot. It connects with a highway not far from here. That's the only risk we'll face if we have to go that way, but if the snow's deep enough, it'll keep the traffic down."

"And what about the truck?"

"It's a good twenty miles from here, but not too far off one of the better dirt roads. He says we can get to it from here without going to the main roads, though I don't see that on my maps. But I discovered long ago that not all the roads are on the maps.''

He drew her against him. "With any luck, it'll all be over tomorrow.''

Chapter Eleven

C.Z. shifted on the lumpy bed as though by doing so she could magically smooth it out. Across the cabin's one large room, Zach and their host were no more than dark lumps in the flickering firelight. She smiled, thinking that Davy Crockett's gentlemanly gesture was misplaced. He'd offered her his bed when the thick bearskins on the floor were almost certainly more comfortable.

Her surprise at the construction of the cabin extended itself to the interior. The furnishings were sparse and old, but the place was immaculate. He had running water after a fashion—a pipe from the little creek that provided a thin stream of icy cold water. Unfortunately, the amenities did not extend to any other indoor plumbing, but the outhouse was better than the woods, which she'd been using since they'd fled Scott's cabin.

But her biggest surprise had been the one that had apparently endeared her to the recluse. She'd noticed several very good cameras and had asked him about them. After a long hesitation and without uttering a word, he'd hauled three well-filled cardboard boxes onto the table, boxes filled with thousands of photographs.

C.Z. had been utterly amazed and then entranced by the pictures of wildlife—deer, bears, foxes, squirrels, bobcats, even rattlesnakes, though she could certainly have done without them. The quality was truly astonishing. She'd never seen anything better. She'd told him so, and had been rewarded with a smile, though it was nearly buried within his bushy beard.

She shifted more, wishing she could take the thick quilt and make of it a more comfortable bed on the floor. But she dared not insult their host and risk destroying the fragile bond between them. She had already decided that when this was over, he was going to become her private special project. If she couldn't persuade him to give up his solitary existence, at least she could visit him regularly and perhaps convince him to allow his wonderful pictures to be exhibited.

When this was over… C.Z. smiled. With any luck at all, this might be their last night as fugitives. She hadn't yet asked Zach how they would arrange the end of this misery, but she assumed that he and Sam could work out something. It was enough for now to know that it was nearly over.

HER EYES SNAPPED OPEN and she was surprised to discover she must have fallen asleep. But what had awakened her? She was facing the wall, and she started to roll over to see if one of the men had gotten up. A hand clamped itself over her mouth, and before she could draw a terrified breath, Zach was bending over her.

"I heard something outside," he whispered. "It's probably only an animal, but I'm going out to have a look."

She nodded and he took his hand from her mouth. She saw that he had his gun in his other hand. "The snow," she whispered. "How—"

"The snow stopped," he whispered. "Mostly, anyway. Don't follow me!"

She nodded. It was an easy promise to make. She had no intention of going out there to confront a bear. Some of the ones she'd seen in the photographs were huge—far larger than she'd imagined bears in these woods could be.

Zach slipped away, then eased the heavy door open almost soundlessly. For one brief moment, C.Z. feared they had human visitors, but she quickly pushed the thought away. Those men hadn't found this cabin when Zach stopped them, and after he'd disabled their vehicle, their only interest would have been in getting out.

The moments dragged past. At one point, she thought she heard a brief cry, but that could have come from their host, who had been making noises in his sleep earlier. She continued to expect Zach to return any moment as she watched the door.

Then something heavy struck the door, rattling it on its hinges. Before she could do more than gasp with fear, something came crashing through the window on the other side of the room.

The smell of gasoline nearly choked her as she stumbled from the bed, but before she could get her feet properly under her, she'd forgotten about the odor. Flames lit the darkness—and they seemed to be everywhere!

Propelled by terror, C.Z. ran for the door only to see flames outlining it. The noise was almost as horrifying as the sight of so much fire, cracklings and spittings and roaring. Panicked, she turned toward the back of the cabin only to remember that there wasn't another door! And then, in a rush of shame, she remembered Davy Crockett. In her terror and her urgency to flee the fire, she'd forgotten all about him.

Although the fire seemed to be everywhere, it hadn't yet reached the hearth, and in the hellish light she could see him, still sleeping soundly while his cabin burned. He'd been drinking earlier, and though he hadn't seemed drunk, no doubt that contributed to his stupor.

The smoke was thick, and she was having trouble breathing. She grabbed a rag from beside the sink, soaked it and held it over her nose and mouth as she zigzagged through the flames to the sleeping recluse.

He was beginning to stir by the time she reached him, and then he was struggling to his feet, coughing and staring wildly around. She grabbed his arm, shouting to make herself heard above the terrible noises of the fire.

"Come on! We'll have to go out a window!"

She ran toward the single rear window, then fumbled with the lock as she continued to hold the rag over her mouth and nose. When she got the window open, cold air rushed in, and she turned, hearing the roar of the flames become louder and knowing that the fresh supply of air must be feeding the flames.

Where was he? She'd thought he would be right behind her, but he wasn't. Her eyes darted wildly around the fiery cabin—and then she saw him. He was trying to make his way through the flames to get to the boxes of photographs he'd returned to a corner. Even in this moment of sheer terror, C.Z. could feel sympathy for him, but she started after him, shouting.

"No! There isn't time!"

He had picked up one box, and she saw that flames had begun to lick at its edges. Then, in a fresh wave of horror, she saw that the fire was causing a heavy wood beam in the ceiling to crack.

For one brief instant, she thought about grabbing another box, but then her instinct for survival took over and she tugged and pushed the reluctant man toward the window.

The cold air felt like ice against her heated skin as she took the smoldering box from him and heaved it out the window, then began to push him through, as well. Just as she swung her legs over the sill, there was a loud crash behind her, and she knew the roof had begun to collapse.

Davy Crockett was on his feet, flapping his arms wildly as sparks and flames leaped from his clothes. C.Z. landed in several inches of snow, then ran to him and tackled him, sending them both thumping to the ground.

The flames on him spread to her, and she rolled them both over and over in the snow until the fire was extinguished. Then she disentangled herself from him and sat up, coughing and struggling to breathe. Barely fifty feet away, the cabin was completely outlined in brilliant fire, and sparks shot into the dark heavens.

For one brief moment, she knew the pure joy of having survived—and then she remembered Zach. How could she have forgotten about him?

"No!" she cried, but the certainty would not go away. The only reason he wouldn't have come to their rescue was that he was dead.

She staggered to her feet, still saying no to herself over and over. It could not end this way! Leaving the silent, dazed man whose life she'd saved, C.Z. ran around the cabin, only to come to a stumbling halt as a large, dark shadow hurled itself out the side window, trailing flames!

Before she could reach him, he had rolled himself in the snow and was getting to his feet. He was still in a crouch when he saw her, and for one long moment, as the cabin collapsed completely behind them, they stared at each other, not moving. Then he straightened and spoke her name in a wondering tone that she could just barely hear above the hellish din.

"I thought...."

"Me, too," she said as they held tightly to each other, coughing and wheezing.

"Davy?" he gasped.

"He's back there. I got him out. He was trying to save his pictures."

Holding tightly to each other, they returned to their erstwhile host to find him sitting dazedly beside the box of pictures. And it was only then, when she saw this harmless, pitiful man staring from the box to the flaming ruins of his cabin, that C.Z. began to feel anger. When she turned to Zach, she saw the rage in his eyes, as well, as they reflected the fire.

They sat beside him and watched the fire begin to die, helped by the mixture of snow, sleet and rain that was falling. Zach told her that he'd gone outside and found two men with cans and bottles of gasoline approaching the cabin. But before he could confront them, a third man had ambushed him. He could remember a blow to the back of his head, then had vague recollections of being picked up and tossed through a window into the cabin.

"I wasn't really knocked out completely," he said, gingerly touching the back of his head. "But I might have faded away for a couple of minutes. When I came to, the cabin was on fire and I couldn't see either of you. So I tried to find you, then realized that you must have gone out the back window. I couldn't get to it, so I dove out the one they'd broken when they threw me in."

"I heard a window break while I was trying to get us out," C.Z. recalled. "But I thought it was from the fire."

"They were trying to make it look as though we'd all died in the fire," Zach said. "But they must have panicked, since they didn't stay around to be sure."

"How do you know they didn't?" she asked nervously, staring into the darkness beyond the glow of the dying flames.

"I heard one of them yelling to the others to get moving.

Big mistake on his part, because I recognized his voice. I never got a good look at them.''

''Harvey Summers?'' she asked, her rage burning as brightly inside her as the fire.

''No, his name's Isaac Neil. They call him Zeke. I know him because I arrested him for a bar brawl. He works for Summers.''

''I'M ALL RIGHT.''

''No, you're not, but I appreciate the effort.'' Zach gave her a brief smile as he polished off the rest of a granola bar.

''Well, I'm all right *enough,* then.''

''Your old English teacher, Mrs. Jackson, would frown on such grammar.''

She paused with her coffee mug halfway to her mouth. ''How do you know she was my teacher?''

''She told me while she was feeding me chocolate chip cookies after I rescued one of her cats from a tree. We were talking about your father, and she mentioned you, as well.''

''I don't believe this! You rescued her cat? I thought that only happened in old stories.''

''I suppose it does, mostly, but Mrs. Jackson thought otherwise. I was on my way home and the desk sergeant called me to see if we were in the feline rescue business. So I made it my first act of community service.'' He frowned at the wrapper from the granola bar. ''She makes really good chocolate chip cookies—and oatmeal raisin, as well. She brought a batch of them to the station later.''

''Could we please talk about something other than food?'' she implored him. If she never saw another bag of trail mix or a granola bar or a stick of beef jerky, it would be too soon.

''I'm worried about him,'' she said, gesturing in the direction of the Jeep, where they'd left Davy Crockett with some food and a mug of coffee. The tent wasn't big enough for all three of them.

"He'll be all right. I told him he can stay at my place until we can get another cabin built. Or maybe we'll put him at Scott's place." He scratched his beard. "The problem is that the cabin was illegal to begin with. It's on state land. But I'll work something out."

She listened to the steady drumbeat of sleet and rain against the walls and roof of the tent. When they'd gotten back to the Jeep, they'd melted snow and heated it on the little stove, then tried as best they could to wash away the stench of smoke. But it clung to their clothes and was overpowering inside the Jeep and the tent.

"We'd better get going," Zach said. "What worries me most at this point is that Summers might have found the truck and destroyed it."

"But if he did that, why would he still have tried to kill Davy?"

"Insurance," Zach said grimly. "I doubt if he's thinking too clearly by now."

"Do you think he believes we're all dead?" she asked, shuddering.

"Probably. But that's all for the better at this point. I doubt if anyone saw the flames, and the chopper won't be up in this weather, so no one's likely to come to investigate. When the weather improves, he'll find some excuse for someone to go out there and discover it. If they found our bodies, they'd just say that we'd been staying there with him and the place caught fire on its own."

"But you think he'll still try to find the truck?"

Zach nodded. "Yeah. He probably hopes to torch it, too. But this isn't a very good day for that, so that buys us some time."

C.Z. HAD NEVER been so utterly miserable in her life. She rather wished she possessed Zach's talent for colorful swearing, which he'd been employing virtually nonstop since the Jeep had overturned.

The rain was coming down in torrents, then freezing on nearly every surface. Mixed with it were fat snowflakes and sleet, as though the weather gods had decided to pour everything in their bag of tricks at them. It was enough to make her believe in the old, capricious gods of the Greeks and Romans.

She shivered inside her oversize poncho, peering from beneath its billed cap as the two men grunted and struggled to right the Jeep, all the while slipping in the semifrozen mud that had caused the accident. Zach was barely recognizable as the rain plastered his dark hair and gray beard to his head.

His nonstop cursing was directed at himself, though C.Z. thought he'd done an admirable job of coaxing the old Jeep over slick, rutted trails and down several treacherous hillsides before reaching the one that had been their undoing.

This was supposed to be their day of triumph, the day they could finally prove what they'd known to be the truth all along. Instead, here they were, miles from their goal in the worst weather imaginable and without a means of getting there.

In truth, she didn't know how far they were from the place where Davy Crockett claimed to have seen the truck. Perhaps it wasn't that far away. It seemed they'd been traveling through the dark and gloomy woods forever.

And in her present frame of mind, C.Z. could easily envision them reaching the truck only to discover that it wasn't the truck they were seeking. For reasons she would never understand, some local men seemed to prefer dumping their used-up vehicles in the woods rather than taking them to a junkyard. In their travels, she'd seen several cars and an old school bus, its roof caved in by a fallen tree.

"Okay, forget it!" Zach told Davy after one last attempt to nudge the Jeep upright. "We'll have to walk."

He made his way cautiously to the top of the bank where she stood, trailed by the silent, stoical recluse. Both of them were covered with mud, which was being washed off by the pounding rain.

"How far is it?" she asked, trying—but probably not succeeding—to keep her misery out of her voice.

"Two or three miles, maybe," Davy Crockett responded, studying her as though trying to determine if she was up to it.

"Then let's go," she said, her determination renewed by his scrutiny. She had to prove she was her father's daughter, even though what she really wanted to do was to sit down and cry.

Zach pulled up the hood of his poncho, then studied her, as well. "Imagine the two of us back in that hospital room. Would you still say yes to me?"

He asked the question in such a serious tone that she found herself smiling. "Yes, I would."

He reached out with a gloved finger to touch her nose briefly. It was an oddly endearing gesture, and one that temporarily drove away the chills that had taken up residence in her bones.

They set off through the woods, slipping and sliding, stumbling and falling and picking themselves up again. Davy was leading the way, and Zach seemed to have complete faith in his ability to take them to the truck. They had stayed on the old roads and trails most of the way, but this part of their journey required them to leave the trails behind.

She was a few feet behind the two men, her head down

to watch her footing, when suddenly she bumped into Zach, who had stopped. He reached around to grip her arm, then pointed ahead of them and to the right.

They had been climbing a gradual rise, but she saw that the land dropped away sharply from the top. And at the bottom, in a dense thicket of blackberry bushes and tall, dead weeds, lay a truck.

It was still upright, but its bed was higher than its cab as its front bumper rested against an ancient oak. Obviously, it had been pushed over the hilltop where they stood.

They stared at it and then at each other, each seeing the doubts that had been silently tormenting them. Then they began to pick their way carefully down the steep slope, seeking footholds among the roots and bushes and rocks.

Up close, the old truck was little more than a rusted hulk, hardly the sort of thing one would choose to pin one's hopes on. And yet, as she stared at it, it seemed to her that it was in better condition than she would have expected after all this time. That thought, of course, led to still more doubts. But Zach apparently had had the same thought.

"They didn't choose their spot too wisely," he commented as he began to pick his way gingerly through the blackberry bushes. "It's actually been pretty well protected in here."

She saw what he meant as she looked at the huge trees that formed a canopy over the wreck, a mixture of oak and fir that would have sheltered the truck from both the summer sun and the winter storms.

Zach reached the front of the truck while she was still making her way carefully through the grasping blackberry thorns. She stopped as he made a sudden sound, not the whoop of joy she might have expected, but rather a quiet sound of satisfaction. When she reached him, it was *she* who cried out in sheer relief.

Only the big front bumper of the truck was touching the tree trunk, right in the center. But the left front of the truck was crumpled—and amidst the dents were traces of paint, the distinctive yellow of a school bus.

They both stared at it as raptly as they might have gazed upon the proverbial pot of gold at the end of the rainbow. Even the rain gave the appearance of having let up under the sheltering trees.

Then C.Z. recalled Mary's story about the spilled bleach and dragged her gaze from the yellow paint to tug at Zach's arm. She didn't have to say anything because she could see that he was remembering, too.

They pushed their way through the bushes to the passenger door. C.Z. reached it first and tried to open it, but the door handle refused to budge. So she stepped aside and Zach tugged at it until the door finally swung open with a loud groan of rusted hinges.

He reached in and picked up the floor mat—and there was the final proof, a large yellowed area where the pooled bleach had washed out the black carpeting. With Mary's testimony, there could be no doubt this was the truck her husband had sold to Harvey Summers.

They backed away from the truck, and Davy Crockett looked a question at them. Zach nodded and clapped a hand on the man's shoulder.

"That's it! You found our proof!"

Davy grinned for the first time, lending an almost boyish quality to his craggy features. "We've got him, then?"

"We've got him," Zach assured him. "Now…"

He broke off abruptly and frowned into the distance. Davy Crockett did the same, but it was a second or two before C.Z. heard it—the sound of an engine, barely audible above the rain.

"Come on!" Zach said, taking her arm. "Let's get out of here and into hiding."

Instead of climbing the steep hillside, they hurried into the woods on the far side of the truck where the ground dropped off gradually. Flinging themselves down on the semifrozen, slick ground, they peered over the top of the bank as the sound of the engine grew steadily louder.

"Damn!" Zach swore as a dark blue vehicle came into view off to their left. "It's Summers himself!"

The vehicle lurched to a stop at the top of the hill at the same place Summers had pushed the truck into its present resting place.

"Nice of them to come along just when we need a ride," Zach observed dryly as they watched both front doors open.

Harvey Summers came into view first, standing at the crest of the hill and staring at the wreck with a look of triumph on his face. His words carried to them clearly.

"I shouldn't have listened to Colby. I knew it was back here."

Then the other man came into view, a small wiry man with a face that immediately made C.Z. think of a rat. Zach leaned close to her ear.

"That's Neil, the one whose voice I recognized at Davy's place. It's going to be a pleasure to put him away."

The two men turned toward their vehicle, out of sight beyond the crest of the hill. C.Z. could hear their voices but not what they were saying.

A few moments later, the two men were back, making their way carefully down the slick hillside, carrying two huge red gasoline cans whose weight made their progress slow and clumsy. She could feel the tension in Zach as he lay beside her, a coiled spring ready to erupt into action. His gun was in his hand. On his other side, Davy stared impassively at the struggling men, but she could sense tension in him, as well.

They reached the bottom of the hill and approached the truck. Summers began to walk around it, putting out a hand to touch the side and then the fender.

"It'll burn. It isn't that wet down here, and this way, we won't have to worry about the fire spreading and drawing any attention."

The other man, Neil, was walking around the truck, as well, and he stopped at the front. "Shoulda got rid of that paint, Harvey."

Harvey Summers glanced at it and swore disgustedly. "We were both so drunk we didn't even notice it. All we wanted to do was to get rid of it."

"Well, that's what we're here to do now," Neil said as he started to the gas cans.

But Harvey Summers continued to stand there, staring at that smear of yellow paint. C.Z. couldn't see his face, but there was something in his stance and his utter stillness that might have elicited her sympathy if he had not gone on to commit further crimes.

As Summers turned toward the gas cans, Zach stood up in one fluid motion that startled C.Z.

"Just stop right there!" he ordered, all hard, cold cop.

Summers froze, then turned slowly, his expression stunned. The other man did nothing except to slowly raise his hands above his head.

"Hollis!" Summers cried hoarsely, then turned to his accomplice. "You said they all died in the fire!"

The other man shrugged, his arms still raised above his head. "We thought they did."

Zach advanced toward them. "If I were you two, I'd watch what I'm saying. I'd read you your rights, but I'm not back on the job—yet." He turned to Davy. "I don't

think they're carrying, but you'd better check them anyway."

Davy Crockett stepped forward and patted both men
down, then shook his head. "Nothing. They might have
something in the Bronco."

"Yeah, you'd better check it, too." Zach stepped closer
to Harvey Summers. "We've got you, Summers. Mary
Williams can identify the truck as the one her husband sold
to you. Maybe you never noticed that bleach stain under
the floor mat."

Summers's gaze went from Zach to the truck, and C.Z.
thought his face was beginning to crumple. His skin was
ashen.

"Then there's conspiracy to commit murder," Zach
went on in a calm, almost pleasant tone. "I think Zeke here
might be willing to talk to save his hide." He turned to the
other man. "Killing a police officer is sure as hell going
to be a capital offense, but if you tell the D.A. Summers
paid you to do it, you might get off with life instead."

C.Z. was confused. She expected Neil to deny that he'd
killed anyone. After all, they were standing there as living
proof that his murderous scheme hadn't worked. But then,
just as Harvey Summers began to speak, she realized that
Zach had said police officer. He wasn't one at the moment.
That could only mean—

"Shut up, Zeke!" Harvey Summers ordered. "He's bluff-
ing. He doesn't know anything!"

"Wrong, Summers. Davy here saw Zeke on the grounds
of Tom Morrison's camp that day—and he was carrying
the same kind of rifle that killed Morrison. You paid him
to do it because you knew Tom was getting close to the
truth."

Zach turned contemptuously to Neil. "And you probably

had a grudge against Morrison yourself, didn't you? I know he arrested you a couple of times.''

Neil's little eyes swiveled from Zach to Summers and back again. ''You telling me the truth? If I say he paid me, they'll go easy on me?''

Summers tried to interrupt, but Davy Crockett stepped behind him and clamped a big hand over his mouth.

''All I'm saying, Neil, is that you should tell the D.A. the truth. Otherwise, you're gonna go down for it and old Harvey here is probably going to get nothing more than a suspended driver's license.''

Neil's head bobbed. ''He paid me, paid me for that and for torching the cabin.''

C.Z. remained silent, her gaze going from Harvey Summers to the other man and back again. Together, they had murdered her father, and yet their only concern at the moment was who would get the blame.

She was somewhere beyond rage at the moment, unable to comprehend the working of two minds that could care so little about having taken a life. She'd encountered such men in her short-lived prison career, of course, but none of them had killed someone she loved.

But it was Harvey Summers who was the focus of her attention, not Zeke Neil, whom she didn't know—even though he had been the one who'd actually killed her father. Neil was little more than a deadly tool for Harvey Summers, and if he'd refused, then Summers would have found another tool.

C.Z. knew something deep within her had shifted, something inexplicable. It occurred to her that some part of her had, right up to this moment, refused to accept Summers's part in all this despite the overwhelming evidence. And if she felt this way when she barely knew the man, how would those who did know him feel?

It was, she thought, betrayal of a particularly repellent sort. This man had walked among them all his life, smiling, helping everyone, demonstrating his concern for the community. The parents of the children who had died because of him had undoubtedly accepted his sympathy, commiserated with him over their terrible loss. Perhaps some of them had benefited from the many small favors he'd done over the years.

The end of innocence, she thought sadly. As a result of his betrayal, people would lose their faith and their trust in their fellow human beings—and they might never regain it.

Davy Crockett returned from his inspection of the Bronco carrying a handgun and a rifle. "Found these," he said. "There's some heavy rope, too."

Zach nodded. "Let's get them in the Bronco, then. You can drive, C.Z., so Davy and I can keep an eye on them. We'll go back and pull the Jeep out first."

She didn't move as Zach and Davy herded the men into the Bronco. Davy got into the back seat between them while Zach climbed into the front passenger seat, then turned around and kept his gun aimed at them. She wanted Zach's arms around her, needed his comfort right now. But she understood, finally. They would have their time, but there was still work to do.

As soon as she had slid into the driver's seat, Zach reached out with his free hand to grasp hers. "Hang in there, Charlie girl. It's nearly over. You're doing fine."

She wasn't, but she knew she didn't have to tell him that. His love and his concern were in his eyes and in his voice, which temporarily lost its hardness.

She drove the big, clumsy vehicle carefully over slick trails and through the woods until at last they reached the spot where the Jeep lay on its side on the icy bank. Their two prisoners remained silent. Once, she glanced in the rearview mirror to see Harvey Summers watching her, his expression unreadable. She wondered if it would make any difference if she could see some remorse there.

When she had brought the Bronco to a halt, Zach ordered the two men to get out. Then Davy used his wicked-looking knife to cut off two short pieces from the coil of rope he'd found, and he and Zach bound the men's feet. After that, he handed her his gun.

"If they cause any trouble, aim at their legs," he told her.

She nodded, though in truth, she didn't think she could bring herself to fire the gun—even at them. She kept her distance from them as they all stood there in the driving rain.

The Jeep was hauled quickly up the slope to the trail, and Zach cut more rope and bound the men's hands, as well, before pushing them into the back seat of the Bronco.

"Davy will ride with you to keep an eye on them," he told her. "I'll follow in the Jeep."

"Where are we going?" she asked.

"Davy says he can get us to the highway pretty quickly—not far from that closed gas station where there's a pay phone. Then we can call Sam."

She had more questions, but it seemed pointless to stand here in the rain asking them, so she did as he asked. It took nearly an hour for them to reach the highway, and the entire trip was accomplished in a heavy silence.

C.Z. kept glancing into the rearview mirror even though she couldn't see Zach's face behind the rain-smeared windshield of the Jeep. How were they going to manage this? What would happen to Zach? She was terrified at the possibility that he might be forced to return to prison until it could all be sorted out.

When they reached the highway, Davy broke the long

silence to tell her to turn left, and within a few minutes she could see the abandoned gas station. She pulled in, her mind busy at work on various scenarios to bring an end to their ordeal.

When she saw the Jeep speed past and disappear quickly around a curve, she was too stunned to believe her eyes. She started to put the key in the ignition, but Davy's big, callused hand stopped her.

"He's got to disappear for a while," Davy told her. "Just till things get settled. He says they'd send him back to prison, and he doesn't want that."

Tears sprang to her eyes. "But they won't! He's innocent!"

"He was innocent the first time, too," Davy reminded her. "And he knows the law better than we do." He paused. "Now you go call that lawyer."

She wanted to go after him, but she realized that Zach had set it up very well, saddling her with the responsibility of their two prisoners, not to mention Davy. Half-blind with tears of anger and pain, she got out and ran through the rain to the phone booth.

Sam wasn't in his office, but when she identified herself, his secretary asked for her number and said that Sam was carrying a pager and would get back to her right away. So she waited impatiently in the booth, trying to get a firm grip on all the emotions that were buffeting her.

Why couldn't Zach have taken her with him? They could have made the call to Sam and left the prisoners with Davy. Then she realized that Zach had done what he'd done out of concern for Davy, as well. He seemed to be okay, but how well could he function when all the police arrived? Besides, the man was homeless now, without anything other than the clothes on his back and the box of photographs that were still in the Jeep.

He could have pointed *all that out to me,* she grumbled to herself as the phone began to ring. *He didn't have to do it this way.*

The moment Sam identified himself, she started talking and didn't stop until she'd told him everything, ending with the fact that Zach had disappeared.

"Good idea," Sam said. "There's no way I could have gotten him out on bail, and it'll probably take a couple of days to get things sorted out."

"But he's *innocent,* Sam!" she protested.

"We know that, but the system doesn't know it yet. If it were just the conviction for attempted murder, I could get him out once they hear our story. But he escaped from prison, and they'd insist on getting him back until it's all cleared up. He knew that, and that's why he did it. I don't blame him."

In LESS THAN half an hour, the state police descended upon them in force. Sam had called them rather than the Ondago County police for the obvious reason that Chief Colby was soon to be arrested, as well, for leaving the scene of an accident, not to mention burglarizing her place.

C.Z. saw very quickly just how right Zach was to be concerned about Davy. He was very uneasy—especially when the officers asked him to produce some ID and he couldn't. She drew the officer aside and explained about him.

"Davy Crockett?" the officer echoed, then nodded. "I've heard about him. I understand that he's been living illegally on state land for years."

"Not anymore," C.Z. said, gesturing to their prisoners. "They burned down his cabin—and nearly killed us, as well."

"Can't he talk?" the officer asked.

"He can, but I think he's decided not to. He'll talk to me, though. Just don't arrest him. He didn't do anything wrong."

The officer swept an arm around to encompass them all. "We're going to have to take all of you over to the barracks until we get this sorted out, but you can stay with him as interpreter."

By the time they reached the state police barracks, some thirty miles away, Sam was already there—and so was Mary Williams. Their presence was reassuring to C.Z., but it didn't prevent her from having to tell her story over and over again.

Then the county D.A. arrived, and she had to go over it all one more time, even though Sam had already talked to him. She was still chilled, despite the cups of coffee that had been provided to them, and the caffeine was kicking in and making her jittery, to boot. More than once, she decided she would have answered differently if Zach had asked her again the question he'd asked earlier. She loved him, there was no question of that. But that love was being sorely tried.

She was asked several times by the police if she had any idea where he might have gone, but when she said she didn't, they seemed to lose interest. When they were alone for a few moments at one point, Sam told her they weren't really interested in finding Zach. They understood why he'd chosen to vanish temporarily.

Finally, they were let go, though she was told that she would have to appear in a special court the next day, together with Davy. Sam had brought Mary with him, and the four of them piled into Sam's car. Mary suggested that C.Z. and Davy come to her home, but one glance at the silent recluse told C.Z. he wouldn't want that.

She thanked Mary for her offer but said she needed to

get back to Stacey's because her clothes were there and because Stacey must be worried about her.

"She knows what's been going on," Sam told her. "She called me a couple of days ago and I told her. Then I called her again at school on my way out here."

"I want to take Davy out to my friend Scott's cabin. He'll be more comfortable there." She turned to the recluse, with whom she was sharing the back seat, and was rewarded with a look of gratitude.

"My name's Edgar—Edgar Wallace."

"Oh! I'm sorry, Edgar. I just didn't know what else to call you."

He smiled, though it was rather hard to see in that big, bushy beard. "This is a nice place. Is it okay with your friend?"

C.Z. explained that Scott was in Europe for a year and had turned the A-frame over to her. With an inner smile, she thought about the long letter she would have to write to him.

"So you can just stay here until we figure out something."

"They won't let me build out there again," he said unhappily.

"No, they won't," she agreed. "We're going to have to get you some land." She frowned in thought. She was sure Scott had told her he owned quite a bit back here. Maybe she'd turn that letter into a phone call.

"How would you feel about building a new cabin somewhere around here?" she asked, trying to brighten his spirits. "My friend only comes here occasionally on weekends, and the same is true of the man who owns that other cabin. They might be happy to have someone around to keep an eye on their places for them."

"I can't afford that," he said, though she could hear hope in his voice.

"Edgar, the man who owns this cabin and a lot of land is a good friend. And when he hears what you've done for Zach and me, I think he'll be happy to give you some land." He probably would, but she'd offer to buy it. "Then we'll see that you get a new cabin. Zach will help you build it, if you like."

The recluse nodded. "He told me that before he left."

"So there you are," she said brightly. "It'll all work out. Now, do you think you have everything you need?" They'd stopped to buy him some clothing and some groceries. "I'll be out tomorrow morning in any event because we both have to appear in court."

"You'll be with me?" he asked uneasily.

"I'll be with you," she promised.

"You're a lot like your dad, you know—even if you don't look like him."

C.Z. SLIPPED INTO the warm, fragrant water with a sigh that was part relief and part regret. Beyond the big windows, snow was falling softly and silently in the dark velvet night.

Her relief was because it was over—for now, at least. After a long day in court, Harvey Summers and all the others, including Dave Colby, had been charged and sent to jail to await trial. The state police had towed the old pickup from the woods, and photographs of the yellow paint and the bleached rug had been shown to the judge.

Sam told her that plea bargains were in the offing for Isaac Neil and the other men Summers had hired to do his dirty work. Dave Colby might be offered a deal, though he would certainly go to prison, as would Neil.

Mary Williams, who had testified, said she'd spoken to the other commissioner and they were prepared to offer

Zach his job back. Sam made some noises about a lawsuit against the county because of Summers's and Colby's lies, which had sent Zach to prison, and Mary said perhaps they could work something out to compensate Zach for his lost pay.

Only the local reporters had been present at the judicial proceedings, but as they left the courthouse, Sam warned her that it was likely the national media would pick up the story and descend upon them soon.

"Who knows?" he grinned. "Maybe you two will become the movie of the week."

C.Z. tried to enjoy his humor, but she was still too close to the ordeal to see it the way he—and others—would see it. She thought, however, that he had a point. It *was* quite a story.

But it wasn't over yet—and that was the reason for her regret as she soaked in the big spa tub. Sam had taken it upon himself to get the electricity turned on at Zach's house, saying she might want a place to get away from it all. And she did.

She sighed. Sam had already begun to work on Zach's situation, but it appeared it could take several more days before he could get the charges dropped. It helped that the warden was being sympathetic.

She had very nearly dozed off when she was jolted awake by a tapping sound at the windows behind her. Terror clawed at her spine as she swiveled around to face them.

She could barely see the face beyond the glass, but somehow, her body recognized instantly what her eyes hadn't quite registered. Without giving a thought to her nakedness, she climbed from the tub and approached the long windows.

"I could use a bath myself," said the familiar voice, muffled by the glass. "And I brought the champagne."

To her astonishment, he held up a bottle. But she didn't say a word. Instead, she wrapped herself in a big towel and ran to the door to let him in.

He was cold and wet with snow, but she didn't complain when he swept her into his arms and carried her to the bathroom. After depositing her gently into the tub, he stripped off his dirty, wet clothes and joined her.

"Where have you been?" she demanded. "And where did you get that champagne? Did you rob a liquor store?" Her body might be eager to have him here, but her brain was a bit slower.

He shook his head. "I gave up my life of crime. I got it from Scott's cabin. I remembered that he had some there, and besides, I figured Davy would be there and I'd check on him."

"Edgar," she said. "His name is Edgar Wallace."

"I know. He told me. He also told me that you're going to get him some land out there, and he told me what went on in court today."

"I'm angry with you, Zach," she said, even though her husky voice belied that. "Why didn't you trust me enough to tell me that you had to disappear?"

"Because you would have argued with me, and there wasn't time for that. I figured you'd understand when Sam explained it all, and you'd realize that one of us had to stay around to be sure Davy—I mean Edgar—was okay." He leaned toward her and kissed her softly.

"It wasn't a question of trust, Charlie girl. You know I trust you."

C.Z. thought she really ought to maintain her righteous anger a bit longer, but that proved to be impossible as Zach's hands slid beneath the water to seek her out.

"Can you really stay here?" she asked breathlessly, knowing she couldn't let him go again, even for a few days.

"Uh-huh. They'll never look for me here because they don't really want to find me."

"Sam said he should have everything straightened out in a few days," she told him, ending with a moan as his fingers found the source of her growing heat.

"Good old Sam. The least I can do for him is to ask him to be best man."

"And he seems to be working out something to get you back pay for all the time you spent in prison."

"Even better. That means we can have a long honeymoon."

"You've got your job back, too."

"That's nice. Are you finished?"

"Yes."

"Good, because I'm just getting started."

'HAVE I DONE something wrong?' Angie persisted, wishing Taylor would emit a sense of camaraderie instead of holding an impenetrable reserve.

'Not at all,' he assured her. 'I would say a lot of things right. You seem to be fitting into our little Outback community very well. I've heard only good things about you.'

'They're nice people,' she said sincerely. Only the Maguire family kept her shut out of their hearts.

'Yes,' he agreed. 'Though I appreciate it's taken considerable effort from you. It is a world away from what you're used to.'

The control Angie had been exerting over her feelings snapped. He wasn't as blatant as his aunt in his prejudice against her but she'd felt it coming through every word he'd spoken and she didn't deserve any of it.

'Don't judge me by your wife!'

His jaw jerked. A flicker of some dark emotion destroyed the steady power of his probing gaze.

'No two people are the same. If you don't know that, you're a man of very limited vision. So I come from the city as your wife did! That doesn't stop me from being an individual in my own right.'

She straightened up, proudly defiant, furiously angry with the situation. 'I'm *me*. Angie Cordell. And it's time you took the blinkers off your eyes, Taylor Maguire.'

Then she whirled away from him, too agitated by the explosive expulsion of her emotion to keep facing him.

The storm outside hadn't yet eased. There was nowhere to go. She stopped at the window, staring blindly at the torrential rain. The thundering on the roof was almost deafening but it wasn't as loud as the silence behind her.

'You want me to go, don't you? You've given me a month's respite and now you want me to leave and channel my energies somewhere else.'

'I didn't say that, Angie.'

'You were working your way around it.' Bitterness at his tactics spewed the suspicion. 'Do you have your first choice of governess waiting in the wings?'

'No. I said I'd give you a chance.'

'Have you?' She swung around to face him. 'Have you really, Taylor?'

He hadn't moved. He didn't move now except to make a gesture of appeasement. 'Angie, I was merely trying to ascertain how you felt.'

'Then let me tell you your cynicism was shining through every word.'

He frowned, shook his head. 'I didn't mean to hurt you.' The blue eyes fastened on hers with devastating sincerity. 'I truly did not come in here to take you down or suggest you leave.'

Her heart jiggled painfully. He might be speaking the truth but the judgements were still there, the judgements that ruled his attitude towards her, that kept her shut out of his life, denied any real sharing with him, denied his confidence and trust. She didn't know why it meant so much to her but it did. It did. And the need to fight for justice from him was as much a raging torrent inside her as the rain outside.